GHOST SOLDIERS

A VINCE CARVER THRILLER

MATT SLOANE

BLOOD &
TREASURE

Published by Blood & Treasure, Los Angeles
First Edition

Cover by James T. Egan of Bookfly Design LLC.

Print ISBN: 978-1-946-00852-7

Matt-Sloane.com

Preface

I'm Matt Sloane, I like great stories, and I hope you do too.

The cool thing about stories is they come in all kinds. Everyone has their opinions and nobody's wrong. (Which must mean I'm right.)

So here's what I like in a story: Smart dialog between characters that feel real. Spurts of action, moments to breathe, and plenty to think about. Complex plots that aren't easy to predict, with realistic twists that don't make your eyes roll. And most of all, a satisfying ending, because you can't cheap out on those.

The Vince Carver books are high action, high intrigue spycraft on the world stage, and I hope they're your kind of story.

If you'd like to get in touch to say hi, offer a correction, talk shop, or otherwise gab, feel free to drop me a line:

matt@matt-sloane.com

Or you can get an email from me every time a book is released at: Matt-Sloane.com

Happy reading,

-Matt

GHOST SOLDIERS

1919

"Who rules East Europe commands the Heartland: Who rules the Heartland commands the World-Island: Who rules the World-Island commands the World."

> • *Democratic Ideals and Reality*,
> Sir Halford J. Mackinder, England

1934

"It is a great mistake, world-politically, to consider borders as unchangeable, rigid lines. Borders are anything but dead—they are living organisms extending and recoiling like the skin and other protective organs of the human body."

> • *World Politics of Today*,
> Generalmajor Karl Haushofer, Germany

2015

"My heart beats with the same rhythm as the heart of my country, my people. I waited for the diastoles and systoles, the ebb and the flow, contraction and expansion."

> • Aleksandr Dugin, Russia

It's one reason I've convinced them to give you a shot."

Carver leaned into the vintage tan leather of his Eames office chair and motioned for Williams to sit across from the desk. If there was one quality he liked about the case officer, it was her straight shooting. "I appreciate the good word, Lanelle. How about we get down to it?"

"This is about the bombing in Rome last week." She sat, somehow looking more stiff in the chair. "Twelve dead after a suicide bomber drove into a crowd and detonated. Terrorists affiliated with the Libyan National Army took credit, releasing a statement condemning cooperation with the West."

Carver knew something of this world. He'd served six years in the US Army's 1st Special Forces Operational Detachment-Delta, much of that time in Africa dealing with various Salafis and jihadis. Officially, the Government of National Accord runs Libya, sanctioned by the United Nations Security Council. In truth the country is a hotly contested war zone. Various sectarians vie over territory and idiomatic influence in a resource-rich state. Larger powers, serving their own interests, back them by proxy. Russia and the United Arab Emirates outfit the rebels while Turkey and Italy support the interim government.

"They call Libya the Gateway to Europe," said Carver, revealing to Williams his knowledge of the area. "Migrants cross into Italy to gain access to the EU. While the vast majority simply want a better life, they don't all have good intentions. You need help tracking a terrorist cell?"

"Interpol has a handle on that aspect. We would like

your cooperation, however, with protecting someone who escaped the blast."

Williams slid a phone over the desk. It was a standard CIA burner, and it currently displayed a picture of a young woman. Carver picked up the screen to study it.

"Her name is Katarina Litvinenko, a Russian figure skater in the Beijing Olympics. She spoke out against the abuses of her country and was ordered to return before the commencement of the games. She refused and eventually received a humanitarian visa from Poland."

Carver bristled. "This kid was the target of a bombing?"

"She's not a kid. She's twenty-three, rich, and has a well-connected family. She speaks publicly about leaving her country, and she barely escaped the blast in Rome as her outdoor speech concluded. Frustratingly, Katarina refuses state protection. She's currently employing private bodyguards in Berlin. Officially, the CIA can't get involved. Katarina is too open about her dealings with government agencies. That transparency is why she's so popular, and why we can't push her too hard. We also can't risk a confrontation with Russian interests that apparently wish her dead."

"But private security like me is okay."

"Off the books, of course."

"More proxy battles," he chortled.

"It's the way today's wars are fought."

There were only three photos of the girl on the phone, and in two of them she was holding a large handbag with a pampered dog sitting inside like an accessory. It was a

Russian toy terrier, which resembled a black-and-brown chihuahua except its ears and mane were fluffy. Katarina's hair was decidedly less fluffy. It was long, blonde, and expensively done. Carver was already yearning for his previously barren work schedule.

"So the largest complication is the client," he summarized.

"In more ways than one. Katarina doesn't publish a planned speaking circuit so her movements are difficult to predict. Her appearances are mostly driven by on-the-fly social media activity. But we did find mention of an important future stop in Kyiv. I don't need to remind you that Ukraine is a non-NATO country and tensions on the eastern border are ripe. The USA's mandate in the region is increasingly specific. We provide military training and economic support, but we're no longer conducting official operations on the ground. The State Department issued advisories clearing out all non-essential personnel. The embassy was relocated to Lviv in the west, and the latest thinking is to move them clear to Poland."

"We're conceding Ukraine to Russia?"

"C'est la vie. Let the powers that be worry about geopolitics. Your mandate is Katarina Litvinenko."

After seeing there was nothing else of consequence on the burner phone, Carver slipped it into his pocket. "Sounds straightforward enough, if a little far-fetched. Why is the girl so important? And how can you be sure she was the target of the bombing?"

"Because her uncle is Arkady Malkin, Russian oligarch

and right hand of the president. He's one of many corrupt businessmen currently sanctioned by the US. His fingers are in casinos, restaurants, and politics. He funded the Internet Research Agency, famous for coordinating sophisticated cyberattacks against us. He also has a hand in running the Wagner Group."

That was the mercenary outfit that took Crimea, nicknamed little green men at the time because of their non-affiliated army uniforms. In reality they were private military contractors with heavy sponsorship by the Russian state. US forces recently skirmished with them over an oil field in Syria. More notably, the Wagner Group put boots on the ground in Libya, training and supporting the Libyan National Army.

"It all comes full circle," said Carver, unsurprised. "Proxies training proxies."

"Just another facet of Russian unconventional warfare. They're brewing a perfect storm of aggression in Eastern Europe. A worsening gas war, weaponized migrants, political assassinations, and an increased troop buildup bordering Ukraine. The Kremlin is cultivating right-wing sentiment to fracture the European Union and protect their buffer states. They're constructing a renewed Iron Curtain."

"When do we start?" asked Morgan.

Very little was able to unsettle the CIA officer, but the silent approach of Carver's coworker to his doorway had a noticeable effect.

"Juliette Morgan," said Williams icily. "How much of that did you hear?"

"It's okay, Lanelle. Jules works for me, and I don't keep secrets from my team. Not anymore."

"There are national security implications at play here..."

"And there's only the two of us. You have nothing to worry about. Jules is the sole member of my security advance party, necessary to secure my arrival, collect and prep my equipment, and perform initial recon of the situation. That includes technical surveillance countermeasure sweeps of our forward-operating bases to protect your secrets."

"I'm aware of her role on your team, Vince."

"Good. Then you're aware that she needs to arrive before I do, which means the sooner you get on board with this, the sooner we can start."

Morgan leaned on the doorframe with crossed arms. Her straight brown hair curved like talons at her chin and framed a sideways smirk. Williams was markedly less amused.

"I can already see I'm going to regret this," she muttered.

"I beg to differ," countered Carver. "You give me your trust, continue being straight with me, and I'll do everything I can to deliver a win. That's what you're paying me for. That said, you're not my boss and I don't take orders. Once you hand this off, this is my show. It's the only way this works."

The CIA handler clicked her tongue. "Such is the price of deniability. Fine, we'll do it your way."

"Thank you. But I need to know the end goal here.

What do your bosses see as the ideal conclusion to Ms. Litvinenko's unofficial protection services?"

A shrug. "It's simple. Katarina is young and thinks herself invincible. She doesn't yet see reason. Your job, while keeping her alive, is to convince her there are only two outcomes in her future: she defects to the West, comes in out of the cold, so to speak, or she's eventually assassinated. The only variable is the timeline."

"The Libyans are coming after her again?"

"We've picked up chatter that indicates as much. Katarina will eventually see the light. We need the CIA in her ear when the revelation hits. Otherwise we're looking at another dead Russian dissident and who knows how much collateral damage."

2

Two days later Carver strolled into a fancy boutique hotel across from the Tiergarten. The oldest park in Berlin originated as a hunting ground and was still densely forested. A tranquil escape from the commercial City West district, Carver mostly thought it nice to see so much green that wasn't converted into a golf course.

As for the hotel, the interior design more than made up for its modest size. There were tasteful marble accents, textured walls and ceilings, and artful lighting to set the mood. It was unironically hip.

Carver was cool but stopped short of being suave. He wasn't especially accustomed to the finer things in life. He didn't style himself a real-world James Bond. Instead, Carver was a military man, pragmatic and able to make do with minimal means. And while he enjoyed relaxing with a good beer or cocktail now and then, he could do without the high society.

But as long as he was being expensed by the CIA...

The room was a complementary blend of grays and browns with an open window of beaming sunlight. A painting on the wall featured what must have been a mythical flower. Below was a basket-weave ottoman he was afraid to put weight on. He drew back the curtains and admired the skyline.

Berlin is a beautiful city without any skyscrapers, giving it an old feel amid plenty of modern construction. The Berlin TV Tower to the east stretched hundreds of meters to the sky like a giant spindle.

Carver unpacked quickly before leaving his room and knocking on the door just opposite. Morgan opened up.

"Not taking in the sights?" she asked as he entered.

"Not without my expensive camera equipment."

"We can speak freely," she assured. "The rooms are clean." She strolled to the bed and rapped an open hand on a black duffel.

Sweeping for bugs on a protection detail seemed like overkill, but Carver had learned how to deal with the CIA: never underestimate their incompetence or assume their good nature. Thoroughness was just as important to their safety as it was critical to their mission. They could not assume their arrival had gone unnoticed. From here on out, it was a good bet they would learn things the Agency hadn't prepped them for. This outlook was especially prudent given the likely involvement of Russian intelligence.

The bag contained a SIG Sauer P320 full-size handgun; an Israel Weapon Industries X95, otherwise known as the civilian version of the TAR-21 assault rifle; an integrally suppressed Maxim 9 with subsonic rounds in Glock mags; and enough ammunition to make it a party. There were also backup blades to the ones he'd checked with his luggage.

Carver zipped the bag closed. "These weapons aren't new."

"Gently used."

"Government?"

"Williams hooked me up with their Armor and Special Programs Branch. They procure weapons from clandestine sources for use by the Special Operations Group."

"I know who Armor Branch is," he said with a nod. "You pick this hotel?"

"Katya did."

Carver arched an eyebrow.

"Our principal goes by Katya on social media," Morgan explained. "It's the source of half our intel so far. She checked in last week." Morgan produced her phone and read a post. " 'So many lives lost,' she says. 'They want me to grieve but stir me to act.' It sounds like she's been keeping her head down since her close encounter in Rome."

"Smart girl."

"For all of five days, anyway. She also announced a speech tomorrow at an event run by One Europe. She's going back into the spotlight."

"Tomorrow? That doesn't give me a lot of time for recon."

"Speaking of which, you can start now. Ten minutes ago Katya live-streamed herself at the hot new Belgian Waffle bistro two blocks from here."

"She's streaming her lunch?"

"Don't get ahead of yourself. She was still waiting in line."

Carver sighed absently. "You're enjoying this, aren't you?"

Morgan grinned. "Bring me back a Duck Fat Sausage Waffle?"

"I'll do you one better. I'll share a video."

* * *

The business of close protection is many-pronged. In some cases it's as simple as a bodyguard towering over anyone in the principal's vicinity, an imposing wall of man or men performing a public show. Other times discretion is preferred, with eyes posted several paces away or even blending into the crowd. If you own the location you run access control, otherwise you're at the mercy of the environment. Professional teams mitigate this by scouting a location first and maintaining a perimeter. The customized formula for any particular client comes down to several factors, the most important being cost, threat, and autonomy.

On the surface of it, Katarina Litvinenko was a girl of means, which meant the price of protection wasn't an issue. Terrorist bombers dialed the threat to the max. This left autonomy as the notable weak link.

Katarina was a newly styled social media influencer, a visible figure by design, who was courageously standing up and speaking against the abuses of her government. Then there were the confounding factors. She was young, beautiful, and headstrong, with an outgoing nature that could be her undoing.

Carver took in the brisk air as he watched the cafe of industrial ironwork from across the street. It was the size of a spacious coffee shop, which was to say not very large, and full of well-to-do thirty-somethings in button-ups and spring dresses. Several small tables were crammed inside but the bulk of the action was on the sidewalk patio enjoying the sun as it peeked between swaths of gray.

Two personal protection operatives waited outside the door. They wore plainclothes except for black ballistic vests that read "Iris Executive Protection" in bold white letters. Carver had cut his chops in the close protection trade in Europe and had worked alongside Iris in the past. They were good at what they did and hired competent operators, mostly French and EU military.

Security companies based in France are heavily regulated and either partner with other outfits or maintain separate identities to fulfill various roles. The black limo and the driver leaning on the hood for a smoke were affiliated with Iris Transport, separate yet together. They were all here for Katarina.

Protection appeared a little light at first blush, but then that was a constant in this business. There was never a such thing as enough. More practically, if Carver were running the show he would single out a rover, often himself, to maintain overwatch from a distant location, likely across the street. His trained eyes didn't spot any such precautions, and he wondered why Katarina's security was far from adequate, given her recent close call.

He lingered across the street, leaning on a lamppost and fiddling with his phone. Sooner or later he had to move lest he appear suspicious, and an update on Katarina's feed presented the perfect opportunity. It was a snap of a waffle stack topped with crème fraiche, chocolate shavings, and apricots. The principal had secured a rare seat at an indoor table.

Carver crossed the street and made visual contact with Katarina. She sat alone with no additional PPOs in the establishment. While the line ran by her table, it started outside, and it would be some time before he advanced to her. Fortunately a separate pastry counter doubled as a takeout station and Carver had already ordered coffee in the mobile app. He unassumingly strolled past Katarina's bodyguards and stopped beside a few others waiting at the caffeine counter. A drawn-out glance at his watch confirmed he was early, which was right on time. Carver leaned his back against the counter and sighed loudly.

It was easy to watch Katarina without drawing attention. She was the only one in the bistro attempting to take a selfie with a dog in a handbag. The toy terrier was black with a scruff of tan on her snout and ears. She wore a pink leather collar with a rhinestone-encrusted bow in front and currently had a dollop of whipped cream on her nose. The poor dog attempted a serious face but couldn't help prematurely licking at the good stuff. Katarina's repeated attempts drew laughs from the surrounding patrons, of which Carver was just another face. It was an opportunity to break the ice.

Iris Security wasn't an issue. The bodyguards had glanced him over but weren't especially alert, no doubt due to Carver's lack of Libyan descent. They were hands off and their mandate was specific. Katarina was a different story.

Carver reached into a glass jar of doggie biscuits for sale, grabbed a couple, and approached the table. "May I?"

Katarina huffed in exasperation as her dog took another gulp of cream. She turned to Carver but had no time to respond before he cracked the dog treats apart and set the resulting chunks on her table.

"This is an easy trick," he explained. "I can show you if you've got a minute to spare."

He offered the dog an empty hand. She immediately sniffed for the treats that were no longer there, giving him the opportunity to pet her. Then he grabbed one of the crumbles and held it out. The dog went to snarf it up, but Carver denied access by closing his hand into a fist. She desperately sniffed at his clenched fingers.

Katarina chuckled. "I'm afraid nobody can teach Anya patience."

"It's not about teaching her patience," he replied. "It's about teaching her that you *want* patience."

He waited fifteen seconds until Anya stopped sniffing and pulled her head away.

"Good," he said, placing the treat on the table beside her. It disappeared into a miniature black hole.

Carver grabbed another treat and held it out. Once again, the dog went for it and he covered it up. Anya pulled away quicker this time.

"Good." Another treat on the table, another catastrophic celestial event.

Katarina watched wide-eyed as he repeated the technique two more times, each reflecting improvements in the dog's understanding. By the time Carver offered the fifth morsel, Anya hesitated without him needing to close his hand.

"Good," he said again, giving her the treat. "I think she's ready. You wanna do the honors?"

Katarina flashed a skeptical frown before scooping a dollop of cream with her finger and applying it to her dog. Anya eyed the next treat in solemn anticipation. Carver held his hand further away this time, but the idea was clear. Anya waited. Katarina squeezed the toy terrier against her face and beamed for the camera as she took a few shots. When they were done, Carver gave up the treat and slid the leftovers into reach too. He rubbed the dog's fluffy ear as her owner giggled in glee.

"That was amazing," said Katarina with a genuine smile.

"Nah, it was easy. She's a smart girl." One of Katarina's bodyguards had noticed the interaction and was heading over. Carver twisted a chair away from the table and pointed. "May I?"

"Ma'am?" asked the PPO, concern in his voice.

Painted nails waved him off. "He's okay, Marcel."

Carver sat as the bodyguard eyed him and backed away. So much for just being another face in the crowd.

"Don't mind him," said Katarina, noticing his gaze on

her security. "They're just looking after me." She set the bag with the dog on the floor to lean toward him. "So you train dogs?"

"Nothing like that. We just have an understanding."

She giggled again, dimples blooming under high cheekbones. Katarina was a beautiful woman, even with her hair messily prepared in a top bun behind the sunglasses on her head. Her eyes were bright and her smile infectious, like she'd managed to bottle all the optimism and excitement of youth.

It was a far cry from the trauma of just escaping a bomb blast with your life. But affability was in her file, and so far nothing was a surprise.

"You must be wondering why I have a bodyguard," she said.

"It's not hard to guess. The pink dog collar is cute, but the bow is studded with more diamonds than a Super Bowl ring."

Her expression tightened. The mention of money put her on guard. It wasn't the reaction he'd expected from the compliment so he decided to move a little faster than he'd planned. This was, as they say, business.

The trick was getting Katarina to cozy up to the CIA without announcing that he was employed to do so. The Agency had already been rebuffed in previous direct approaches. The girl didn't think she needed the government and that was fair enough, so long as an opposing government wasn't gunning for her. There were some things you couldn't do alone.

"Vince," called a woman behind the takeout counter. Carver stood and retrieved his coffee in a paper cup, leaving a few dollars for the dog treats before returning to the table.

"Vince," Katarina repeated. "It's nice to meet you. I'm —"

"Katarina Litvinenko," he finished, earning only mild surprise from her. "I confess, I know who you are. You've been in the news."

Thin lashes fluttered and she splayed her hands toward her bodyguards. "Then you know why I have to put up with this."

"It's a good cause," said Carver, "and there are people who believe in you."

Katarina may have been intelligent, but she was susceptible to flattery. She puffed her chest and sat up straighter. Her posture and long neck gave off a regal impression. "I didn't ask to be in this position, but now that I am, it feels like something I need to do."

"I understand. And to be completely forthcoming, it's the reason I'm here." Her brow tensed as he leaned in to speak at a discreet volume. "My employer sponsors dissidents fleeing their home countries, like you."

She hesitated for an invisible moment before her charming smile returned. "And who says I need sponsorship?"

"It's the opposite, in fact. We're interested in your outreach. You're a symbol of change. A success story sharing your success with others. We can help each other."

"How is that?"

He shrugged matter-of-factly. "Changing the world costs money."

"Do I look like I need money?"

"Not at all, but we both know it's better to spend someone else's than your own."

Again, Carver was surprised money was a sensitive issue to the woman. She had grown up around a lot of it, that much was clear. Less certain was how much funding she had access to after splitting away from her uncle. Carver tried another angle.

"Even harder to resolve are the logistics of moving people and getting them situated. My employer has experience in this area and possesses vital contacts throughout the European Union who can facilitate safe placement."

Any good fisherman learns to recognize a real bite from a nibble. Katarina wasn't hooked yet, but she was getting hungry. She ran her tongue along her teeth in deliberation. "You... help immigrants from my country find a home?"

"Not me, my employer. I'm just a guy talking and looking for someone to listen."

She studied him with calculating eyes, reminding Carver that appearances could be deceiving. Katarina was playing a part for the news cameras and social media feeds. It was the nature of the game, he supposed. Now he needed to uncover the nature of a young woman who had turned down the CIA.

"You still haven't told me who your employer is," she pointed out, "and I suppose that isn't by accident."

Carver graciously showed his teeth. "You're obviously a clever woman, Katarina. I can explain the priority business moguls place on privacy and the sensitivity of this line of work, but it would just be an excuse to talk to a pretty girl longer. The bottom line is we can form a unique partnership that assists dissidents escaping the new Iron Curtain."

The edges of her lips upturned. "The new Iron Curtain," she said with a wry smile. "I like that."

"Just a little line I came up with," he said with a shrug.

She sighed at her barely eaten waffle stack. It didn't offer any input. "Spending someone else's money sounds appealing, but we both know help doesn't come free."

"Isn't that the definition of charity?"

She harrumphed to show she wasn't amused. Carver knew the cover was thin. It didn't need to be solid or specific. It was merely a means to get a foot in the door.

"What does your employer want from me?" she asked.

"Just that you be open-minded and receptive to discussion. My employer is not yet convinced you can deliver on your promise."

"I never made any promises, Vince."

"I'm referring to your potential." He placed a business card on the table. It was plain white with only the number of his burner phone printed on it.

She scoffed. "I'm not here to prove I measure up."

"It's not like that. We're just observing in order to make a sound investment. Call it due diligence, and it goes both ways. I expect no less from you."

Katarina stood and hefted the blue handbag to the table. "No thanks. When an offer sounds too good to be true, it usually is." She patted Anya on the head before zipping the top shut. The dog repositioned to the roll-up window on the front. "Thanks for your help with Anya. I'll call you if I need to post more dog tricks."

"As long as you call," he said, standing politely to see her off.

Katarina Litvinenko paced away. She was a bit of a mystery. Usually an offer for backing and support would be met with optimism. Curiosity at the very least. Perhaps the girl was world weary after running away from home and being bombed. Still, while her attitude was outwardly dismissive, she hadn't hesitated to pack his business card into the pocket of the blue-patterned handbag.

Carver strolled to the window with his to-go cup and watched the security team escort her to the car. They pulled away without fanfare, and no other roving guards or cars followed.

The meeting hadn't gone perfectly, but Carver had accomplished what he set out to do. Katarina now knew his cover legend and would regard him as a familiar face. He could safely orbit her atmosphere, even nose into her affairs, whether she liked it or not. And rather than be suspicious, she would expect it.

3

The City West district is a bustling commercial sector that hosts heavy vehicle and foot traffic. It was near enough to Carver's hotel that walking greatly simplified matters. He had scoped out the neighborhood earlier in the morning and made several passes of his target, the Stilwerk building.

A long block of windowed storefronts topped by four stories of brown metal, the design complex ran to a corner of sleek rounded glass that reflected the cityscape. Part skyscraper and part expo center overhung a small corner plaza with a steady stream of visitors. By this point Carver was in stakeout mode, getting to know the ins and outs and general flow of movement in the area.

The building itself was too large and multipurposed to ever truly be considered secure. There were multiple entry points including a garage and fire escapes. There were various tenants and shopkeepers who hosted countless customers and art displays. According to Katarina's social updates, she was speaking on immigration rights at an events space on the rooftop.

Carver peeked inside the lobby, saw what he needed to know, and continued down the street grumbling. It was sixty seconds to the nearest outdoor cafe where he sat down at the table where Juliette Morgan was enjoying her tea.

"You didn't order me a coffee," he said.

"And you never got me my waffle."

"You're not still mad about that. Only hipsters wait in line for breakfast. Besides, if that Rorschach of syrup on your plate is any indication, whatever you just ate was twice as filling."

She ignored him and turned her attention to a thin newspaper she must have picked up on the street. "Can you believe this? NATO and Russian warships are playing chicken in the Black Sea."

"They're just for show. The real fight is on the ground."

"You think it will come to that? Ukrainian NLAWs against Russian armor?"

"Doesn't seem like the smart play, does it?"

He twisted in the seat to check the corner of the Stilwerk building before deciding to slide the chair to the side of the table for a better view.

"There's a joke here about spies reading newspapers in cafes," he said. "Next thing I know you're going to pass me a gun in the sports section."

Her eyes didn't rise from current events. "No, those are in the bag at my feet. You sure you don't want them?"

"I can't. Event security is a local company, not the one Katarina hired. They're using wands on all guests."

"And there's no better way in?"

He shook his head. "The locals know the venue. They probably work it every week. It's better to play by their rules until I know what we're dealing with."

As he answered, the same Iris Transport car Katarina had used the day before drove by. They watched as it pulled into the building's underground garage.

"That's my cue. Enjoy the tea, you traitor."

Carver headed back to the busy plaza. The transpo vehicle was no longer in view but he knew where the occupants were headed. The more important detail was that they weren't followed in. He took a post at a corner lamppost and kept an eye on things as he played out the next ten minutes in his head.

A beat-up red hatchback drove through the intersection and past. It caught his attention because the passenger window was cracked and the blare of auto-tuned raï music reminded Carver of his time in North Africa. Something about the occupants seemed off as the car slowed by the plaza entrance before resuming normal speed and moving on.

It wasn't until they circled the block and came back around that they truly earned Carver's suspicion. The red hatchback pulled to the curb beside a bike rack. Carver kicked off the lamppost and tailed a couple of pedestrians heading toward them on the sidewalk.

The passenger door opened and a man in a suit exited as Carver passed. Through the half open window, he could make out a bearded driver saying something in Arabic. The sun glared off the back window and obscured the figure in the back seat. Carver turned to get a better angle, but the hatchback sped off.

Carver watched in disbelief. He was no language expert, but the flavor of Arabic resembled a dialect spoken in the Benghazi area and western Egypt. While he had no luck parsing out a translation, his time in the region made him confident that these men were Libyan.

The smartly dressed businessman made for the Stilwerk entrance at a brisk pace. Carver considered going back for his weapons but there wasn't time. This man didn't look like a terrorist, but speaking Libyan Arabic was too much of a coincidence. Carver set his jaw and followed.

Pushing into the glass doors, he found the man some way ahead. The large lobby was spread out and afforded multiple paths of ingress. Signs for the charity event by One Europe funneled guests toward a corner elevator where a pair of guards searched bags and scanned guests with a handheld metal detector.

The businessman faltered at the sight of the admission checkpoint. Carver spun to a wall painting as the man looked around. He was nervous. After a moment of shuffling feet, he detoured across the room toward a rear hallway.

Carver resumed pursuit at an innocuous speed. The man was likely searching for a rear entrance but wouldn't find one. Instead of heading to the stairway or main elevator bay, however, he turned into a men's room.

Carver increased his pace. He reached the door and pulled it open a hair, putting his eye to the narrow opening just in time to catch the man in the suit dropping a pistol in the trash can. He muttered under his breath in what was definitely a North African dialect before spinning to the door.

The sudden turn gave Carver no choice but to act. Since this was a public restroom, the least suspicious option was to simply finish opening the door. He pulled it wide and stepped in, acting surprised to see the sweating man.

"Morning," said Carver as he approached the sink.

The businessman was stiff as a board, but he didn't stay that way. Despite not having used the sink, he dispensed several lengths of paper towels, wiped his hands with them, and stuffed them in the trash to ensure the hardware was out of sight.

Carver turned on the tap and washed his hands, idly glancing over at the man staring at him. Another nod before asking, "You speak English?"

The man frowned and shook his head. "No."

He started toward the door as he fiddled with his jacket. Carver moved to the paper dispenser and wiped his hands. As the man reached for the door handle, Carver said, "Hold on a second."

The man tensed and slowly faced him. Carver ripped one last paper towel away and approached the man holding it out. "Your head," he said, pointing to his own crown. "Sweat."

The man swallowed. He accepted the paper towel and dabbed perspiration from his forehead with a stiff nod. "Thank you."

"I figured you're getting ready for a job interview or something. You look nervous, you know? You should look your best."

The man nodded and gave a clipped, "Yes."

"So am I right?" Carver prodded. "What are you here for?"

The man blinked at him. Instead of speaking he shook his head.

"No need to sell yourself short. Your English comprehension is pretty good, am I right?"

Still no reply.

"Yeah," he continued, "I bet I am. That will make it easier for you to understand your big problem."

Carver grinned helpfully at the man, who now furrowed his brow, swallowed, and asked, "Problem?"

"Yeah. You see, you just dumped your gun in the trash can, but you're going to need it in about two seconds."

The man in the suit watched him icily for a second and a half before he scowled and lunged. The attack was telegraphed and wild, the act of a man more desperate than prepared. The Delta training kicked in and Carver easily redirected his momentum into the nearest stall. Instead of a hard bounce, the sturdy door slammed open and the man tumbled inside and sprawled sideways onto the toilet.

"Are you Libyan?" Carver asked. *"Shen tebbee?"*

The man's eyes widened and he tried to get up. Carver planted a hand on his neck to hold him down. He reached into his jacket. Carver grabbed the arm and landed a couple of punches to his cheek to soften him up. The man covered his face with one arm while the other continued digging into his jacket.

Carver tightened his grip around the man's throat while

his other hand fought against the grab. "Let go..." he urged.

The man refused to submit. Though he had already dumped the gun, Carver couldn't risk him grabbing another weapon. He kept the pressure on both the neck and the arm, putting his full weight against the man splayed on the toilet. No longer taking punches, the Libyan attempted strikes of his own. Carver broke the man's neck to end it.

Slowly, he withdrew the empty hand from the jacket and shifted the dead man on the toilet. He closed the stall door for privacy and opened the jacket.

The man wore a makeshift bomb vest. This was it, just like the incident in Rome. A Libyan terrorist was targeting Katarina Litvinenko. Though he was alone at the event, two fellow plotters had dropped him off. There was a cell in Berlin. Carver wasn't sure of the timeline, but he guessed the terrorists would know something had gone wrong with their plan in about twenty or thirty minutes.

The bomb material appeared to be notorious Libyan Semtex, invisible to metal detectors. It was a light load that wouldn't be noticed by its bulk, not meant to cause structural damage to the building but to inflict casualties. This was an assassination disguised as a terrorist plot.

Carver pulled the detonator but left the bomb in place. No one knew where it was. He exited the stall to toss it in the can before returning and shutting the door. He checked the man's pockets which had no other weapons or genuine identification. He did find a lanyard with a badge to the One Europe event.

Carver used the burner to snap photos of the terrorist, a

wide shot and a close-up of his face. He would send it to Williams later via the discreet web platform run by the CIA. For now, his operating orders were to maintain distance and deniability. The United States officially had no assets on this. Besides, he was now on a ticking clock and the Agency would only slow him down. Operatives of Detachment-Delta were encouraged to make decisions in the field and this situation was no different. In fact, it presented an opportunity.

The badge had the name Mark Watson with no matching picture. Carver slid it around his neck. After some adjustments to the dead man's sitting pose, he exited the stall, closed the door, and used his plastic room key as a screwdriver to lock it from the outside. He washed his hands again and used a paper towel to wipe down the faucet, dispenser, and stall and bathroom doors before strolling back into the lobby, refreshed.

4

The security guard with the wand caught Carver red-handed with a belt buckle and a watch. There was no pat down, which meant the bomb vest would have easily walked in. He was ushered to the elevator which was then directed to the fifth floor.

On the way up, alone, Carver tested the buttons for the other floors. They didn't remain lit as he depressed them. There were certain to be similar obstacles at other entrances, whether electronic or kinetic. Security had locked down access to the event.

The doors opened at the top floor to a makeshift lobby. The main hall was cordoned off and greeters funneled guests toward a separate stairwell and elevator that only went to the roof. Carver took the stairs so he could study the layout. As expected, security guards prevented cross-traffic with the rest of the floor. It wasn't that they were impossible to force past, but doing so would blow any semblance of disguise at the event.

Upstairs, a modest glass-walled room housed a bar and lounge area. An entire wall opened up to the true destination outdoors. The terrace was a long stretch of white tables dotting a wooden deck. A glass wall offered an unobstructed view of the skyline and greenery of the distant Tiergarten. Scaffolding supported crisscrossed string lights intersecting a light-blue sky, with speakers on the columns delivering the address from the stage at the far end. The events space was swanky, stunning, and cozy, and surely hosted a number of weddings every year.

The party was jammed. The inside was crowded, the bar packed, and all the tables and chairs taken. Carver couldn't immediately locate Katarina but figured his first order of business should be fitting in. He lingered at the bar, keeping his eyes on everything and nothing at all, and ordered an old fashioned with rye.

Somewhere in the middle of that process, Katarina Litvinenko took the stage to mixed applause. Some recognized her recent celebrity status, though it was obvious that many in the audience weren't sure who she was.

Katarina's speech was a string of platitudes one would expect at an event like this. Everyone was part of the same human race, Europe was stronger together, yada yada yada. She spoke of a collective cooperative spirit more than she mentioned immigration reform, but she did remind everyone of her personal story.

Katarina had traveled to Beijing to represent her country in the Olympics. She'd wanted to make them proud despite her reservations. Then the fateful day came when her idealistic platitudes didn't go over so well with the motherland. In a pre-commencement profile, Katarina shared her distaste for fighting and the buildup of troops on the border with Ukraine. Russian authorities demanded she quit talking to the press, cease her involvement in the games, and return home immediately.

She made other plans.

The young woman felt alone in a wide world. She characterized the events as happening *to* her, as decisions made without her consent, but she was careful never to refer to herself as a victim. Self exile wasn't a choice because it was the only humanitarian option, yet she owned it as part of her personal mission. And, with the support of the community, she was no longer weak, no longer alone. It was a clever analogy to Europe as a whole.

She winked at the audience and walked offstage blowing kisses amid thunderous applause. If Carver hadn't watched it himself, he would have assumed it had been quite a show.

He mingled on the deck, still not quite sure what the girl brought to the table. Was she just a symbol, a face on a movement? Was it enough to publicly denounce Russia and advocate for human rights? This was important to somebody, otherwise there wouldn't be a dead Libyan wearing a bomb downstairs.

Italy was one thing. Many Africans crossed there into the EU. These terrorists were taking it a step further and tracking her across the continent. It barely made sense.

Then again, bombing every party she hosted might be message enough. Moscow was many things, but subtle wasn't one of them.

Carver advanced through the crowd, passing a long table where a staff member lit a series of candles on an elongated birthday cake. He zeroed in on Katarina doing a victory lap with an Iris PPO in tow. He approached, cocktail in hand, but an older gentleman got there first.

"Inspired stuff!" boomed the obvious Englishman. "I have to say, Ms. Litvinenko, you almost make me wish we didn't leave the EU. *Almost.*"

He said it in jest and the joke landed. Katarina laughed heartily and joined the man at his standing table with a handshake. "I would like to think my words transcend bodies of government and trade organizations, Mister... ?"

"Mathers, miss. Henry Mathers. And right you are. Issues of currency should be left to the state, but you speak of a humanitarian crisis."

A bodyguard posted behind her with clasped hands, eyes roving over the immediate vicinity. He wasn't one of the ones at yesterday's breakfast, indicating she rotated teams or had stepped up protection today. The PPO's trained gaze spotted Carver's approach.

"Hearts will never be at rest while they live in fear," explained Katarina.

"And borders?" asked Mathers.

"It isn't the borders I wish to embolden."

He chuckled and held a glass of wine up in salute.

Carver leaned an elbow on the table. "Sounds nice, but what's the value of words without action?"

Mathers responded to the challenge with raised eyebrows before flicking his gaze to Katarina. Her cheek twitched at the sight of him. "Greater than the value of action without words." She glanced at his badge and showed her teeth. "Mark, is it? What brings you here today?"

Carver flipped the badge around to hide the name even though it was too late. "Protecting an investment," he answered opaquely.

"I hope you mean an investment in our future. And that is what words bring forth. Words come *before* action, because action has no moral basis without them."

Mathers nearly choked on a gulp of wine before mirthfully slapping Carver on the shoulder. "She's got you there, man. Quick-witted, she is." He took a step away from the table to admire her. "An inspiration, wouldn't you say?"

"She inspired me to get waffles the other day," he said flatly, putting the old fashioned to his lips.

Katarina's eyes narrowed to slits.

"I personally approve of what she's doing," disagreed Mathers, oblivious of the subtext. "Ms. Litvinenko is a very stirring figure, even more so up close. If anyone can get the world's attention, it's her."

"Really?" challenged Carver. "Because I see a lot of talking but not a lot of doing. Are high-minded ideals your sole contribution while leaving the dangerous work to everyone else?"

"Come now. Go easy on her. She's just a girl."

The Russian dissident's face went red. "I am NOT just a girl," she snapped. "And I'll have you know, while you look down on me as some pretty, helpless thing to pity, I have nothing but scorn for people like you. Only interested in the appearance of caring, and only as long as it protects your wallet!"

She did a one-eighty and stormed away, earning the men a stern glance from her bodyguard before he followed. Mathers blinked in stupefied speechlessness, gaze flicking to Carver for support.

"Don't look at me," he said. "You were the one defending her."

They watched as Katarina disappeared through a door beside the stage.

"Yes, well," rejoined Mathers, mustering his dignity, "you know how temperamental Russians can be..."

Carver scowled, upset at himself for pushing her so hard. Katarina could be hotheaded, it seemed. She was young and impulsive. The combination of guilt and the Englishman's blathering nearly prevented him from noticing a man wearing a gray hoodie at the stage door. His back was to the crowd, hands in pockets, as he spoke to event security. He was following Katarina and, surprisingly, was allowed access to the exit.

Carver stepped away from the table as the door shut behind the mystery man. This was the end of the terrace opposite the bar. It made sense for there to be a rear exit. His thoughts battled between protecting Katarina and preserving his cover.

He could go back down the stairs the way he'd come. There was a good chance Katarina was heading to the same place, or at least to the back hallway. There was nowhere else to go on the roof. But then he'd be faced with the same problem of having to bypass the event's access control. And there was only one guard at this door as opposed to two below.

Carver grabbed the Englishman's cocktail napkin and stepped away without a word, collecting others on every table he passed on the way to the birthday table. He discreetly snatched the disposable lighter and moved to a metal garbage can along the glass balcony wall. With his back to the guests, he lit the bundle of napkins on fire before dumping the evidence into the bin. He strolled to the stage before risking a backward glance and was rewarded by the sight of smoke.

"What's that smell?" someone asked.

Carver backed toward the security guard.

"Fire!" someone screamed.

A wave of panic spread from the pinpoint, and the guard from the back door slapped a strong hand on Carver's shoulder. "Excuse me, sir." He pushed him to the side and hurried to the garbage can as flames licked out from its opening.

"You're excused," Carver muttered under his breath, slipping through the back door while all eyes focused on the fire.

He was in a small green room, just a table and chairs and water dispenser. It connected to a back hallway that Carver peeked around. They had gotten too much of a head start.

Rather than head towards the entrance, Carver found a stairway in the back. He quietly descended and listened at the door. When he didn't hear anything, he went inside. He was in what looked like office space, flush with windowed doors and walls. Katarina's voice winded through the hallway. She was arguing with someone.

Carver moved with purpose, standing back and slicing the pie as he breached the next corner. An Iris Executive Protection officer turned out of sight ahead. The office space joined the rest of the building, a sprawling design hub with cement floors and open lofts. This was past the purview of event security.

He hurried forward as Katarina's voice spiked. She spoke Russian and grew more heated. He increased his pace and was ambushed by the gray hoodie in his peripheral vision.

Carver rolled away, avoiding a tackle but getting grabbed from behind. He threw an elbow that connected with a grunt. The man reached for a choke and Carver ran backward into the wall. The grip loosened and a fist pounded the back of his head. Carver disengaged, dizzy, and spun around with a punch. The man with the beard blocked it. Carver batted the arm down and raised his fist again. Both men froze.

"Nick?" said Carver in shock.

Shaw was ready to go with his own punch, but he too held back. "Vince? What the hell are you doing here?"

5

Shaw glanced up and down the hall before lowering his fists. The operative was many things. A former Navy SEAL. A boy from the Kentucky backwoods with a thick mahogany beard. He was gruff, abrasive, and, most important of all, a damn good friend.

Carver's threatening posture relaxed. He grabbed Shaw with a quick rap on the back before pulling away. "You're working for Iris again."

"That's exactly what I'm doing, brother. The question is, what are you doing?"

Carver pinched his nose. He'd gotten into trouble by keeping secrets from Shaw before. He didn't want to risk his friendship again. The difference this go around was that Shaw wasn't part of the operation. Not the CIA side of things, anyway.

But if he was on Katarina's security detail, he was inextricably involved. Carver wondered whether that little personnel detail had anything to do with Williams volunteering him for the job in the first place.

"I'm on another op," he admitted. "National security and all that."

"No shit? That little venture of yours working out?"

"I guess that depends on what happens with Katarina. Were you around for the bombing in Rome?"

He shook his head. "Negative. The principal didn't enlist close protection until after that incident. We've been with her for a week."

Carver couldn't help but smile. "Roving, huh?"

"Just like you, Vince. Working the job from a distance."

"Didn't see you at brunch yesterday."

Shaw practically hissed. "You were there too? We were lucky she had anyone at all. She tried to sneak out. But I only go rover at planned events like this. Though, I have to say, all these visits of yours begs the question. What does the Agency want with Katya?"

Carver pulled out his phone and brought up the picture of the terrorist on the toilet. "You know this guy?"

Shaw frowned at the sight of the dead man. "This your work?"

"Not exactly my magnum opus. The Libyans are determined to finish what they started in Rome. This guy's strapped with explosives and I'm wearing his pass to the party. You haven't seen him before?"

Shaw shook his head. "Can't say that I have."

"Two members of his cell dropped him off before driving away. They're still in town."

"If this is still an active threat, I need to warn my principal."

"Just keep me out of this side of things. I don't want to move too fast with her."

Shaw pulled a radio to his chin. "P One this is Team Leader, how status?"

The reply came after a few seconds. "This is P One. Principal is still on the phone. We're holding at the top of the garage elevator."

"P Car, how status?"

"P Car is running and ready. Area is clear."

"Copy that. All teams, wait on my go."

The teams echoed their affirmatives as Shaw slipped the radio back on his belt.

"Keep a lookout for a beat-up red hatchback," Carver added.

"Will do, but it was probably a junker."

Carver nodded as he studied his friend. It was odd seeing him without the backwards cap and sunglasses, but those weren't the only missing items. Shaw was only equipped with a pistol.

"You don't have heavy hardware for this job?" asked Carver. "Isn't that a little unprepared against terrorists?"

His buddy twisted his lips. "The principal isn't worried about bombers. We were hired primarily to protect her from spies. Sound like anybody you know?"

Carver's brow furrowed.

"She thinks she's in danger of being kidnapped and extradited. You know anything about that, Vince?"

"I'm only here to keep her safe and convince her to come in on her own. She's probably worried about her Russian uncle. Has she mentioned Arkady Malkin?"

"I know who he is, but she hasn't been very forthcoming

on that front." Shaw chewed his lip. "American intel says he's involved?"

"You can follow the dominoes from Malkin to the Wagner Group to the Libyans. Just keep my involvement need-to-know."

"Copy that, Spy Man. The intel's appreciated so I'll return the favor. We're on a train to Warsaw in the morning. Only staying a night and then it's on to Kyiv, I think. I don't know more than that. Katya isn't one for planning."

"Can you keep her safe?"

"Brother," he said with a self-assured smile, "what could possibly go wrong?"

As if the statement was a challenge to fate, the building's fire alarm went off. Harsh buzzing grated their ears and discordant red lights strobed. They locked eyes for a millisecond before snapping into action and hurrying down the hall. Shaw issued commands on his radio, and after a few bends they rejoined the security detail. Katarina's concern was evident on her face, as was her surprise at seeing Carver again. It would be difficult to put that cat back in the bag. It was the opposite for Anya. The terrier ducked inside Katarina's handbag, eyes wide with concern at the braying alarm.

"I don't like being followed," said Katarina.

"He warned us of a threat, ma'am," interjected Shaw. "We need to evacuate. Hanz, take the lead down the stairs."

With pistols drawn, they marched down the stairwell as a unit. Carver felt useless without a weapon. An incoming text gave him something to do, and he read the message from Morgan.

"Juliette's outside," he told his friend. "The police have the building surrounded. There's been a bomb threat."

Between rounding each flight of stairs and the alarm and the news, Katarina bobbled like a boxer on the ropes. She welcomed the guiding hand of her PPO and quietly let the tide take her. If only all clients were as cooperative.

They burst out into the elevator bay on the ground floor where a police officer blocked the exit to the garage. The security team holstered their weapons and funneled into the main lobby with everyone else. The crowd thickened and the scene through the exterior windows was just as hectic.

"The *Landespolizei* have this place locked down," said Shaw.

If the authorities were already here, they must have triggered the alarm to evacuate the building. A large dark-blue Survivor R blocked the middle of the street. The armored vehicle had scores of *polizei* around it directing foot traffic and vetting evacuees on the way out. Some of them checked IDs against event badges, which was a problem.

Carver slipped his badge into his jacket and grabbed Katarina's elbow. "Let's get you outside, ma'am," he said with an authoritative boom. Shaw snorted as the crew marched outside.

Carver headed to a police officer of his choice, a young guy who looked too green to deal with any real threat. Luckily he seemed to know who Katarina was. He nodded the team through as the crowd grew more massive and unmanageable.

"There," announced Shaw, pointing down the block.

Their driver had managed to escape the cordon by moving as soon as the alarm triggered. Once the foot team was past the first line of police, they were as good as free. They rushed to the vehicle.

Katarina, still held close, gave Carver a sideways glance. "Charity work, huh?"

He stopped outside her black car and shrugged. "I told you, I'm protecting an investment."

She didn't get a chance to respond as the Iris Executive Protection team secured her inside the vehicle. Shaw lingered by the open passenger door. "I trust you can manage from here."

Carver saluted as Shaw loaded up and the team sped away.

6

The river Spree bisects Berlin from east to west. It runs along the north boundary of the Tiergarten and right past the modern glass and steel *Berlin Hauptbahnhof*, otherwise known as Berlin Central Station.

The overcast sky changed the character of the city. The stifled sun injected tension into the crisp air, a kind of battle fought out of sight but felt on your skin. Yet that ever-present anxious tickle was no match for the excitement of a new trip. Katarina Litvinenko was going to Poland today, and she wasn't going alone.

A team of four Iris Executive Protection officers was at her side. Carver and Morgan too, trailing some ways behind. They made up the knowns. The open question was who else would be in tow, and Carver thought he had an idea. Katarina was concerned about being kidnapped, but twice she'd narrowly escaped bombs. He could only hope she was taking the threat seriously now.

"Can you believe it?" fumed Morgan as they strolled along the river walkway. "Frank says I'm not committed to being a mother. This is the man whose idea of a balanced dinner is McDonald's with orange soda."

"Don't knock it till you try it," said Carver with a grin.

"I have tried it, Vince. Three days a week. I get sick just thinking about it."

He was used to Morgan bitching about her husband. It was a sort of game for them to pick him apart before putting him and her relationship back together, but the vitriol was more forceful these days. Kids getting older, work moving into international arenas... Change is a constant wildcard in life. It can ameliorate or aggravate. Just about the only constant is the help you get from the people around you. And listening was Carver's contribution.

They started up the riverside ramp to street level.

"This work," said Carver, "it's more demanding when we're called upon, and for good reason. Everything else is our time. Didn't Frank appreciate the last two months of R and R?"

Morgan's elongated sigh put the answer into question. But her lips twitched, like the sun fighting to peek through the pall, not fully formed but hopeful. "The kids loved it. I can tell you that much."

"That's all that matters then, Jules."

She snorted. "Unfortunately, that's not how the real world works, and you of all people aren't one to believe in such platitudes. Frank's opinion and satisfaction are a huge part of the equation. Family can't live in a house divided."

Carver grinned. "You get that line from your new marriage counselor?"

"He's the worst. You know he actually gave me homework?"

"Brushing up on the Pythagorean theorem?"

"No, it's much more patronizing than that. Since I was a Green Beret, he told me to think of my marriage as an operation. He asked me to come up with a mission statement of how I would save the relationship."

"Yikes."

"He's trying the philosophical approach. You know, a whole lot of talking about ideas without mentioning the problems. Frank likes it because it keeps the focus off his screwups."

"If you need someone to be more direct, I can talk to him for you."

"Vince, no offense, but the last fucking thing I need is you involving yourself in my personal life. You haven't met a problem you didn't want to punch."

"That's not true," he laughed. "I shoot them too."

They crested the incline below the glass towers of Berlin Central Station. A large plaza stretched before them. Dozens of groups crisscrossed in and out of the impressive structure, its clean lines a testament to the efficiency of the rail.

They entered at ground level. Shops lined the walls past an information booth.

"Look," said Carver, pointing to a McDonald's. "Vitamin C."

Morgan punched his arm and headed to the escalators. It took Carver a few seconds to scan the signage printed in German and English. The lower levels led to underground platforms, but their destination was Platform 11 up top.

Two flights later found them beside a picturesque rail beneath a curved glass dome.

Carver's vigilance didn't only take in the sights. Travelers filled the platforms, and he did his best to scan each and every one. Security was present but sparse, which was more or less standard at these Euro stations.

They watched Katarina and her escort load onto the train first. The BWE traveled to Warsaw in under six hours. The Polish rail operator cars were white with a horizontal blue line. The six coach cars were headed by an aging pink locomotive. While it was impossible to study every passenger boarding the train, he watched for anything out of the ordinary, remaining on the platform for another ten minutes.

Satisfied, he and Morgan strolled into a separate car on the same train. Rows of blue upholstered seats paired on either side of the central aisle. Their car wasn't first class so they didn't have immediate eyes on their charge, but that problem could be solved once the trip was underway.

Morgan set her computer on her lap while Carver watched the train car's occupants as they carried luggage aboard. It only took a minute to be interrupted by a troubling grunt.

"The One Europe coordinator got back to me," announced Morgan after checking her email. "Yesterday's event sold out last week."

Carver frowned. "Why is that relevant?"

"Because the event badge you pulled from your boy on the toilet wasn't a forgery. The terrorists acquired a legitimate ticket." She shrugged. "Easy enough with a small donation and some lead time."

His eyes narrowed. "At least a week's lead time if they purchased admission. But how is that possible if Katarina only announced her speech three days ago?"

Morgan nodded along. "It could mean Mark Watson is a real guy who had his ticket stolen. I did a quick search for him but couldn't zero in on anybody specific, and I don't know how much more I can get without access to a privileged government database."

"Or dedicated legwork."

The boarding process had a quick turnaround and the train headed out with little fanfare. The carriage itself was older but charming, and their pace not especially fast but steady. Carver looked out the window as the glass ceiling disappeared and the city of Berlin moved on a reel.

"I think we need to roll with the punches on this one," he said. "Keep moving. We can't get sidetracked with Mark Watson, even if it may end up providing a valuable lead. Why don't you pass the information to our case officer and see what she can dig up? Maybe we get lucky."

The online go-between they had access to was a prototype CIA messenger. It allowed the sending of encrypted drops of data back and forth, but the exchange was indirect. Even if the messages were uncovered and decoded, they couldn't be linked to the CIA.

Carver continued watching the window. His slate eyes were a reflection of the burgeoning clouds, but they brightened when he spotted the parked car half a block from the train station.

"We have a problem," he said.

Morgan moved to the window and followed his pointed finger. "Red hatchback. That's the car the Libyans used. That's not long-term parking."

"Nope. It's unattended and the windows are down. How much do you want to bet the keys are sitting on the dash?"

She began typing a message. "They're dumping the car."

"Which means they don't plan on coming back. A little ominous when you're dealing with suicide bombers."

She took a moment to finish her message before clicking it away. "Maybe our friends can recover it in time. Tell us something we don't know about these guys."

Carver didn't bother shooting down the idea. A lead wasn't much good if the Libyans were coming to them.

Morgan noticed the concern painted on his face. "We don't know that they're on the same train."

"We don't have proof that they are or they aren't."

"There are twelve other trains to Warsaw today."

He grunted dismissively. "They already ditched the car. You don't do that in a public place like this unless you're on the move."

"It could be misdirection. Dump the car at the nearest train station. Give the authorities a million places to look."

"It's awfully coincidental. I doubt that car's been sitting unnoticed since their failed attempt yesterday. It was dumped today."

They both when silent as they pondered the point.

"Okay," she conceded. "There were a few trains that left

before ours. Maybe they took an earlier train."

He nodded. "What I'm trying to work out is why? Katarina doesn't have a public engagement in Warsaw. The Libyans couldn't have followed us. We walked through the park and along the Spree. They must have already been parked."

Morgan chewed her lip. "We're not sure their destination is Warsaw. Maybe they know about Kyiv."

He grunted again. Both Williams and Shaw had mentioned the capital of Ukraine. It was certainly possible that the terrorists had keyed on the same hints. This explained why Katarina kept her schedule close to the vest. But Shaw was on the inside, and the CIA had plenty of clandestine methods to garner information. If the Libyans knew her destination before it was announced, it meant they had an alternate source of intelligence.

That was a problem.

The good news was the terrorists had no cause to suspect American agents were in play. The *polizei* hadn't released details regarding the foiled bombing. With their show of force in the streets yesterday, it was easy to assume they uncovered the plot on their own. The only witness to Carver's involvement was a dead terrorist. That saving grace preserved room for him to continue operating covertly.

That said, the more he interacted with Katarina and remained in her atmosphere, the more likely anyone following would eventually notice him. He was a big American who didn't speak the local language and had special forces written all over him.

Everything is secret until it isn't. The trick isn't to remain hidden forever, it's to take decisive action before the other guys do.

"Keep an eye out."

Carver grabbed the backpack and headed into a private bathroom. He equipped himself with a couple of Glock mags and slipped the Maxim 9 holster under his jacket. The built-in suppression didn't render the weapon completely silent—that was impossible. However, combined with the subsonic ammunition, its report was a sharp clacking of metal rather than an ear-drumming explosive discharge. It wasn't perfect but it was as good as it got.

He returned to the train car, dropped the bag with Morgan, and went to do a little recon.

7

As theirs was the second-to-last train car, Carver decided to start at the back. Standing at the rear door's window, he had a full view of every single passenger in the last car. All the seats were forward facing and the bathroom was unoccupied.

He was searching for the two men he'd seen in the red hatchback. While the driver's face wasn't cemented in his mind, he did get a decent glance at him. The man in the back seat was a different story. Carver could only say he was vaguely Egyptian maybe, just like his cohorts.

Libya is ninety-seven percent Arab and Muslim. Of course, the majority of males fitting the description on this train were just like everybody else. They had a family, a job, and good intentions. Carver was banking on the fact that, if he ran into the terrorists, he would know them by sight.

The rear car was clear and everybody aboard his had already been scrutinized. Carver advanced at a casual pace, taking in the Spree outside the window and slowly passing each guest before sliding open the glass door at the front of his car. He proceeded through the twist and entered the next door.

This was a compartment car and appeared older. The thin hallway ran along the left side of the train. Each compartment was a cluster of six faded green-and-yellow-print seats, three facing forward and three facing back. Even though the cabins were sealed, they weren't private. The sliding glass doors didn't lock, and they offered a clear view of the odd assortments of passengers, some in familiar groups and others with complete strangers.

Carver smiled politely as he turned to each of the passengers, gray eyes never lingering more than a fraction of a second, always passing over the view of the city outside. Blue curtains were drawn over one of the compartments. This could mean anything from its occupants being up to no good to them simply desiring a little privacy and rest. Carver made a mental note of the location and moved ahead.

The next car was the same. More compartments and no suspects, only this time there were two cabins he couldn't see inside. A man approached in the walkway holding a chocolate bar. Carver squeezed against the window to let him pass. The man opened one of the curtained doors and was greeted by his wife and young sons excited for candy.

Not bad. Four out of six passenger cars had been searched and there were only two questionable compartments.

Passing through the next set of doors, Carver found himself in the restaurant car. Full-service tables lined the windows, four-seaters along the left side and two-seaters on the right. The chairs were bright red and had paper covers on the headrests with a message. Judging by the extreme application of accent marks, he assumed it was Polish. Taking up the far corner of the train car was a small rounded bar. The restaurant was newer and brighter than the previous cars, and passengers were already trickling in for a meal.

On his immediate right, a woman in her fifties sat alone with a bowl of soup and a paperback with the word Girl on the cover. In the center of the car was one of the Iris Executive Protection officers. He sat on a four-top while one of his coworkers spoke to the service attendant behind the bar. At the final small table furthest from him, a man in slacks and a polo waited for his food. He seemed innocent enough, yet somehow familiar.

The driver of the hatchback had a bushy black beard while this man's was neatly trimmed to his chin. Aside from that and the nicer clothes, his appearance was remarkably similar. It was possible the man shaved as a precaution in the wake of a high-profile failure. Carver would need to get a closer look to be sure.

He strolled down the center aisle with the intention of stopping at the bar for a look at the menu. The plan was perfect until it made contact with the enemy.

"Excuse me," came the voice of the seated close protection officer.

Carver avoided eye contact and walked past the man.

"One moment!" insisted the man in a French accent. He hopped to his feet and the bottom of his seat retracted to its folded position with a thud.

Carver sighed and made a half turn so he could look both ways with a swivel of his head.

"I know you," said the CPO. He was the same guy from the first day in Berlin. Strong jaw but small forehead, black hair gelled forward. The man squinted and gave a single smug nod. "You were at the waffle cafe. I never forget a face."

"Good for you... Marcel, is it?" The man's cheek twitched and Carver smiled. "I never forget a name."

Marcel blinked calmly in return. "Touché. It is curious, no, to see you on this train? What are you doing?"

"I'm on my way to Poland, Marcel. What about you?"

"Cut the bullshit!" he snapped. The word sounded funny in his French accent.

The stern voice drew the attention of the car's occupants, and a glance towards the head of the car confirmed his prime suspect was staring right at him. Carver took a step toward the CPO and lowered his voice in an attempt at cooler heads.

"Listen, Ms. Litvinenko and I are discussing business. I was at the terrace yesterday too, though I didn't run into you?"

The question was meant to put Marcel on the defensive, make him explain himself, but he steamrolled past it. "What kind of business?"

The man at the head of the car quietly took to his feet and carried his briefcase to the far door. Carver muttered under his breath and moved to follow.

"Wait a minute," demanded Marcel, clamping a hand on

his shoulder.

Carver shot back a fierce scowl. "Your job is to protect your principal, not stop me from going to the bar in a public restaurant car."

Marcel narrowed hard eyes. "Tell me my job. One more time. Tell me."

"Slow your roll, boys!" called Shaw, entering from the first-class car ahead. Carver's suspect disappeared behind while his friend wearing military fatigues approached. "If you two are gonna fight, at least wait till we place bets." He backhanded the shoulder of his coworker at the bar. "What do you say, Hanz, Marcel with the KO?"

Hanz grinned. "Just like Lyon." The man did a mean Schwarzenegger impression. He was built like him too.

"Lyon?" snorted Shaw. "Not a chance. The Belgian was half his size. No, I'll give you three to one that Vince takes him."

Marcel's face scrunched, unamused. "You know this guy? You vouch for him?"

"Well now, knowing and vouching are two different things. But I do know him, and I advise you to remove your hand from his shoulder if you intend to keep it."

Marcel thought it over a second before doing as he was told. "He's following us," he glumly explained.

"Yes he is. He's the one who tipped us off about the threat yesterday."

"Okay, but what's he doing here?"

Shaw stopped, dramatically crossed his arms over his chest, and sized Carver up. "Yeah, Vince, what *are* you doing here?"

Carver impatiently blew air through his lips. "Does this whole production usually make an impression on people?"

Shaw's beard tweaked with his smirk. "Can't rightly say. People are usually smart enough not to follow us." Hanz chuckled in the background.

"Just give me a second, will you? I'm not interested in Katarina right now."

Carver brushed past Shaw and Hanz, the latter being the more difficult maneuver due to mass, and marched to the head of the car. Marcel's mumbled complaints faded into the drone of the train on the rails. The next car was the final one to search, and it was first class. Full of six-seat compartments as well, but the seats were bright blue, with more cushion, more space, and larger tables. Carver bit down when he encountered a hallway that was empty except for Katarina exiting her compartment.

He hurried over, scanning the cabins on the way. First-class tickets weren't much more expensive in the scheme of things so the seats were packed.

"Where did the guy go?" Carver asked.

Katarina's brow furrowed. "Which guy?"

"A man with a briefcase. He just walked in."

She twirled, looked up and down the car, and shrugged. The last Iris bodyguard remained seated inside her compartment with the dog. Anya barked once upon seeing Carver. She crawled out of her bag and took residence on her owner's vacant seat.

"Really, Vince, I told you I wasn't interested." Katarina

put a firm finger on his chest. "You should respect when a lady says no."

Shaw waited by the open door between cars, watching the exchange. Carver noticed that, despite the principal's objections, she hadn't removed her finger from his chest. He sighed and backed against the window so she could pass. He continued down the rest of the car to check the other compartments. Each was more than half full, none were blocked by curtains, and none of the passengers were his suspect. The glass door at the head of the car offered a clear view of the attached locomotive. Even if the door hadn't been locked, there was no entry into the locomotive's rear end. It was impossible to continue.

He was halfway into a frown when the bathroom door at the opposite end of the car creaked open. The man with the briefcase stepped out, all eyes on him like he had floppy ears and had just been pulled from a magician's hat. The man's stringy eyebrows were familiar. He swallowed uncomfortably and tried to squeeze past Shaw to return to the restaurant.

Carver rushed over and swooped past Katarina. Once his body was between them, he focused on the man.

"Who are you?" he demanded. "What do you have in there?"

The man had failed to dance past Shaw and shielded himself with his briefcase. "What is this?"

Katarina rolled her eyes and disappeared into the bathroom. Carver yanked the briefcase away and opened it. A sheath of papers seemed to be... banking documents.

There were no weapons or bomb components. The slimline case had no room for false bottoms.

"Were you driving a red hatchback in Berlin?" asked Carver. He immediately realized his mistake in not being authoritative enough.

The man straightened. "I have a driver," he said indignantly.

"What's your business in Berlin?"

"I don't need to answer that." The man held out a waiting hand for his briefcase.

Carver skimmed the contents one last time before folding it closed and handing it over. As the man attempted to organize the papers, Carver patted at his slacks. It was easy to tell by sight alone that there was nothing under the polo.

"Excuse me, sir. What do you think you're doing?"

Shaw eyed him with a wary smile that only tightened as Carver failed to find anything.

The bathroom.

Carver turned and rapped on the door. "Katarina."

The sound of running water stopped. "You don't quit, do you?"

"Katarina, this is serious. Open up."

"What? Why?"

"You might be in danger."

Shaw watched the door and the man, unsure what to think.

"Katarina," said Carver. "Just trust me and—"

The door folded open. Carver pushed in. It was only

slightly more spacious than an airplane bathroom, maybe enough for one and a half people. That was average people, anyway. Carver was a large man and his presence had Katarina cowering around him. He checked the sink, the toilet, and the counter. The top of the window was open and it smelled like someone had been smoking.

"Can you let me out please?" she asked.

He grunted and stepped out. The man was already heading back into the next car for his meal. Shaw chewed his lip without comment. Carver went back into the bathroom to finish searching it. Every second vastly decreased the chances of finding a bomb.

"Win some, lose some, Vince," muttered Shaw. He directed Katarina into the restaurant car and held Carver's eye an extended moment before following.

Carver took a breath. He was sure he'd seen the man before. It had to be him who was driving the hatchback. While he wouldn't bet his life on it, it was damn well worth being embarrassed over.

Except the man seemed to check out. He didn't have the beard. He didn't have a bomb. His English was flawless. Carver stood alone in the hallway and ran through the possibilities. He did another sweep of the bathroom, peeking out the window at the fast-moving countryside. He then retraced his steps along the first-class car. He scrutinized every passenger and every bag through the glass doors.

Another point against him was that there was no second man. Not in this car, not on this train. Once again at the rear of the locomotive, Carver sighed and leaned against the window.

Shaw was never gonna let him hear the end of this.

There was nothing to do but suck it up and remain vigilant, which was now easier said than done. Carver had overplayed his hand. Katarina was already suspicious about his cover legend—now the possible suspect knew to watch out for him as well.

If anything, those two facts meant he could operate in the open without all the pretext. There'd be *some* pretext, of course. He couldn't go blabbing about the CIA. But if he had to be public about keeping an eye out for terrorists, so be it.

8

Carver stepped into the restaurant car with the grace of someone stepping in dog shit. What had been a lively conversation went silent. He flashed a conciliatory grimace as the man with the briefcase shied into the wall at his table. The Iris officers watched him: Marcel smug, Hanz baffled, and Shaw with a flat expression.

The saving grace was that two of them were between the principal and the suspect. Shaw was too experienced to chalk the whole thing up as a false alarm. Carver may have come up empty, but his friend had a job to do. He would keep his team alert.

Carver continued to the second-class compartment cars. By this point he was done with etiquette so he slid open the first curtained cabin he hadn't checked. A couple sleeping upright jolted awake.

"Sorry," he said.

He moved to the next car and opened the last mystery door. Four teenage girls sharing earbuds glared at him. He waved and moved on.

Morgan eyed him expectantly as he approached, but he completed the circuit to the end to check the trailing car again. He could now say with one hundred percent confidence that the only person on the train who was a possible match for the red hatchback was the man with the briefcase. At least that was something.

He returned to Morgan and plopped into his seat. "I think my cover's blown." He proceeded to go over the sordid details.

"I wish I had seen the driver," she bemoaned. "I could give you a second opinion."

"All we can do now is watch him."

The man was in the restaurant car, but he had a seat somewhere and likely possessed luggage. Finding that was the next priority. Chances were he was in first class since he had used that bathroom. The problem was, unless you purchased the whole block of six seats as Katarina had for her security detail, the compartments weren't private. Each had several passengers. He couldn't easily walk in and rummage through everybody's luggage.

"Maybe we can get CCTV of the hatchback in Berlin," suggested Morgan. She went back to her laptop. "If our friends can isolate a photograph of the driver, we can compare it with your suspect."

"You place a lot of hope in 'our friends.' We're supposed to be persona non grata, remember?"

"*We* would be personae non gratae, plural."

He just stared at her. Language specialists.

"Anyway, this is the kind of thing they'll be looking into without us. We're not guiding their investigation, we're just asking them to give us a peek."

Carver sighed and consented with a nod. She was spot on and he was just in a bad mood. Working through existing channels wasn't asking much of the CIA. All of Europe and NATO wanted these terrorists caught.

"While you're at it," he said, "go ahead and tell them we found a possible suspect."

"You're sure you want to bring the police down on him? How positive are you he's the driver?"

Carver worked his jaw as he pondered it. "Tell them eighty percent likelihood."

"Will do."

He turned to the window and rapped his fingers on his knee. People like him were wired for action and sitting still was tough. It was one thing to be lounging on the beach with a beer, but another entirely to be stuck on a train with a possible suicide bomber.

He stood up. "You want lunch?"

"It's too early. I'll wait a couple of hours."

"Probably for the best. You might still be anonymous in this."

He made the trek through the train again. A few more dining tables were being served now and the mood of the car was convivial. Carver was about to sit next to the woman reading the psychological thriller when Shaw called out.

"Vince, come sit by us, brother."

His friend sat alone at a two-top on the right side of the train. At the large table beside him across the aisle sat Katarina, with Marcel and Hanz squeezed opposite. Carver joined Shaw. He sat sideways, back to the window and facing Katarina.

No one said anything.

The attendant swung by and he ordered a pierogi plate.

"He'll have a beer too," said Katarina.

Carver arched an eyebrow. "It's early."

"We're on an international voyage surrounded by beautiful scenery." She stuck her lower lip out like a precocious toddler. "Come on, they won't drink with me."

The Iris staff didn't have a single drop of alcohol among them. Maybe Shaw had turned a new leaf. Carver nodded to the waiter and Katarina clapped her hands. When the bottle of Polish lager was delivered a moment later, she clinked it to his across the aisle.

"*Nazdarovia!*"

He downed a refreshing gulp. Although the ice had been broken, the security staff still watched him as if waiting for an explanation. Behind Shaw, the man with the briefcase glanced his way.

Marcel huffed impatiently. "If nobody else will say it, I will. What was that all about?"

"Now, now," chided Katarina, "I won't have any of you bothering my drinking buddy. That is the American way to say it? Drinking buddy?"

Carver hiked a dismissive shoulder at Marcel. "You got it."

"Good."

"But," protested her bodyguard.

"I won't hear any more of it. Vince is simply concerned for my safety."

Carver appreciated not having to answer questions, but it didn't feel right to completely move on. "If I may," he said, "you seem especially nonchalant about safety given the circumstances."

"Nonsense. I'm surrounded by so many big, strong men. What could happen to me?"

Carver didn't miss Shaw's knowing glance. It was the same one they shared every time a principal made security pronouncements to their trained close protection officers. Katarina was every bit as obstinate as his intel implied.

"Why don't we talk about more pleasant business instead?" she suggested.

"Yeah," grinned Shaw, "because Vince is a real pleasant guy."

Katarina clicked her tongue a few times. "He says he works with immigrants less fortunate than me. That he places them in homes and offers them financial support. Is that right?"

Carver sighed. "My employer does that, Katarina. I'm just a guy."

"You're not just a guy, you're my drinking buddy. And my buddies call me Katya."

The waiter delivered a plate of boiled pierogies that must have been cooked already. Carver took a fork to one. The pork was nicely salted and blended with carrots, onions, and garlic. It was surprisingly good for train fare.

Katya sipped from her bottle. "So what have you concluded?" she prodded. "About your investment?"

Carver downed another dumpling before answering. He

wiped his chin with the back of his hand and said, "That you're reckless."

Her neck stiffened. "That's it?"

"That's all I know. There are people trying to kill you and you're going to parties. On top of that, you're dragging these poor guys around with you."

Shaw's eyebrow arched in amusement but he was otherwise unreadable.

"Don't bring my staff into it. They're well paid."

"And the innocent bystanders?"

She huffed. "I expected more from you. If your employer has the resources you claim, you know more than you admit. 'That's all I know' is not believable. If you ask me, there are no immigrants and there is no employer." Her eyes narrowed in mirth. "All this is a pretense for a date."

Shaw snickered outright now. Marcel enjoyed the dressing down, Hanz clearly had trouble keeping up, and the man with the briefcase minded his own business. He'd finished his meal and now had his nose buried in banking documents.

"The thing of it is, Katya, that until you decide to sit down and discuss brass tacks, our relationship can't go anywhere."

Another sip of beer. "We're sitting down now."

Carver swallowed the last pierogi and slid the plate aside. "Then tell me. You talk a big game about wanting to help, but do you get your hands dirty? Are you interested in assisting other dissidents? Because that's the kind of work that requires a pipeline, and that's what my employer can provide. We'll let you be the face, and you'll get a slew of extra hands. You just need to tell us what you need."

His speech had pushed her a little too hard. Katya took obvious offense at the mention of her contribution to the cause. "This may be difficult for you to understand, Vince, but I'm not just a pretty face." She winked. "I have pretty legs too."

She stretched a foot out showing off spandex jeans and over-expensive tennis shoes. He had almost forgotten she was an athlete. She moved with limber grace and knew it. Katya retracted her leg and layered her voice with venom.

"I'll have you know I *am* fighting for the people. I'm meeting a notable activist in the Ukraine. We're going to the opera. If you want to talk brass tacks, as you say, you'll have your chance to show me and Pavel Shishov what you can do. Then we'll see who puts their money where their mouth is."

Carver raised his eyebrows and nodded. "I guess we will."

It was good to have further confirmation of their destination. Despite the opening the conversation presented, Carver didn't want to get more specific in the presence of the man with the briefcase.

"Does it scare you, Vince, to go Kiev?" She said it with the Russian pronunciation.

"A hundred fifty thousand Russian soldiers lined up at the border? Now why would I be scared?"

Katya blinked at him, cheeks flushing some of the red away as she seemed to grow a genuine smile. "Oh but look at me, giving my drinking buddy a hard time. I'm sorry."

She stood and transferred to his lap, one arm around his neck and the other holding her bottle. The move was quick and decisive, like a magnet snapping into place. She kissed his left cheek then his right and then back to his left.

"Will you ever forgive me?" she asked with a pout.

She was acting, playing a part, and being overly silly, but damn if their eyes didn't hold a silent but fully understood exchange. She wiggled in his lap, face aglow.

"Thank you for your concern in Berlin," she said, more seriously. "I may keep you around for that gesture alone."

The train slowed and a monotone announcement came over the intercom. They were arriving in Frankfurt (Oder) on the German side of the Polish border. The man with the briefcase took that as his cue to return to the first-class car.

Katarina returned to her seat and ordered another beer. The service attendant delivered her bottle and explained there would be a temporary suspension of food service. The train pulled to a stop beside a red Baroque Revival building and the attendant debarked.

9

Carver didn't like waiting without eyes on his suspect. The train was stopped at one of the platforms between two sweeping canopies. He figured there might be a customs check before entering Poland. That wouldn't be a problem. Officer Williams had provided him and Morgan with false documents.

After several minutes, nothing appeared to be developing. Katya grew bored and her crew made for their compartment. Carver tagged along to reacquire visual contact with his suspect. In the first-class car, he found him leaving his cabin, briefcase in hand. Carver paid no outward attention as the man passed the group and disembarked the train. Carver waited half a minute before excusing himself and following outside.

Frankfurt (Oder) Central Railway Station consisted of Spartan cement platforms. It was a far cry from the layered groundscaping of more refined cities. A traditional metal canopy covered the platforms, featuring a pair of skylight strips, but they were more or less still outdoors. The main building connected to the awning, and the man with the briefcase headed into a railside restroom.

The fact that he exited the train was concerning. If he

was a terrorist, it could mean his plan was complete. While the suspect was otherwise occupied, Carver walked to the locomotive where the conductor waited outside with a cigarette. She was a stout middle-aged woman with kind features.

"Do you speak English?" he asked.

"Yes."

"I'm sorry if I missed the announcement, but why are we stopped?"

"We wait for the Polish crew. They are late."

Carver kept his gaze on the bathroom exit. "How long do you think we'll be here?"

"They always do this. Twenty minutes, maybe."

"Okay, thanks."

He boarded the first-class car. Katarina was busy kissing her terrier but the Iris crew watched warily as he passed on the way to the compartment his suspect had come out of. He slid it open and greeted the two men and woman inside.

"Hi. I'm the driver of the man who just left. He lost his cell phone somewhere. You know, his mobile? Has anyone seen it?"

As he spoke, he shuffled at the luggage in the overhead. They shook their heads and said they hadn't seen anything.

"Maybe it's in one of these bags?" he asked, patting a leather satchel. "Is this yours?" Between polite questions, he kept glancing at the railside bathroom.

One by one, he matched the bags and belongings to the passengers, including whatever was stowed beneath the seats. Every item was accounted for. The man hadn't left anything behind.

"Sorry to trouble you," said Carver. "Thank you for your time."

Next he proceeded to Katya's compartment.

"Really quick, guys, are there any bags in here that don't belong to you?"

"What now?" complained Marcel.

"Just humor me. Katya? Could anyone have slipped a package in without you noticing?"

The fourth PPO who hadn't gone to the restaurant car said, "I've been here with the dog the whole time. No one came in."

Anya barked excitedly. Carver leaned in to rub her neck and she licked his palm. No treats today.

"What about the bathroom?" Carver asked. "Did you step away for even a second?"

"Not a chance."

"No suspicious activity?"

"Just you nosing around."

While he was leaning over, Carver peeked inside the blue-patterned handbag. There was nothing inside but loose fur and a mangled chew toy.

"Sir?" the PPO pointedly asked.

"Sorry. I'll get out of your hair."

As Carver exited the compartment, the man with the briefcase strolled out of the bathroom. Instead of returning to the train, he circled toward the back entrance of the building. Carver waited until the man went indoors before hopping onto the platform and following. A quick peek confirmed the conductor still waited trainside. It was risky to walk away from a train at a stop, but he only needed a few measly minutes.

Foot traffic within the hall was modest so he stayed back a ways to avoid being spotted. The inside of the station was more contemporary than the exterior, well lit with sunbeams and recessed lights. A handful of shops ran along either wall. Carver passed a Burger King, a hair salon, and a doner kebab place. A single bend led to the main lobby area with its massive ceiling and arched windows. The old touches of architecture were out of reach of the modern world below.

The man with the briefcase walked into the storefront by the main entrance and took second place in line. English wasn't plastered everywhere as in Berlin, but it was easy to determine it was the ticketing counter.

Carver pivoted behind a large directory and checked his watch. If his suspect was purchasing a new train ticket, it could be because his changeover was unplanned. It was far from a sure thing, but it lent credence to Carver's theory. If the terrorist planted a bomb and ditched the train, he might have already had a ticket for a planned escape route. If, instead, their unexpected confrontation spooked him, he could be aborting the operation.

Carver pulled a pair of brown leather gloves from his pocket and slipped them tightly over his fingers.

After several minutes, his suspect exited the shop holding a new ticket and headed back toward the platforms. He passed while Carver waited on the opposite side of the directory. The man was on his phone now, speaking Arabic. The accent seemed a little haughty. It could have been Libyan but just as easily Egyptian. That made it Western or Northern Arabic, probably, but something with an African twang. It was another open question.

After affording a sizable distance, Carver pursued at a pace matching his target, who walked back to the rail and boarded a different train. Carver pushed forward and hopped on as well. He didn't have a ticket but those were rarely checked until the trip was underway. He followed the man to a private sleeper compartment. Before the solid door could fully close, Carver stuck his boot in the jam. He pushed inside.

"What are you—"

Carver shoved him onto the bed. He shut and locked the door. They were alone.

"Where's the bomb?" he asked plainly.

The man swallowed and furrowed his brow. "What are you speaking of?"

Carver pulled the curtain over the window and withdrew the Maxim 9 from his jacket. "I was the one who killed your friend in Berlin."

The man's eyes widened.

"You were the one driving the red hatchback."

The man's gaze didn't leave the weapon. "... I don't know—"

"I was twenty feet away when you dropped him off. You're part of a terrorist plot. You know how serious this is."

Silence.

"Where's the bomb?"

The man began to gather his wits. "Who are you?"

"You first."

He reflexively shook his head. "You're American."

Carver sighed impatiently and wagged the gun in the man's face.

"There is no bomb!" he cried. "I don't know what you're going on about. Look for yourself. Search me." He flipped open the briefcase. He tossed his papers to the floor. Then his pens.

"You don't need to do that," said Carver.

"Apparently I do," he fumed. He upended the briefcase and shook it, losing the last few paperclips and business cards. Then he went to his pockets. "My wallet." He spilled bills out and tossed them to the floor. "My mobile." He palmed his phone and smashed the glass face a couple of times into the metal window frame.

"Shit." Carver grabbed the phone.

While they were close, the man pulled a knife. Carver hopped away from the slash, kicked his boot into the man's forearm, and put two bullets into his chest. The reports were similar to the sound of the smashing phone, only louder. Carver sat on the opposite bed a moment, staring at the seat across from him. The man blinked slowly, his eyes sagged downward, and then he was dead.

Carver scowled. These guys were true believers. They refused to be taken alive. He put the gun away and, still wearing the gloves, proceeded to go through the man's possessions. There was nothing there. No bomb, no vest. The phone was junked. With access to local assets the data could be recovered, but the thing was too incriminating to hold onto. Carver didn't want to risk it. It was better to leave the phone in the sleeper with its owner. When the authorities discovered him, the evidence would find its way into official channels. If the Agency wanted to investigate, they would have access to it then.

Carver picked up the pair of bullet casings and slipped them into his pocket. He straightened his jacket and listened at the door. When the sound of footsteps faded, he slipped out and exited to the platform. The conductor for his train was no longer waiting outside. The Polish crew had already boarded. Carver rushed over and climbed inside as the train groaned.

In an ideal world, he would convince Katarina to wait for the next train to Warsaw, but his was leaving now and he needed to put distance between him and the dead body before someone found it. There was very little chance a bomb had been planted on this train. Carver was sure of it.

The trip got underway without incident. Deep blue filled the windows as the train navigated the bridge over the Oder River. In a minute they were officially in Poland without an ID check. Carver strolled into his car, heart still pounding in his eardrums, to find Shaw sitting in his seat and sharing a laugh with Morgan. He sat in the aisle seat across from them.

"Thought we left without you," chuckled Shaw.

Morgan grinned pointedly. "It would be just like Vince

not to tell anyone."

"Relax," said Carver. "I'm keeping you in the loop, aren't I?"

"Depends what just happened," countered Shaw. "I know that look."

Carver worked his jaw and his friend interlocked his fingers in his lap.

"Hey Vince, you sure about this suspect of yours? That he's a threat?"

Their train car didn't have many passengers, and they were seated far enough to speak freely.

"He's not a threat anymore," said Carver. "He entered permanent repose in a sleeper compartment on another train."

Their faces deflated.

"Jules, you might as well inform Williams. Amend our threat to an investigation. There's a smashed phone over there that might have something on it."

She nodded silently and began composing another message.

"Hell," muttered Shaw, "more spy stuff." He shook his head at Morgan. "Some guys have all the fun."

"Don't look at me," she countered. "I'm fine right where I am."

He snorted. Shaw was different from Morgan. She was a green beret so she'd been embedded in some gnarly situations, but her expertise was as a combat interpreter. She had never taken the kinetic aspect of the job as far as Carver and Shaw. Nick had been a SEAL, and he felt the same rush from action that Carver did. More than him, probably. It was why they should have been working together.

"Are you cleared for this kind of thing, Vince?" he asked. "Wetwork, I mean. I don't want the full force of the Agency coming down on you."

"No need for concern. I'm authorized for whatever extra-judicial work I deem is necessary. No one will burn me over another dead terrorist."

"Amen, brother. But how does that umbrella of protection hold up if you get caught?"

Carver shifted uncomfortably, face forward. "Nature of the job."

Instead of objecting, comprehension overtook his friend's features. No, not just comprehension. It was kinship. Nick Shaw had waded through the same trenches before.

After they passed whatever Polish city was on the border, the train sped through dense forests. Dark greens and browns filled the windows, and the grass ran all the way up to the tracks. Although still winter, there was no snow in sight. After a few minutes of sustained silence, Morgan sent her dispatch. They still hadn't heard word back.

"So what are we dealing with?" asked Shaw. "Have you found another bomb?"

Carver shook his head regarding the last nagging doubt. "I'm sure it's out there somewhere. I just can't fill in the whole picture yet. This guy was the driver in Berlin. That's a fact. What he was doing here, without a bomb, is anybody's guess."

"You must have spooked him," said Morgan.

Shaw laughed. " 'Course he spooked the man. Hell, he spooked me."

It struck Carver that he had never searched the restroom at the train station.

"And the third guy?" pressed Morgan. "There's one more out there."

Carver nodded. "All I can say is he's not on this train. I checked everyone. It's possible he went ahead earlier, that this guy was headed to meet him. At the station, the driver had a phone conversation in Arabic."

"That settles it," concluded Shaw with a clap of his hands. "Katya's staying locked down in Warsaw."

"You're going to have a hard time reining her in."

"That's a fact but it has to be done. I'll tell you what else. I'll steer her away from Kyiv if I can. This is a bad time to go to the opera. Not that there's ever a good time."

"Here's hoping she's as sensible as you."

"What about the train?" he asked. "Is it safe? Any chance your guy planted the bomb before he disembarked?"

"I searched the car and compartments and bathroom. I don't see how he could have."

Shaw scrubbed his beard for a moment of deliberation. "Okay. I'm going to transfer the principal out of first class just in case. We'll bring her back here. It's open. There's plenty of space to spread out. Katya will complain but we're in charge of her security, not her comfort."

Carver reclined his seat with a grin. He couldn't wait to see the look on her face.

10

Iris Executive Protection secured Katarina's exit through *Warszawa Centralna*. The train station was newly remodeled, with retro-futuristic lights above a mezzanine ceiling that swooped down into the wall of an open-area coffee shop. As much as Carver wanted the caffeine, he and Morgan followed the security detail toward the exit, a window-front that featured a beautiful backdrop of Warsaw.

Across the street, a curved glass structure balanced above a concrete plaza. In the distant cityscape, it was impossible to miss the Palace of Culture and Science. The high-rise was a 1950s-era landmark of towering masonry stacked like a giant Soviet wedding cake. It culminated in what was at one time the tallest clock tower in the world.

A host of ultra modern glass skyscrapers echoed the nearby plaza, including one that reached higher than the symbol of Soviet generosity. The view made for a different feel from much of Europe. It was a skyline borne out of necessity, the city having been almost completely razed during German occupation.

It must have been strange for Poland to endure the height of the German empire, to have revolted and to have lost, to have seen their city reduced to ruins, only to then have it taken by the Red Army. That had been Stalin's fait accompli. Now, with the Warsaw Pact in ruins but the city rebuilt, the world was again talking about Russia's expansionist policies in regards to Ukraine. It is said history must be remembered in order not to repeat it, yet many of today's wars result from that very inability to forget the past.

After taking in the view from a distance, Carver was jarred back to ground level by the uninspired square parking lot of Warsaw Central. A raucous crowd of protesters pressed against metal barricades and chanted anthems of national pride. They held signs, some in English, that read, "Poland is under attack," and, "Polish patriots united." The chaos was just barely held back by a row of police officers.

"What's this for?" grumbled Carver.

"You watch the news?" asked Morgan.

"I try not to."

"Look," she said, pointing to a sign in Polish and translating. "Strong border, strong Poland. They're anti-immigration demonstrators."

Carver bit down as he scanned over every close protection officer's nightmare. Here he was, waxing poetic about Russia's incursion into Ukraine, but that was far from the extent of it. Belarus, impossible to describe as anything but a Russian puppet state, had been flying in tens of thousands of migrants from across Iraq and the Middle East. The second they touched down in Eastern Europe they were redirected to the borders shared with Poland and Lithuania and forced to make the journey without supplies.

In the Polish winter, it was a legitimate humanitarian crisis.

The protesters waved Poland's red-and-white national flag and brandished a coat of arms with a crowned eagle. They were nationalists reacting to an unprecedented flow of Middle Eastern migrants that were of Minsk and Moscow's making.

And Katarina Litvinenko was either a symbol for immigration or for the motherland that had orchestrated the growing state of emergency on their border.

An empty bottle smashed on the asphalt a few yards short of Katya. The Iris officers deftly responded, covering up their principal and rushing her out of harm's way. In an environment like this, there was no fighting back or bringing perpetrators to justice. The safety of the principal was the only motivating factor, even at great risk to a close protection officer's own body.

Objects pelted the ground as they scurried toward a waiting company car. Shaw loaded in with Katarina and the rest, and the tires squealed as the car fled down the lane cordoned off by police. The protesters applauded and sang in solidarity to their hollow victory.

"I guess we're walking," muttered Carver.

Once clear of Warsaw Central, the city made good on the promise made by the view. The air was crisp and it was a pleasant late-afternoon walk, even if the sun mostly hid in the overcast sky. In a little over fifteen minutes, Carver and Morgan lugged their bags into a small hotel. A walkway flanked with modern art led to a central white desk attended by a white-haired woman with sharp cheekbones.

Morgan halted Carver with a finger and approached the desk alone to put her language skills to the test. The women shared an exchange with only minor difficulty while he examined the finer points of an entirely red canvas. Two minutes later they were strolling to the elevator with key cards.

"I knew you spoke Russian," said Carver, "but Polish too?"

"She was speaking Polish; I stuck with Russian."

"They're compatible?"

She pushed the call button and shrugged. "It's a matter of Eastern versus Western Slavic. They're not the same languages but there's a decent amount of overlap. The pronunciation's difficult to keep up with, but I got the gist of it."

"Color me impressed."

"I haven't gotten to the impressive part yet. I told her Katarina was my associate, on business from Russia. We're now booked on the same floor as her."

The elevator opened before he could complete his smile. Shaw and Katya stepped out, in heated disagreement, with Hanz in tow. "Just getting dinner, Vince," said Shaw. He marched past them and to the car on the curb.

"Should we follow?" asked Morgan.

Carver took a breath. "Better give them some space. Nick's with her. But dinner does sound good and I could use some red meat." His eyes lingered on the gloomy interior of the attached restaurant and bar. "Meet you down here in an hour?"

"You got it."

His room was traditional, clean and simple with a comfortable bed. The third-floor window overlooked the street entrance and some office space opposite. There was a pharmacy on ground level and what looked like a closed jazz bar. He took a shower and shaved and put on jeans and a brown jacket. He cleaned his gloves. He also cleaned the Maxim 9 and reloaded it. The bullet casings had been dumped in a trash can on a random Warsaw side street on the way to the hotel.

Sometime later, the sun set as they polished off their meals and ordered after-dinner beers at the table.

"So have you figured out our strategy here?" asked Morgan after she had run out of complaints about her husband.

"Well, I've neutralized two terrorists so far. I was thinking of going for the hat trick."

"Of course we're prioritizing Katarina's safety, Vince. I mean beyond that. At what point do you ask her to play nice with the CIA?"

He frowned. Protection was what he was good at, but it was no longer his sole business. He had more subtle concerns now. They were the reason for all the pretense to begin with.

"Katya plays on hearts and minds," he started. "I take that as a means to an end. It's not what internally drives her. She's a practical person."

Morgan chewed her lip and nodded at the assessment. "I don't disagree, but getting blown up isn't very practical."

"No argument from me. She thinks she's invincible. If I were a more coldhearted operator, I might allow another bomb to go off in her vicinity."

"Sounds like the alphabet agencies to me."

"Exactly. Good thing they hired us instead." He sipped his beer. "The thing is, I don't think fear will convince Katya to do anything."

"You sound like you admire her."

"I can't stand her. On the flip side, I do admire her *taking* a stand. Her uncle is practically a nefarious Disney villain. It takes guts to go against him."

"With an undisclosed amount of his money."

Carver canted his glass to make his point. "If that money runs out, things get about as practical as they can. Like you said, though, we don't know how much she has left. But we do know that making a difference is far from free. She's meeting an activist in Kyiv. I've looked this guy up. Pavel Shishov. He's not a militant, but he's not the type to sit on the sidelines either."

"He's rumored to smuggle dissidents across the border."

"That's exactly right. He's a hero to many. And in the back of Katya's mind, I think she wants to be a hero too. But in order to get involved, she'll need money, support, and connections. No one hits that trifecta better than the CIA."

"Look at you," said Morgan with a grin, "barely out of spy school and already grooming assets."

Their window table offered an evening view of the street, and Carver was palpably relieved to see the Iris Transport car return. Shaw and Hanz unloaded holding shopping bags.

Katarina managed Anya in the blue handbag, bright-pink collar reflecting passing headlights. Shaw dismissed the driver with a rap on the roof. It was his way of keeping his commitment to lock Katya down, if only partially. She seemed a little heated over it and spoke curtly.

Shaw was unusually restrained and scanned the street for threats, quickly noticing Carver watching him. They moved inside and he sent them ahead before detouring into the restaurant.

"What was that about?" asked Carver.

"Creative differences, Vince. What do you think?" Rather than join them, he stood by the table.

"Just going to dinner, huh?"

Shaw shook his head as if reviving an hour-long argument. "She insisted on going to the mall for Anya. I watched her drop six hundred bucks for a dog carrier with a fancy label."

"What's wrong with the blue one?"

"It's more than a few weeks old, I guess. You know her type, Vince. Spending money is a coping mechanism."

"You wanna sit?"

"Nah, I ate my full." He cleared his throat. "But I wanted to pass on an update. We booked the InterContinental Kyiv two days from now. Tomorrow we board the Kiev Express at 5 pm. It's an overnight."

Carver sat back and stretched. "Looks like we have a day to kill in Warsaw."

"That's what I'm afraid of," he said. "You two stay sharp. I'm gonna get some rest." He left them sipping their beers in silence.

Morgan brought up the Polrail site on her phone. "That's a long train ride," she eventually said. "Over sixteen hours. If you don't mind, I'll fly instead. Get there ahead as your advance party. Kyiv's where the action will be."

"Good idea. You'll be a half day ahead of us at least."

"The only catch is I'll need to leave the hardware with you rather than attempt to sneak it through the airport."

"Trains are awfully efficient at smuggling contraband, aren't they?"

"Just don't get caught."

It was the kind of thing people said that was a given. "What about the grapevine?" he asked. "Did we hear word back?"

Morgan snorted. "Not a peep. Was I fooling myself by thinking this relationship would be more than one way?"

"Is there an answer that isn't either cynical or naive?"

She chuckled and killed the last half of her beer. "I think you just found it. Nick has the right idea. I'm headed up."

He waved her on and took a slower approach to his beer, pondering it for long moments between every sip. Carver hadn't wanted to give voice to his feelings, but something about Officer Williams resonated with him. It was like he knew her. Knew how she operated anyway. Their responsibilities were different, their skill sets and approaches to problems vastly so, but they seemed to share the same beliefs about what constituted justice in this world. There was something to be said for that. And, Carver believed, if they handed her a solid piece of intelligence, she would reciprocate by getting back to them.

Eventually.

He lingered for a while, eyeing the window until his beer was warm, and then headed up to the second floor.

The ding of the elevator announced his arrival and he stepped out to find Marcel sitting in one of those decorative chairs beside the elevators that nobody actually uses. They swapped uninterested glares and Carver checked up and down the hallway.

This wasn't a Taipei situation with billionaires paying men to stand guard outside their doors. Shaw was aware of the threat level and was likely the only reason a PPO was in the hallway at all. Having seen Katya's growing frustration at her security concessions, Marcel by the elevator was probably the best they could get without further upsetting her. It was a workable compromise. Shaw and the rest of the team were one call away.

Carver continued to his room. He wasn't leading this particular group. Besides Shaw, he knew nothing about them. He just had to ride things out as best he could. Same as anyone.

Settling into his room, he made the mistake of sitting on the bed and kicking his legs up too soon. Only afterward did he consider the minibar, but by then it was too late. His body objected to moving.

It was surprising how taxed he found himself after the day's events. The shooting wasn't that big a deal. Carver had participated in enough protracted firefights that this one hardly rated. He decided the stress of sharing a train with a potential bomb for six hours was the culprit.

He sighed, staring at the minibar, willing it to tumble over and roll a bottle of whiskey out. It was a fierce battle of wills and neither him nor the fridge budged. Carver sighed again and resigned himself to his fate. He briefly wondered if Williams would come through with an update, but no dice on that account either.

11

Carver flinched awake to his phone buzzing. It was midnight and the call was from an unregistered number. He had passed out on top of the comforter still wearing his boots.

"Vince's Fluff n Fold," he answered in a groggy voice.

"Isn't it a little late over there to be so damned sardonic?" grumbled Lanelle Williams.

"Sorry, I didn't check the time," he lied. "You have some dirty laundry for me or what?"

"The line's secure enough, Vince. I ran down that Mark Watson ID. The identity's completely fabricated. It's not tied to a real person and One Europe doesn't vet the names on their list. It's a dead end."

"It means the terrorists have inside knowledge of Katya's schedule. They purchased the ticket before she posted her plans to social media."

"Do you think it could be someone from her security team?"

"I'm not sure they know a whole lot either, but about that... It's funny you failed to mention Nick Shaw was employed by Iris Executive Protection again."

"I didn't?" she asked coyly. "I figured you kept in touch."

"I don't think the CIA figures much."

"Do you trust him?"

"I do."

"Does he still trust you?"

"No thanks to you, but it seems so. Is this connection the only reason I got the job?"

She scoffed. "You're not getting sensitive on me now, are you?"

"I'd just like to know," he insisted in an entirely not sensitive manner.

"It's a foot in the door, Vince. Whether you open it up the rest of the way is up to you."

He stifled a laugh. "Sounds like something my dad used to say."

"How old do you take me for?"

"Now who's sensitive? What else did you dig up?"

Williams sucked her teeth and moved on. "Mixed results so far. We didn't find the red hatchback. After being missing for the better part of a day, we can assume it's either chopped up or we'll find it a week from now in the wilderness burnt to a husk. There's a low chance of it delivering actionable intel."

"You said mixed."

"There's some good news too. Berlin is one of the most surveilled cities in Europe. We don't have the physical car but we pegged it on CCTV. We isolated a clear picture of the driver."

Carver sat up on the bed. "The man on the train."

"It was the same guy, Vince. Excellent job running down

a ghost. You might have saved lives today."

Although he had been sure he did the right thing, confirmation was always welcome. "What about the third guy? There's one more out there and he wasn't on the train."

"We couldn't get an image of the passenger in the back seat. Running down actual identities of the John Does hasn't scored any hits yet so we can't track known associates either."

"What about any intel recovered on the driver?"

"The briefcase documents were printouts from the internet. They weren't meant to fool anyone with more than passing interest. The phone is still in analysis."

"The phone's important, Laney."

"Well, you broke it, you bought it. I put a rush request on it, but German authorities are running their own investigation. I'll send word directly if anything comes through."

Williams took a turn asking some questions about Carver's version of events in Berlin and on the train. She wanted a quick rundown and surprised him by not giving him a hard time.

"And what about Ms. Litvinenko?" she asked. "I notice you're using her nickname. Do you have an in with her?"

"I'm set up as a potential benefactor. I'm not sure she buys it, but that's not a requirement. I've earned enough goodwill that she expects me around.

"That's good."

"It seems you were right about Kyiv. She's lining up an

opera with Pavel Shishov. That info wasn't online. How did you get it?"

"How do we ever?"

Ask a stupid question, he grumbled to himself. "Regardless, I think I'm going to give her the push there. I'm appealing to her activist ego by promising a pipeline."

Williams seemed to frown through the phone. "It could work. The situation there is rapidly deteriorating. I'll look into ground assets for you, but no promises. I think that's it for now."

"Okay. What about this number? Should I call if I get anything?"

"No, this number will be disconnected as soon as I hang up. Keep the phone, continue radio silence, feed us intel through the messenger, and I'll reach you." The line clicked dead.

Carver rubbed his eyes. A certain amount of cloak and dagger was expected, but things seemed more sensitive than usual. Was there ever a usual in this business? He supposed it was a measure to avoid sparking World War Three. The truth was, the secrecy only complicated his job if he needed something immediately. So far he and Morgan were doing just fine on their own. And thus far the government had lived up to their end of the deal. He was running the show on his terms. Whatever that cost, he would gladly pay it.

He stood to stretch his legs. A glance out the window revealed a quiet night interrupted by the occasional car. The day-long threat of rain had finally materialized. It was drizzling and the road was covered with a sheen. The jazz club that had in the day appeared shuttered was open now, its neon saxophone reflecting off thousands of slick droplets.

The thought was tempting and reminded Carver once again of his stalwart enemy, the minibar. He dug a snack-size bottle from the fridge and set it down beside a glass. Maybe it was the crick in his back, or maybe the room was too small to pace in. Either way he grabbed the ice bucket and trudged out to the hall. He strolled past the elevator bay, stopped in his tracks, and slow-walked backwards.

The elevator chair was empty.

He moved closer to check it out but Marcel didn't magically reappear. There was no evidence of any wrongdoing. No note scrawled with a "Be right back." Just a ring from a paper coffee cup on the mirrored tabletop.

Carver set the ice bucket down and quietly moved down the hallway, listening for a CPO pacing the halls or using a bathroom. He didn't know which rooms belonged to who, much less which was Katya's, but the floor wasn't that expansive.

He opened the door to the stairwell and looked up and down. Everything was still, just like the hallway. No need to panic, he assured himself. If something had happened, the Iris Executive officer would have made a heck of a lot of noise.

Carver cursed under his breath when he figured it out. Katya was a party girl. She had convinced her bodyguards of the importance of going to a Warsaw nightclub or something equally stupid and they had begrudgingly but dutifully followed her. Damn it. He took the elevator down and strolled into the lobby.

The hotel bar was recently closed—he wasn't that lucky. But his eyes strayed to the jazz club across the street. The idea had merit. Her team had sent away the car for the night and would want to keep her close.

A wash of refreshing cool hit him outside. The rain was omnipresent yet intangible, and he managed to make it across the street with only a wipe of his face. Carver entered the dark bar. It looked like something out of a fifties noir flick except for the complete lack of smoke. A long bar started from the near wall before giving way to a wider area for tables and booths in front of a stage. A duo of young guys handled drums and keys while an old dog blew on some brass.

The blonde bun was easy to distinguish. Katarina Litvinenko sat at the bar alone. He frowned as he searched up and down for the security team. They weren't around.

Carver slunk to the near corner, figuring he'd be less obvious away from the door. He leaned against the wall so the bartender would leave him alone. One minute turned into several, and still he couldn't wrap his head around the situation. If Katya had snuck out, Marcel would still be waiting by the elevator. If they had escorted her away, someone would be in sight. Yet Marcel didn't emerge from the bathroom. Shaw wasn't lingering on the outskirts.

As he waited, Katya glanced to the door a few times. Perhaps she was expecting them. It wasn't obvious if she was looking forward to company or doing her best to avoid it. When she checked her phone for the third time, Carver casually sat on the stool beside her.

"I hope no on had the gall to stand you up."

She twirled on her perch, smirk only half disguised. "Are you following me?"

"Someone has to. Where's your security team?"

Her lashes fluttered dismissively. "I'm a big girl, Vince. Is that your real name?"

"All right, don't be dramatic. I'm looking out for you." With the music going, they had to lean close to speak.

Katya set her jaw. "I'm not isolating myself in that hotel."

"Fine, I'll join you." Carver waved the bartender close. "Old fashioned with rye."

Katya's lips curled. "Drinking buddy..."

He couldn't tell how many she'd belted down so far, but she was definitely enjoying a buzz.

"I'll be honest with you," she leveled. "While I'm surprised to see you here, it is a nice surprise."

"That's a start, I suppose. It's nice to see you here too, instead of kidnapped or worse."

She snorted delicately. "Still playing the curious business partner?"

"You have me mistaken, Katya. I'm in security. The business partner is my boss."

"The anonymous one?"

"Yes, the anonymous one. That can change the moment you get serious."

She turned to her drink, something bright red, and took a sip. The bartender meanwhile hand-carved an orange peel before delivering a glass tumbler with a single ice cube.

"That's something, I guess," said Katya.

"Getting serious?"

She snickered and leaned in. "You told me something new about yourself. You work in security."

Carver tasted his drink and hiked a shoulder. "That shouldn't come as a surprise."

"Whose security are you interesting in, yours or mine?" She swayed closer and he could smell her perfume.

"I do my best work in pairs."

She grinned and laughed. "You're very sure of yourself, aren't you?"

"It's a job hazard."

She blinked at him. After a moment of chewing her lip, she grunted and pulled away to order another drink.

A muted TV behind the bar showed news clips of warships building in the Black Sea. A number of Russian vessels, including amphibious ships filled with marines, were enjoying an unprecedented run of the Black Sea. Despite talks by the Royal Canadian Navy and others about bolstering the area, the last time there was any NATO naval presence in the region was over a month ago. US ships were patrolling the North Sea and the Mediterranean, ensuring they did not occupy any waters bordering Russia.

It was a whole lot of delicate political maneuvering as various states vied for supremacy of hearts and minds, but the warning signs were there. Eventually, the kinetic option would be called on.

"Where is Nick Shaw, Katya? He doesn't strike me as

the type of guy to let you bar hop on your own."

"You're right about that. He didn't want me to leave so I fired him."

It took a second to process that statement. "You what?"

"Iris Executive Protection is no longer employed as of"—she checked her phone again—"twenty-seven minutes ago. Although I fired them before that. They were only paid through today."

"Katya, that was an extremely reckless thing to do."

"Says who?"

"Says me, talking to you right now. Do you know that man on the train was an associate of the terrorist who tried to blow you up in Berlin?"

She was stupefied. "That's ridiculous. How would you know such a thing?"

"You watch the German news?"

She scoffed. "The *polizei* are chasing their own tails."

"They're very capable at what they do. There's a real threat and you're ignoring it, damn it! Are you trying to get yourself killed?"

Her eyes flared at his outburst. Carver didn't take himself for the emotional type, but this woman was driving him crazy. She slowly slid to her feet and put a hand on his shoulder. "You actually care, don't you?"

He breathed hard, unsure what else to say. Her eyes were blue, and they softened.

"Vince..."

"Would it kill you to let yourself be looked after?"

She rubbed his arm. The scar on his left shoulder

burned, the vestigial wound that would never go away. Katya was a girl who was unaware of these things. Not naive, exactly, but overconfident. She leaned in and kissed his cheek. "I'm going to the restroom."

He stood and walked with her. She huffed in protest but his attention turned to the patrons of the bar. He checked every face for interest, every posture for readiness. He looked for anyone not having a good time.

In the back hall was a single unisex bathroom. She tried to push in ahead but he barred her with an arm and went in first. There was a small wash basin with two stalls, the first without a door. He opened the second to ensure it was empty.

"My hero," she mocked. "You know, this is the second time you've followed me to the bathroom. Is this your kink?"

Katya strolled into the stall without a door and pulled her spandex pants to her knees.

Carver spun away as she sat. "I'll just—"

"No, stay. You make me feel safe."

His brow furrowed as she started peeing.

"Can you pass me some toilet paper, Mr. Hero?"

"This isn't a game, Katya."

Carver stepped outside and waited by the door. She was out half a minute later. They returned to their stools and she leaned on him again.

"I feel as if we shared an intimate experience," she said. "We had a breakthrough."

"Laugh it up. If it means you're safe, I'm happy."

"Does that happiness mean you'll let yourself have a little fun?"

He paused with the old fashioned at his lips. "You've made your point." He frowned when he noticed powdery grains in his drink.

Slowly, Carver turned in his seat to once again inspect the crowd. No one was watching them. No one specifically stood out. It was possible he was being paranoid, but that was just another word for cautious.

He grabbed Katya's drink as she reached for it. He leaned over the bar and upturned both glasses into the sink.

"Hey!"

He set hers back on the table and put his to his lips as if he had just downed it. Hopefully nobody was watching too closely.

"You're in danger," he whispered. "We need to get out of here." He withdrew his money clip. "Hey," he called to the bartender. "How much do I owe you?" He placed three twenties on the counter.

"No, no. Too much," he said.

"Keep it." He turned to the door. "Let's go."

"I'm not going anywhere."

Carver clamped his hand wholly around her arm, just under her shoulder where there wasn't a lot of room to wiggle. He gripped her tight, pulled her body into his, and squeezed. "You listen to me," he graveled, lips to her ear. "I am taking you back to the hotel right now, and I will use whatever force you make me. Tell me you understand."

Defiant eyes glared back. He squeezed her arm tighter

and she squirmed.

"Tell me you understand."

She shivered under his relentless will. She deflated, averted her eyes, and hastily nodded. "I understand. I'll go."

"Don't try me."

He loosened his grip but still held her as they walked outside and into the street. The rain had picked up, reducing visibility. He thought he saw movement in a parked car a block to his left. Brake lights disappeared down the other side of the street, and a couple huddled under an umbrella in the distance. Carver's brisk pace had them entering the hotel in a little over ten seconds. They didn't see anyone on the way to the elevator.

Katya slicked water off her arms. "You can let go of me now," she hissed, once the car was going up.

He walked her out. She tried to go left but he pulled her right and into his room. There he grabbed the Maxim 9 and slipped it under his leather jacket. They returned to the hall and then to her room.

"Is that legal?" she asked, digging into her purse and referencing the gun.

"Define legal."

She was nervous as she fumbled for her key card. Inside, her dog let out several yips.

"Poor baby," said Katya. "She must need to pee."

Carver impatiently checked the hall and wondered if Anya would pee in the shower. A shuffling noise in the room was followed by growls. There was something else too. A low scraping sound. And someone shushing the dog.

Katya clicked her key with a beep and Carver pushed her aside. He flung open the door and entered, leading with his gun. Anya lay in the center of the room, chin on the floor and whining beside a yellow puddle. Carver swept the room with his weapon and Katarina entered behind him. Rain pattered the window with increasing tempo. He completed his circuit in the bathroom before returning to Katya.

No one was here, which was concerning because he had definitely heard something. He cleared the closet next, and then went to the bed that was still stacked with shopping bags. No one was beneath it.

"You're scaring her," said Katya, making pouty lips as she grabbed her dog.

Anya's blue bag was in the corner on the floor. It was empty and smelled like the dog had urinated there beforehand. That explained the shopping trip. Just when he was about to write the whole thing off as an overreaction to a terrier with a weak bladder, movement from the curtain caught his eye. It was too sheer to hide behind but was swaying gently for some reason. Carver slid it aside. He hadn't realized the window was a sliding glass door. It was barely ajar and allowing some breeze in.

"You have a balcony?" he muttered.

It was a dumb mistake. He had assumed since his room didn't have one, hers didn't either. He opened the glass door. The balcony was clear. A pair of headlights cut through the pattering rain. A sedan idled in the middle of the street. Carver peeked directly below and caught a man climbing down the brickwork, almost to the ground.

12

Carver slid the door shut and locked it.

"Don't open up for anyone but me," he ordered.

Rather than attempt the precarious feat of scaling two floors to the ground in the rain, Carver raced out of the room and into the stairwell. He took the steps four at a time, sprinted through the lobby, and burst out the glass door into a growing deluge. He made a beeline for the sedan, a dark-blue Mercedes, but the passenger door shut and it peeled away.

"Shit."

He turned to the curb where a pair of taxis had waited earlier. He held the pistol under his jacket and waved, but he wasn't sure anyone was inside the car. Before he could stomp over, the black Iris Transport car skidded to a stop in front of him. The window rolled down and Shaw said, "You gonna get in or what?"

Carver ran around and got in next to his friend. The retreating Mercedes turned a distant corner and Shaw hit the gas.

"Real good," said Carver, wiping the rain from his face and hair. "Leaving her alone like that."

"I was watching the building. What happened inside?"

"I took Katya home and somebody was in her room."

They sped through the dark streets, wipers on full speed. The Mercedes was out of visual range. "I saw that much," Shaw hissed.

"Did you also see your principal go to a bar by herself?"

"I was watching the street, Vince. The question is what were you doing in her room?" He turned the corner. No Mercedes. They were too far behind.

"What do you mean?"

"Don't think I didn't catch the way you looked at each other when she was on your lap on the train."

"What does that have to do with anything?"

"Don't sleep with the principal, Vince. That's rule number one."

"She's not my principal. You're the one on the job, not me. At least that was the case before you got canned. Where's the rest of your team? Are you really leaving her out in the cold like that?"

"I'm here, aren't I?"

Both men cursed under their breath. Shaw sped to the next intersection. Taillights faded several blocks up and he turned to follow them.

Tempers were flaring and for good reason, but the situation was salvageable. They had prevented someone from getting to Katarina and were hot on their trail.

"You should have had someone in the hallway," said Carver.

"She's the boss, Vince. If she stops paying, I can't

convince the others to hang around for free."

"But the hallway."

"Look, I knew Katya was leaving the hotel so I opted to wait outside and track her. I had no way of guessing she'd just be across the street."

Carver grimaced. Waiting a block up in the parked car had been the right call, even if it meant missing the intruder who had almost definitely taken the lobby entrance or back door. The balcony was a desperate escape attempt, a last resort. It would have been too risky to break in that way in full view of the public. Especially since Shaw would have noticed.

The rain was pouring down in sheets now, which made everything in the dense city a hazy glare. Now on a larger street, they had eyes on a few vehicles which could be their target. As they neared, one of them rolled a red light.

"That's them," said Carver.

Shaw slowed at the intersection. After a short wait, he ran the light in a safer fashion. They were now following the Mercedes, but this chase was anything but high speed. If they were lucky, their target didn't even realize they were there. The weather, beginning to resemble a monsoon, provided plenty of cover. Their target moved at a brisk pace but had no desire to attract the police, so Shaw could follow at an innocuous distance and speed. Without a hostage or other aggravating circumstance to raise the stakes, simply keeping the bad guys in sight was good enough.

"This doesn't track," muttered Carver.

"Your terrorists?"

He shook his head. "Two close encounters with Libyan bombers, and Katya fires her security staff and goes out for live music?"

"Warsaw was just a random stop with no appearances. Ten to one she has a new security team in Ukraine. I get the feeling our girl doesn't trust anybody. Might be what's kept her alive this long."

"Might be what gets her killed."

His friend canted his head. "Say what you want, but she has good reason not to trust you. She's cleverer than you give her credit for. She might have put together that we know each other."

Great. Shaw was implying his firing had to do with Carver's involvement. It was another added to a long list of possibilities. They drove for a minute in silence, tracking their prey by the taillights.

"What are we doing here, Vince? Right now we're two dogs chasing a car. What happens when we catch it?"

"I'm still considering that."

A turn indicator blinked ahead. The Mercedes slowed and turned under a gas station roof with a red banner.

"Hold back," instructed Carver.

Although the two no longer worked together and Carver was no longer his team leader, they instinctively fell back into old habits, operating in lockstep. Shaw killed the lights and pulled to the curb a block before the gas station. Two men exited the blue vehicle. As they scanned the distance, Shaw turned off the windshield wiper too. Beads of water mutated into blobs that streaked the glass. It offered them a muddy picture of events while keeping them hidden.

After a brief exchange, one of the men went inside the quick mart while the other pumped gas. As their attention was turned away, Shaw flicked the wipers once to clear the view.

"Window are tinted," he noted. "Impossible to see if anyone's in the car, but it doesn't look like it."

Safe under the awning, the remaining man lit up a cigarette two feet from the pump. His eyes searched the street.

Shaw chuckled. "That's not very smart and possibly illegal."

"I don't think these guys play by the rules," said Carver.

"Don't think any of us do, if we're being fair."

Carver said nothing in response as he continued scoping the scene. He agreed with Shaw's assessment of there only being two tangos.

"We can intercept them while they're split up," suggested Shaw, reaching to his belt and checking his Beretta M9. The old-school pistol was out of favor these days but, with the proper magazines and maintenance, it was a durable, dependable, and battle-tested firearm.

"I don't know. He looks pretty jumpy."

Shaw nodded. "He's favoring a weapon in his jacket."

"Let's hold off a second and see where this takes us."

The only answer was a grunt.

Operations like this involved constant risk assessments. It could be safest to move in now, but that safe strategy might provide the smallest gain. If these men were working with someone, covertly tailing them could yield the larger truth.

"Should I mention the obvious?" asked Shaw.

"What's that?"

"This guy isn't a Libyan terrorist. He's white as snow."

Shaw clicked the wiper again and the picture momentarily crystallized. Carver hadn't caught the race of the first man, but he highly doubted the smoker had been in the back seat of the red hatchback.

"Makes you wonder," said Carver, "what involvement they have with Katarina."

"We could go ask them."

"Or we could stay back and see if they lead us to an actual Libyan bomber."

Shaw combed his beard with his fingers. "How do you know they're tied together?"

"I don't. This could be related, it could be something else."

The reaction to the statement was an obvious snort. "How much trouble is our girl in anyway?"

Carver wondered if these men had stolen something from her room. There was also Katya's fear of being kidnapped. She was currently alone. The more time they spent on this, the more she'd be vulnerable.

He idly checked the door frame and knocked on the window. The Iris company car was equipped with ballistic protection. "Are you allowed to be driving this for extra-curricular activities?"

"Not even a little," muttered Shaw.

The driver exited the building and returned to the island

just as the other finished pumping gas and set it on the hook. Instead of getting back in the car, they lingered outside, chatting. The driver accepted a cigarette and they checked their phones. They almost seemed to be stalling.

"I think they made us," said Shaw.

"They might have."

"We should have moved in before."

"Nothing to do about it now but relax."

They waited another two minutes, not daring to touch the wiper again. It made discerning what was going on difficult, but the distance pretty much took care of that anyway. The two men finally loaded in and hit the road. Shaw waited as long as he could before pulling after them.

A minute later the Mercedes took the ramp onto the S8 Expressway, with slightly more regular traffic and longer, straighter lanes. It allowed them to hang farther back than usual. Even though they were aboveground, the drive took them under a curving skylight structure that enveloped them in glass. The rain suddenly cut out and the distant skyline was beautiful. The Palace of Culture and Science was dramatically lit in purples and blues.

The Mercedes slowed suddenly enough that Shaw quickly closed the distance between them. Their target shifted two lanes and took an exit at the last second, slowing even more.

It was a test to see if anyone was following them. Instead of hitting the breaks, Shaw released the gas and let the car gradually slow. As the Mercedes turned around the ramp, Shaw guided his car out of sight, pulled over to the emergency lane, and stopped. Carver counted to twenty in silence as three vehicles passed. Then Shaw resumed toward the exit. It was a careful balancing act. Move too quickly and the waiting Mercedes might clock them, but stop too long and they would be impossible to follow.

Their timing hit the sweet spot. The Mercedes turned onto the street just barely in sight as they rounded the exit. The chase was still on.

The drive took them past the restored Old Town Market Place. Colorfully painted buildings formed looming walls of European charm. Cobblestones supplanted asphalt, and Shaw had to ease off to avoid being singled out at this lonely time of night. They were starting to stick out like a sore thumb but had to balance that against the risk of losing their prey.

The Mercedes paused before twisting down an alley. Shaw pulled to the edge slowly. The Mercedes stopped half a block in at a wall. It was a dead end. Shaw twisted the steering wheel.

"Wait, don't go down there," warned Carver. "I don't like it."

Shaw worked his lips. "They're trapped in. No way out but through us. No need for us to hop in the cage too."

Shaw drove past the alley and made a U-turn so he could park on the curb across the street from it. They now had an unimpeded view of their target.

As with the gas station, two men got out. They were more relaxed than before, talking and sharing a laugh instead of fingering their weapons. They moved toward a building and disappeared behind the right corner.

"Is there a side alley behind there?" asked Shaw. "A walkway maybe?"

"No way to see from here." Carver zoomed the car's map closer. "There's nothing on the navigation."

"This could be the end of the line."

Carver nodded. "I need to get eyes on them. You stay here, I'm going in."

"Vince, this is dangerous."

"Welcome to the jungle, brother. If you've seen one, you've seen them all. Cover my six."

The street and alley were clear so Carver slipped out and hurried across. Once safely in darkness, he slowed his pace. The rain had subsided some and the close buildings filtered out much of the remaining spray, but it was still wet enough to annoy him. On the plus side, the noise helped cover the sound of his advance. Carver glanced up at the curtained windows, found no snooping faces, and drew the Maxim 9.

While the suppressed weapon was ideal for clandestine operations in urban environments, he wished he'd had the foresight to bring his SIG. He had more confidence in the P320 in a drawn-out firefight against multiple targets, especially considering the weather. In the end, though, one bullet was almost always as good as any other, subsonic or otherwise.

Voices slipped through the pattering rain. The men were speaking, still outside, voices muted. The words were too muddy to decipher. Carver continued on the cobblestone, careful to avoid splashing through puddles. Fifteen feet away from the bumper of the Mercedes, a voice rang out.

"Who are you?"

Carver dove sideways to a gray dumpster against the opposite wall. He ducked behind and readied his gun. The voices had stopped. Carver positioned with half an eye peeking around the steel edge. The Mercedes was motionless. The men hid behind the building corner, also a dead end. Perhaps there was a door, but they were otherwise backed in.

A man stepped out wearing a heavy navy overcoat. The driver, a white guy Carver didn't recognize from the train. He was a stout figure, not especially tall but built like a truck. He had short brown hair and a graying mustache and scraggly hair following his jawline. "I know you are there," he said. "Who are you to follow me?"

The accent was Eastern European maybe. Carver figured it was better tactics to keep his gun hidden. Make them wonder if he was unarmed and find out the hard way.

Carver leaned out from the dumpster and called over the rain. "What's your interest in Katarina Litvinenko?"

The man's sharp eyebrows went up. "Who?"

"Don't play dumb. I was there."

A beat. "That was you at the hotel. How did you track us?"

"Trade secret, asshole. Tell me what you were doing there and maybe we can work something out."

He grinned. On opposite sides of the alley, with the car and rain between them, thirty paces away and in a dark alcove, the man was confident of his safety. "Nothing to worry. We can work out," he said, a break in his English. "Who are you to Ms. Litvinenko?"

This could be another stalling tactic. The last thing he would do was ease off the trigger or forget the second man, out of sight but pinned in the alley just the same. There was still no motion in the car.

"It's pretty simple," said Carver. "I'm paid security, just doing my job. Now you."

The man frowned. Something Carver had said was unexpected. "My name is Roman. I am no one. A messenger."

"You broke into my client's hotel room. Were you there to steal something? To plant something?"

"We just wanted to talk."

"Well now's your chance. You better get to the point real quick unless you want me to come over there."

Roman showed his teeth. It was the expression of a guy who wanted to pound someone into ground meat and maybe grill them up afterward. "We were there to talk business, I swear to you."

"If that's all you want, why don't you come over here and make an appointment?"

His jaw tightened. "Ms. Litvinenko is, how you say, a hero. We cannot speak openly."

"Who do you work for?"

"I am sorry, I cannot say this. Who do you work for?"

Carver scowled and stood a little straighter out of cover to get a better look at his surroundings. Although he was deep in the alley, the twisting rain was finding a way through, soaking his hair and face. "Listen to me. The only way you're getting to Katarina is by going through me. If you have legitimate business with her you need to address it to me. Otherwise I'm afraid I need to treat you as hostile."

"That would be a mistake," he warned, water streaking past his stern smile.

"I'll tell you what's a mistake," started Carver, but that was as far as he got. The second man swiveled around the hood of the Mercedes holding a pistol.

Carver was ready in a wide stance. His arms snapped to the threat, hand bracing the Maxim 9. The slide clicked three times and holes opened on the target. Chest, neck, headshot.

"*Blyat!*" cursed Roman.

Most definitely Russian.

Roman pulled his own gun with deft speed. Carver could barely duck behind the dumpster as bullets clanged off it.

He checked the Iris car, parked all the way at the end of the alley, dark windows hiding Shaw's reaction to the gunfire. Carver glanced left and right, wondering if he could squeeze between the dumpster and the wall to advance to the cover of the Mercedes.

Before he could return fire, a black Land Rover swerved into the alley. The wheels navigated over a pothole, splashing water as headlight beams scraped down and up until they fixed straight ahead onto him. Blinding him briefly, the vehicle drifted to a stop at a slight diagonal, blocking Carver in the alley. All four doors opened and men leapt out holding rifles.

The damned dead-end alley. It wasn't the Russians that were trapped, it was Carver, and the ambush had been executed to a tee.

13

The Maxim 9 clacked as Carver fired at the incoming operatives. The metallic report and subsonic rounds worked against his intent to suppress, and he had no chance of hitting his targets with the lights in his eyes. But the men were experienced and recognized the ricochets of lead well enough to buy Carver a few extra seconds.

He started to twist around the dumpster, but the driver of the Mercedes fired and forced him to retreat. Carver's position was untenable. Four men with long guns and a straight shot down the alley, and another guy around the back. The driver was protected by the brick building so his friends could open up without fear of friendly fire. And besides, Carver couldn't rely on the humanity of his enemy.

He was caught in the crossfire with a handful of seconds to live.

The semiauto bark of an AK echoed off the alley walls. Rounds pelted the cobblestones at Carver's feet. He fired at the shooter, but there were three more where he came from. Carver was about to be mowed down. His only chance was taking on Roman.

Carver braced his back against the dumpster and heaved.

For a second the steel obstruction seemed rusted in place, but with great effort it budged. The Maxim 9 clicked empty as Carver leg-pressed the dumpster into rolling. He ran backward as bullets cascaded around him. Sparks flashed and a loud clang of metal nearly blew out his ear.

Roman fired at the shifting cover but didn't have a line on him. The hunk of metal banged against the front fender of the Mercedes, and Carver spun around it, nearly tripping over the guy he'd killed. He hit the mag release and reached for a new one at his belt.

Roman lunged, swinging the butt of his empty pistol. Carver flinched backward and batted the arm away. Leaning down, Roman reached for his dead friend's pistol. Carver kicked it through a puddle and it hit the brick wall.

The Kalashnikovs stopped firing. Their target was behind cover and mixed up with a friendly. Nice to see they cared. The complication would only hold them off a moment.

Roman swung a fist. Carver turned to take the blow in the side while he wrapped his palm around the spare mag and punched the guy in the jaw. Roman staggered backward. Carver tried to slide the mag in but the Russian set his foot and charged, catching a shoulder to his gut and lifting him off the ground.

This guy was strong. Short, able to maneuver under Carver's guard, and with the muscles and know-how to do something once he got there. Before being slammed into the wall, Carver elbowed the back of his neck hard, making him stumble. Carver's boots returned to the ground and he threw the Russian sideways. Roman barreled into the wall, but so did Carver's spare magazine.

Well-placed fired forced Carver to duck. The other operatives were advancing in formation. Until now Carver had been dealing with amateurs, sloppy militants ill-prepared for his brand of precise violence. These guys were different. Appearing out of the blue, they were well-trained and packed real hardware. Carver had to regain the initiative.

Roman pushed himself a little slowly off the wall. Carver kicked his chest, slamming him back again. The Russian bounced like a boxer off the ropes and tried to smother Carver. This guy was a ground fighter, attempting to use his wide frame to control his opponent.

As Roman grabbed the right hand holding the empty Maxim, Carver reached for the blade on his left hip. He pulled the Colonel out in a gun grip. The Russian tried to grab that too but a quick slash cut open his hand. Roman grunted in pain and Carver quick-punched it into the man's heart.

The blade twisted out of his hand and Roman staggered backward. Carver waited for two seconds until Roman hit the wall with the knife protruding from his chest. It hadn't gone deep enough. Carver rolled low to the other guy's pistol, switching the barrel of the Maxim into his left palm, and fired the new gun twice into Roman's chest. He sagged to the ground, his bloody hand staining a water puddle.

Carver immediately spun and fired at the oncoming Russian hit team.

They scattered and opened fire. The Mercedes ripped apart as Carver cowered behind the wheel and engine block. Safety glass sprayed and chunks of brick chipped off the rear wall.

Carver leaned under the car and fired at the men's feet. He barely missed, but the threat was enough to make them dance back toward their vehicle. They had superior firepower but no cover, but that would only last so long. Carver slowed his fire to preserve his ammunition as best he could. When the gun ran dry, he dropped it and reached for his last Glock mag. He loaded the Maxim and faced down the regrouping team of Russians. He was pinned down, heavily outgunned, and they knew it.

A new pair of headlights roared down the alley. The Russians twisted around as Shaw's car slammed the front corner of the Land Rover, shoving it aside just enough to speed by. One of the shooters bounced off the car's hood as the others dove away.

"Nick, you beautiful bastard," laughed Carver.

He rose to a crouch and hurried around the trunk of the Mercedes. A grunt pulled his attention to the wall where Roman struggled to his feet and yanked out the embedded knife. The bastard was wearing a vest, which explained the Colonel twisting from his grip. Carver raised the Maxim but Roman dove behind the gray dumpster. Irony.

Shaw scraped to a stop. Carver scowled toward the hiding Russian but he had four other operatives and his friend to worry about. He jumped in the passenger seat, slamming the door just as a barrage of fire pelted the trunk and rear windshield.

"Tell me this is armored in the rear," he said, staying low.

Shaw sat up in his seat with little regard for the fire. "What do you take me for, an amateur?"

Shaw slammed the car in reverse and took it back up the alley. The Russian operatives sidestepped and kept their fire trained on the car. A side window spiderwebbed but prevented penetration. The car raced past the shooters and scraped the brick wall to avoid the Land Rover. A shower of sparks filled Carver's window. They reverse-fishtailed onto the street. The Russians sprinted for the Land Rover as Shaw sped away.

"So much for not walking into a trap," muttered Carver.

"What the fuck is this, Vince?"

Shaw's usual dispassion was gone. The Land Rover peeled out of the alley and gassed after them.

"Don't kill me," said Carver, "but I think they're Wagner Group."

"Russian black ops?"

"Sent by Arkady Malkin. It looks like Katya's fears were well-founded. This is why I need to get her to the CIA."

Shaw swerved around a corner, but the right wheel was knocking against something. On an open street, he had trouble pushing the car past fifty without incurring a worrisome wobble.

"Katya hates the CIA, Vince. She'll never go for it."

"You ever have to choose between shit and a shit sandwich?"

The Russians turned into their rear view and accelerated. Shaw made a series of quick turns with the intention of losing them, but it wasn't happening. The Land Rover expertly maneuvered around each bend, gaining on them.

"We have a problem," said Shaw. "Our car is fucked. We're outnumbered two to one, and we don't have military hardware."

He turned onto a wide bridge. The city lights across the river reflected on its surface and conveyed illusory tranquility.

"Should we go to the police?" Shaw asked.

"I can't get caught."

"It's better than dead, Vince. I could tell them Iris was recruiting you. Leave the alphabet agencies out of it."

Carver bit down as he watched the Land Rover close on them. He didn't think it would be so easy to trick Polish authorities, but maybe Shaw had a point. He wasn't acting illegally here, anyway. If going to the police meant saving his friend's life...

Carver sighed. "Nick," he muttered, "I don't think we're gonna make it to the police. Brace for impact!"

The Land Rover slammed their back bumper, skipping the car forward. They swayed side to side. Shaw fought the wheel and steered them straight, but at the cost of slowing them down even more. The Land Rover pulled on their right side, the glint of the river beyond them.

Carver threw open his door, pointed the Maxim 9, and emptied the mag into the windshield. Though the 147-grain rounds were heavier than most 9mm ammunition, they were hollow points meant for stealth applications and weren't famous for their stopping power. The bullets mushroomed on the laminated glass, and Carver missed his SIG all the more. The driver flinched behind the fractured glass. Perhaps a round had gotten through but he couldn't be sure.

"Give me your gun," he barked.

But the Land Rover turned into their fender, jerking the ass of the car sideways in a PIT maneuver. Skidding out of Shaw's control, the car veered sideways and careened into the bridge wall. The airbags snapped open in less than a blink, disorienting them as the vehicle tore through and the wheels lost asphalt. They were suspended in nothingness for two seconds before the hood contacted water. They rocked forward. Carver had removed his seat belt to shoot out the door, and his left side hit the dash with a crack.

The collision had forced his door into him, but it remained open enough that water flooded into the cabin in a wave. The car sank fast. Carver couldn't find his gun.

Shaw unbuckled and they looked at each other. They were both okay considering, but they were still in the shit. The hood of the car went under.

Gunfire erupted over their heads. Plinks and plunks hit the car, and holes popped into the ceiling.

"Down!" screamed Carver, squeezing his large form into the floor and shielding his head with his arms.

A round skipped through the edge of Shaw's thigh and punched into his seat. "Argh!"

"The roof's not armored!"

"I wasn't planning on fighting off helicopters!"

The vehicle pitched forward as it took on water up to their knees. A mixed blessing, sinking provided cover as the butt of the car rose above them. The bullets still relentlessly pounded the vehicle, but the ballistic armor on the rear did its job.

"We're safer in the car," said Carver.

"For now."

Shaw reached over the back seat with a cry of pain and grabbed a kit. He opened the box, removed a splint, and wrapped it around his upper thigh.

"How are you, brother?" asked Carver.

"Just a scratch."

Carver pulled the seat lever and forced his seat back into a reclined position so he could crawl into the back seat. His hopes were dashed when he didn't find any weapons complementing the medical supplies. As the water overtook the front seat, he helped pull Shaw up to him. The bullets stuttered and stopped, leaving the bubbling water their main priority. The black car descended into the depths head first.

"They're not shooting anymore," said Shaw. "That's something."

"They're still up there," replied Carver, watching between the cracks of the beat-up rear windshield. The Land Rover was parked at the broken wall and three operatives looked on, ready with rifles. "The second we peek out of the water, they're gonna rip us to shreds."

"We need to swim for the underside of the bridge. They'll have no shooting angle and they can't hang out forever."

The water lapped at the top of the back seat. The car had launched away from the bridge through the air, and its sinking trajectory was taking them further still.

"It's a good distance," said Carver. "We might have a chance if we're deep enough."

They squeezed their heads to the cracked glass as the car went down.

"This glass is punctured," said Shaw, eyeing a fatal crack. It won't hold in any air."

"Do you have oxygen tanks in the trunk?"

"Who do you think I am, Batman? Deep breaths. Keep them steady."

The former Navy SEAL breathed in and out to a measured rhythm. Carver didn't have the underwater conditioning and dive training so he imitated his more experienced friend. Their preparation culminated with a final intake of air as water crawled up their neck and over their mouths. The beautiful lights of the city seemed like a dream as they faded into a watery sky.

Carver and Shaw switched to hand signals, waiting several excruciating seconds as they descended from the view of their pursuers. A few stray rounds arced through the water, forcing them to hold off longer. The bullets could only penetrate so deep, though, and soon they signaled each other to move.

Carver tried his back door but it was stuck. With the car full of water, there was no pressure differentiation to hold the doors shut. He struggled with it a moment before remembering it had scraped against the alley wall. He turned and found Shaw swimming out from his side. Carver followed.

The car bumped against the river floor in a slow motion collision. Carver lost his footing and fell against the front seat, spitting out a gulp of air. No matter how well trained you are, dark tendrils of panic creep into the margins of your mind when you begin to run out of oxygen. Shaw paused, seeing him in trouble. He returned to the car and helped Carver exit.

They were now deep enough that the water would've been black if it weren't for the headlights, taillights, and cabin lights of the sunken car. A glowing yellow Shaw waved Carver forward, but his lungs weren't feeling too hot. He didn't think he was going to make it to the bridge before resurfacing. Either outcome would be a death sentence.

Carver pulled close to the tire and pressed the air valve. Bubbles shot outward and he put his lips to the nozzle. Putrid oxygen filled his lungs and somehow it was the best thing he ever breathed. Shaw waited calmly as Carver pulled away and gave him a thumbs up. His friend nodded and they both swam along the river bottom and made it under the bridge.

They surfaced quietly, protected by the shade of the bridge arches. There was no more shooting, no more clipped talking. The two didn't move until they heard the approach and retreat of another car. It took a minute to reach one of the bridge's supporting walls. They grabbed the slimy brick and waited. They couldn't see who was on the street just as nobody up there could see beneath it. After another minute they were sure the Russians had fled.

At the riverbank, they climbed out, dripping wet.

"You see that tire thing in a movie?" laughed Shaw.

"I'm just glad they weren't filled with nitrogen," he replied. "Are you okay to walk?"

"I'll manage."

In the distance, a police siren encouraged them to hurry. Shaw favored his leg as he walked, and Carver braced his shoulder under his friend's.

After putting the bridge behind them, Shaw asked, "Were we just neutralized?"

"Hopefully the Wagner Group believes that. But they might also realize American involvement now."

"Good thing you're dead."

Carver's phone buzzed and he pulled it from his pocket. There was water in the screen, but it had mostly survived the water. He wiped it as best he could and checked the anonymous text message.

"This must be Officer Williams getting back to me about the terrorist's phone they recovered from the train."

"Yeah? What does the collected intelligence of the US of A declare?"

"The last phone call the Libyan made, back at the train station, was to a number in Warsaw. She says someone else knows I'm here."

Shaw hocked a loogie and spit it on the sidewalk. "You don't say."

14

The smart thing would have been to disappear, to stay off the grid, but with Katya's life on the line, they couldn't risk playing it safe. Unfortunately, when Carver tried to shake the water out of his phone, it must have shaken into a place it didn't belong because the screen went out.

"What are you doing?" badgered Shaw. "You're supposed to put that in rice."

"Yeah, and your leg's supposed to be on ice, but here we are."

He grunted. "Here we are."

Unlike Carver, Shaw wasn't stranded in the city without backup. He called up Marcel, who had taken his newfound liberty over to one of Warsaw's famed nightlife spots. He put a rush on picking them up in a rented Volkswagen Polo. It didn't have ballistic armor.

"What happened to you guys?" he asked over the electronic music working out his speakers. "I left a cute woman high and dry for this."

Shaw lowered the volume and said, "I'll fill you in when I figure out what story I want to tell. It's better you don't get involved. Just drop us at the hotel and you can be back to wetting your lady's whistle in no time."

Marcel did as instructed with a notable glare Carver's way, as if the father of teenagers had singled out the bad influence. They unloaded from the car at the side of the hotel to check if anybody had eyes on the place.

Marcel saw his boss limp out. "Nick, are you hurt?"

Shaw glanced at the wet stain over his wound. "Blood's not stopping, is it? You mind waiting a few minutes for me?"

"Whatever you need."

Once they passed the front desk, Shaw rested his palm on the pistol on his hip. They detoured to the stairwell and hopped up two flights. The hall was clear and they didn't hear anything at Katya's door. Carver knocked and she let them in while cradling Anya in her arms. Suitcases stood ready by the door. The new dog bag was red, with a similar pattern and label as the last, and a new chew toy inside.

"Going somewhere?"

She hiked a shoulder. "I didn't know if you were coming back." While her breathing and posture were calm, she was still wide eyed. "Why are you here?" she asked Shaw.

"Relax. You may have cut and run on us, but Iris has a professional responsibility, not to mention reputation, to maintain. I just want to see you safely to the train."

She frowned in response to the added inconvenience but didn't go so far as to object. A stranger had been in her room. "Please tell me you caught the bastard."

"In a manner of speaking," said Carver, "but he had a lot of friends so let's just call it a push. Listen, Katya, it's time to consider a change of plans."

"What change? My train tomorrow is booked."

"You can take the financial hit. These guys mean business. They were sent by Arkady Malkin."

She shot daggers at Shaw. "You told him?"

"Everyone knows who you are," he said defensively.

"The point is he's here for you," stated Carver.

Her response was an indignant snort. "I'm not a child."

"No one is saying you are, but these guys aren't social services. They're state-sanctioned killers."

"Just like the both of you were, I bet. Were you Army buddies?"

Carver sighed. She was closer to the bullseye than the boards. "We both did military and met up afterwards in private employment."

"It figures."

"I'm not beholden to anyone but myself now. Everything I do, I do because I agree with it. That's a promise."

She set the dog down. After a quick sniff at Carver's feet, Anya hopped into her new bag and curled into a ball.

"I appreciate the concern..." she started.

"Apparently not enough."

Dimples bloomed beneath her cheekbones. "Vince, I don't know your last name. I don't know where you came from or who you work for. What I do know is I can make a difference. My appearance in Ukraine is important. It's an announcement to the world, and it's what my uncle wants to stop. If I give up now, he wins."

"So this is some family spat to you?"

"I'll be safe once I go public. Otherwise I'll always be looking over my shoulder. And what about Pavel? His activism opposes the separatists in the east. The least I can do is meet him for a press event in Kiev."

Carver muttered under his breath and paced to the window. Katarina was every bit as headstrong as advertised, but she was braver than he could have known. It explained the pestering fearlessness. The live fast, die young mentality. Discounting various combat theaters, he couldn't deny having had similar moments in his youth.

"Are these suitcases for now?" he asked.

"They were in case I needed to leave quickly."

He nodded, watching the empty street through the window. "I think it's best if you stay in another room tonight."

"I already told you, I don't know who you are."

"You could use mine," cut in Shaw. Carver eyed him and he shrugged. "You came to me, Katya. You know I'm on the up and up."

She chewed her lip. "And you want me to stay in your room."

"I'm not using it anymore. I need to hook up with the police anyway."

"You're turning yourself in?" asked Carver.

"I have a gunshot wound that needs stitching. There's a river with a car in it that's registered to Iris. The driver knows I borrowed it, and he works for a separate sub company so I can't count on him to cover for me. Nothing for it but to face the music."

Carver worked his jaw. "I don't suppose you did anything illegal."

"I was the victim," he said. "Don't worry, I'll keep both of you out of it. I was technically off the clock, anyway."

"Okay."

Carver wanted to offer help from the government, if needed, but he couldn't mention that in front of Katya. Not two sentences after he told her he was independent.

They walked to Shaw's room, Katya handling the bag with Anya and Carver with the heavy stuff. Katya said goodnight. Shaw handed Carver his extra key card and went inside to set her up. Ten minutes later, back in his own room at his own window, Carver watched Shaw get into Marcel's car. He wondered what he had talked to Katya about, but he mostly kept an eye on his friend as long as he could to make sure he didn't have a tail.

Knowing the Russians, they would go to ground after nearly being exposed. But they were regrouping, not retreating. Their operation in Warsaw was done, but Kyiv was a blank slate.

Carver was on the opposite side of the same coin. They believed him to be dead, but that assumption only protected him so much. Roman had seen him up close. Maybe the driver of the Land Rover too. Also, there was no telling how much damage was done by the Libyan terrorist's phone call. The description of a large American might be all they needed to single him out later. It was at best a fifty-fifty proposition. Heads they win, tails you lose.

Sleep was difficult. Carver couldn't remember the last

time he had come so close to dying. He'd seen recent action in Taipei and Spruce Pine, but he'd been better armed and on the offensive. Tonight he had been caught flat-footed by a Russian hit team. The truth was he was lucky to have made it.

He pulled a love seat to the window and dozed between bouts of staring outside, passing out, and jerking awake every hour to make sure the quiet of the night wasn't breached. He dreamt of tranquil city lights, always on the horizon.

It was dawn when he brought Morgan up to speed. She was pissed he hadn't immediately woken her up, and she was right to be, but the few sharp words didn't manifest as an argument. It wasn't her style, and they had a long day ahead that turned into a slog. Neither of their departures were until late afternoon.

Carver camped in the hotel to discreetly watch Katya. She was overly energetic and bored but mostly stayed put so he gave her as much room as possible. He drew the line on two points: he would be by her side whenever she walked Anya, and she had to eat in. It was a delicate balance that seemed to work wonders. Either that or finding a stranger in her room had scared her straight.

During some downtime, he and Morgan strategized their next moves. Where to stay, where to recon, and what to look out for. He saw Morgan off to the airport. While there he purchased a new burner phone and transferred the SIM card from the waterlogged one, which he properly destroyed and disposed of.

He ended up away from the hotel longer than he would have liked. By the time he returned, Katya was gone. A note on her nightstand said she was stir crazy and had to get out before being cooped in the overnight train. She said it was nice knowing him.

Carver studied the note. It seemed legitimate. Reckless, of course, but legitimate. Another case of Katya's spontaneity getting the better of her. There were not a lot of options to get to Kyiv and he was confident she would be on the train. At this point he had no time to do anything but head to the Warsaw East station himself. He wore a hoodie and sunglasses to disguise his appearance.

The Kiev Express still used the old spelling. The destination country had only recently started a campaign of convincing English-language organizations to use the Ukrainian Kyiv over the Russian-derived Kiev. Carver supposed Poland wasn't a priority. The Kiev Express was a night train, direct to the city, and while distance was only a third more than that of Berlin to Warsaw, the travel time was almost three times as long.

He boarded as soon as the train hit the station. It was an older model from the seventies or eighties. The cars were all sleepers with private compartments. He quickly found his and parked by the window to keep an eye on the passengers filing in on the platform.

Shaw was a no-show, which could only mean he was tied up with authorities. Katarina approached with Marcel in tow. The CPO appeared hungover but alert. Hanz and the other guy weren't around. Guess you can never predict where real loyalty and duty lies.

Carver watched their conversational back and forth, knowing it was one last push by Iris Executive to extend a contract with an intractable principal. Katya denied further services, and Marcel was powerless to veto the decision. He waved her off. Katarina took in the length of the train and Carver leaned away from the window so he wouldn't be spotted. She pet the terrier in the bag on her arm and boarded one car ahead of his.

15

His sleeper compartment was a single, with a chair that converted to a bed and a luggage rack overhead. A corner table folded up to reveal a sink. The small space was something close to musty due to the radiator beneath the window.

Carver leaned on the open door and lingered halfway in the corridor. His compartment was the last in the car. He could look through the window to the next and watch Katya's door. After a few minutes the conductor stopped by with a disapproving look.

"It's a little hot," he explained, pointing to the heater.

The man nodded and asked for his ticket in what was probably Ukrainian. Carver handed it over. The conductor peeked at his passport for good measure, and Carver had the feeling it wouldn't be the last time his documents were checked on this particular trip.

After he left, another man peeked in and asked, "*Chay?*"

Carver's brow furrowed until the man wheeled up a tea cart.

"You don't happen to have coffee, do you?" The request was lost in the abyss of the language barrier, and he happily accepted the hot drink as a consolation prize.

Anya yipped twice when the conductor reached Katya's compartment. The terrier was easily spooked but quickly quieted. Watching the hall some time after the conductor and tea man were through, it became clear there wouldn't be anything interesting happening for a while.

With the heightened security on this leg of the journey, it would make sense for Russian operatives to make themselves scarce. Ukraine was a country divided, arguably a taut rope gripped at opposite ends by the US and Russia playing tug-of-cold-war. Carver didn't fool himself. Just because the current administration pulled with the Americans didn't mean the entire population did. It meant, once they were in the capital, tensions would be high.

The Kiev Express had no public cars. This kept interactions more or less contained. There was a downside to the increased privacy. Sealed doors made it difficult to keep an eye on Katarina. Carver could only watch the hallway off and on. It wasn't all bad, however. The doors made clacking sounds as they slid open. Even though she was a car over, he was confident a careful ear could detect a passenger switching cars or walking by, at least when the track noise wasn't too loud. Then there was his early-warning system. Anya was territorial when confined in small spaces. Her bark was unmistakable. Carver rested while he could.

Several hours passed. He opened his eyes as the train slowed and stopped on the Polish side of the border. Officials boarded to check passports again. Carver watched just out of sight as Katya opened up for the first time amid stifled barks. It looked like she had been sleeping. An older man with a long coat opened the next compartment over and waited by the door, just like Carver. They eyed each other without a word before turning to the officials and showing their IDs. In a few minutes, they were on their way to Ukraine.

After a momentous hour of watching the moonlit countryside, there was a knock on his door.

"Yeah?"

No one answered. For a moment he wondered if someone had rapped the wall on the way past. Then there was another, more intentional knock. Carver wondered why he hadn't heard the door to his car slide open. He drew his P320 and held it behind him as he opened the door.

It was Katya, wearing a fur coat and holding a bottle of vodka.

"Funny seeing you here," she said with a lilt.

"Am I that obvious?"

"All men are."

She pushed past him inside. Carver checked up and down the hall. No one else was out. He slid the door to a quiet close and watched Katya to get a handle on her.

"This is a small cabin. I have three beds in mine. I booked the whole thing." She sat on the seat, keeping the coat tight. The radiator had been turned down so his room was probably cooler than most by now. She looked tiny wrapped in the puffy mass, long legs of spandex ending in fuzzy slippers. Her hair was let down though her makeup was freshly done.

"How's Anya?" he asked.

Her pink nails drummed the bottle in her lap. "Trains put her to sleep. They put me to sleep too. It's so boring."

He crossed one arm over his chest, the other at his side with the weapon. "You're here because you're bored?"

She rolled her eyes and patted the bed beside her. "Sit. Drink with me, drinking buddy."

Katarina twisted the bottle open and took a swig of vodka. It wasn't a large swig but it was confidently done. A sign of experience without the need for show. She offered the open bottle to him.

Carver twisted around and sat beside her, careful to place the pistol on his left while she sat by the window to his right. He took the bottle and sampled it. Vodka in general didn't have enough flavor for him, but the quality was there. It went down smooth and had a pleasant burn that hugged his lungs.

"Good stuff," he said, handing the bottle back. "I guess if there's no party, you have to make one."

"I'm twenty-three. If I'm not having fun at this point in my life, it's not worth living."

"I see your point," was what he said, but all he could think about was his time at twenty-three in Detachment-Delta. He'd just completed the Operators Training Course at Fort Bragg. Close-quarters battle, close-target reconnaissance, free-fall parachuting, and offensive driving. Fun was one way to describe it.

"How old are you, Vince? I don't think you ever said."

"Thirty-two."

"So your years of fun are behind you?"

"Is that your hot take?"

"... Maybe."

He snatched the bottle back and grinned. "If you really thought that, you wouldn't be here right now."

She smiled as he took a gulp, but then her eyes narrowed defensively as she caught the implication. "Don't get ahead of yourself, big guy. You have too much confidence."

"No one's ever said that before."

"Maybe they have and you just haven't listened."

"Is this a Schrödinger's cat thing?"

He placed the bottle in her lap and she clasped it with both hands, fingers brushing his. He held the position for a prolonged moment of eye contact until she pulled away. How was that for confidence?

Katya cleared her throat and glanced out the window. "You said you wanted to discuss... how serious I was."

He arched an eyebrow. It was an unexpected turn in the conversation, but he wasn't one to shy away from an opening. "What's your business with Pavel Shishov?"

She spun to him a little too quickly. "Wow, you get right to it."

"I'm direct too."

She smirked. "Straight and to the point."

Carver set an elbow on his knee and leaned into her. "Well?"

She took a breath that ended with a shrug, an evolving decision arriving at its conclusion. "I don't technically have any business with him. Not yet. It's an exploratory meeting."

"Because of what he stands for."

"Because of *who* he stands for. Pavel is from Donbas in Eastern Ukraine. A lot of Russians live there."

"The rebels."

"Not all of them. Russia has a mighty history. Uncle— Arkady always said we were only half a country. Moscow is the head, but Kiev was its beating heart."

"Except it's Kyiv now."

Her lips tightened, but the tension was released with a laugh. "Arkady always believed us to be the inheritors of civilization. Moscow is the Third Rome, after Constantinople before it."

"That explains the military failure in Lithuania in 1991. Large-scale conventional operations against sovereign states invite unwanted scrutiny. Russia made the same mistake in '94 in the First Chechen War."

"Some war is justified," she said meekly.

"You must be talking about the intervention in Georgia. Russia brought journalists into the theater of war, vilifying Georgia as the aggressors and accusing them of genocide. Classic *spetzpropaganda*. It's taught in the Military and Foreign Languages Department of the Ministry of Defense."

She stared at him for a cool half minute. "How do you know this stuff?"

Carver hiked a shoulder. " 'Information is cheap, it is a universal weapon, it has unlimited range, it is easily accessible and permeates all state borders without restrictions.' That's from a Polish political scientist out of Warsaw. She was writing about Crimea."

"You're having fun with me."

"Some people pee in toilets."

Her cheeks flushed red and she looked to her lap. Finding the bottle a sufficient distraction, she took two large gulps of the clear liquid.

"You need to understand," she said without meeting his gaze, "in order to properly hate my country, I must first love it."

He sighed. It was a nuanced sentiment for someone whose developed moral beliefs clashed with her fervent upbringing. What would anyone think under such circumstances, and did that really make them wrong?

"If you're so studied," she countered, "you should know the famous words from the English geographer Mackinder. He who controls East Europe controls the world."

"Close enough," said Carver. "And I'm officially impressed. That idea laid the foundation for the next century of geopolitics. It's the Heartland theory."

"It's a Western warning about the danger of allowing Russia to control their own natural resources."

"You're not wrong. The twentieth century was dominated by oil. But the United States promotes market diversity against a Russian monopoly. That's not as heavy-handed as marching troops over borders."

"Isn't it?" Katarina huffed and shook her head dismissively. "Anyway, we're not speaking of war."

"There's a damn lot of overlap, Katya. Those guys back in Warsaw, they're Wagner Group. They're the same paramilitary contractors who strolled into Crimea under the implicit threat of violence."

"Does it not count that violence was avoided?"

"That just means the enemy was sufficiently cowed."

Her eyes hit the window again. She stared without looking at anything specific, seeming to question her reasons for coming to his compartment. He wasn't sure why he was being so hard on her. She deserved it and then some. Then again, she was already speaking out against her country's actions. It wasn't that she fully supported NATO or that she fully detested Russia, it was more that it was complicated. But here she was, trying to get a discussion going, and Carver had derailed her to prove a point.

It was time to soften up. He held out a palm, flashed a winning grin, and asked, "Are you going to drink it all, or can anyone else have a sip?"

Her stoic expression broke into a resigned chuckle. She handed the bottle over and he made a show of knocking it back to turn that chuckle into a full smile. He wiped his mouth with the back of his hand and let her forget about her troubles. For a few minutes they chatted about everything that didn't matter. The weather, the countryside, the vodka. She asked if it hurt to be punched and then slammed her fist into his arm as hard as she could. It hurt her, all right. He checked her fingers but they weren't broken or swelling. After a minute they both realized he was giving her hand a massage. She held her breath, and he let her go.

"So... you were saying about Pavel..."

She cleared her throat. "Yes. We haven't met yet. He's a secretive person. He receives more death threats than I do, you know. He preaches a message of peace. That his home Donbas is both Russian and Ukrainian, you understand? He doesn't fight for liberation or for conquest. He believes in a world where everyone can be civil to each other."

It was a nice sentiment, but Carver didn't believe in that dream. He had years of hard proof that said it was a fairy tale. A pleasant story where all conflict is forever wrapped up in the end.

The real world is a physical one. The powerful run circles around the weak. Kinetic violence is merely an extension of it. Carver didn't believe violence should be the preferred option, but in his bones he knew it was a necessary one. *Tertia optio.*

"You don't want to meet Pavel because of what he says," deduced Carver. "It's about what he *does*."

She watched him as a mouse might a wildcat, without so much as a blink. "What is it that he does?"

"Come on, Katya. It's not like this is privileged information. His home is a war zone. His father was killed in the violence. He wants what everybody wants, which is to live with opportunity and without looking over his shoulder. And these aren't just empty ideals. He's doing the dirty work, helping smuggle Ukrainians and Russians away from the conflict region and even out of the country. This is a man who personifies everything you need. You can be a voice for him, but you can also be a client."

She didn't speak for a moment. She didn't say whether she had decided to help the cause or disappear with its help. Katya grew nervous and must have realized it because she grabbed the bottle and downed so much that Carver pulled it away. She almost growled as it burned her throat, but it was a good, hungry growl.

And yet, she wouldn't cross the finish line and simply talk to him.

"Why did you come here, Katya? I already knew you wanted to meet Pavel. You're not telling me anything I didn't already know."

"I just wanted to—" She froze as her eyes met his. Whatever automatic excuse she'd had lined up dissolved into a wisp. She frowned, took a long breath, and said, "I feel safer with you."

He nodded and, as earnestly as he could, said, "Now we're getting somewhere. There are a lot of people after you."

Her pink nails rested on his hand with unexpected warmth. "It's like you said. If I'm being chased, it's better to stay in a room that isn't mine."

Their eyes held and her fur coat rose and fell with the swell of her chest. The sound of her breathing pounded his ears, and he leaned down and kissed her. Her head fell onto his shoulder as her mouth opened, her hand tightening on his. For the briefest of moments, he was that wildcat and she was that mouse. Timid, meek, shy. Then something predatory awakened in her and she swung her knee over him and sat in his lap.

Carver scooted over so her leg had room. He shuffled the P320 to the table in the corner. He wrapped his arms around her as she cradled his jaw, her tongue slowly exploring. Then she suddenly drew away.

"Do you have ulterior motives?"

"What?"

"Can I trust you?"

His hands pulled her hips, but she resisted. He studied her pout and realized she was no longer playing. "You do know I'm doing my best to protect you?"

She nodded. "I do."

"Then let me."

She hugged him. His hand squeezed her back. Her fingers tickled his chest. She pulled back again, this time pulling the top of her jacket open and exposing snow-white breasts. Katya giggled and stood, lifting each leg to remove her slippers before sliding her skintight pants down. The fur coat still covered most of her, but she was a sight.

The whole thing was such a production that Carver was wary she would suddenly go for his gun. Hell, the coat itself was puffy enough to hide a shotgun. But when her teeth pulled at her lower lip and she opened the coat all the way, he saw firsthand that it wasn't hiding a damned thing. Instead of going for the gun she went for his belt.

"Have you been dreaming about this?" she asked with a kiss.

He canted his head. "I've never slept with a rich girl before."

His belt came away with a snap and she wasn't done

pulling. He laughed when she had trouble pulling his shirt over his head, and then her coat fell to the floor and he forgot what was funny. She straddled him with a moan of pleasure, smirking and staring deeply into his eyes as they felt every wiggle and bounce of the old train.

"Who are you?" she whimpered into his ear.

"I've told you all I can."

A long cool shiver rode up her back. "Are you CIA?"

The rest of his body stiffened. She pulled her head away to appraise him, nails digging threateningly into his neck and shoulders. Her breasts rocked up and down as if on open water.

"If I was CIA," said Carver, "you'd be extradited right now."

"Extra what?"

"I'm not going to take you away against your will."

"But you do want to take me, Vince?" She seemed driven to conversation now. Excited by it. She bucked and dug her nails in. "Are you going to grab me again, like you did in that bar? Are you going to kidnap me? Lock me away somewhere dark?"

He squirmed under her relentless assault. She was driving him wild and he no longer knew what she wanted him to say. All he knew was there was a hint of manipulation in everything she did. Teasing. Taunting. Coming to his room under the pretense of confiding and being safer with him while wearing fresh makeup and no underwear.

And yet, her forwardness was irresistible.

"Tell me what you want," he said.

Her hips stopped and she rocked gently with the train again. Her smirk was boastful now. A challenge to resist. "No, no, no, Vince, I want you to tell me what *you* want. Do you like me here? Do you want to keep me?"

She settled her cheek on his shoulder. The more her body relaxed, the more it drove him crazy. This whole thing was a game. She was no longer bored all right, but this was more. Maybe it was fair play after the thing with the Polish political scientist. Carver's hands traced over her glistening body, imploring her to continue.

The brakes of the train squealed. Katya spun to the window and hopped off him as if ejecting from an attack helicopter.

"The border check," she said, flinging her coat over her shoulders. "They're going to visit compartments." She nodded toward his gun on the table. "You should put that away." She nodded at his crotch. "That too."

Carver scowled as magnanimously as he could and put his clothes back on. "That was a cheap trick."

"I am anything but cheap." Katya bundled her slippers and leggings in her hand and opened the door. Then her bravado softened. "Sorry. Bad timing."

She blew him a kiss and left him high and dry.

Carver packed the SIG deep in his bag. Authorities boarded the train and a thin, balding man wearing a coat two sizes too large came to his compartment and asked something in guttural Ukrainian.

"English?" asked Carver.

The man nodded. "Tourist?"

"Yes."

He glanced over the compartment and left. A minute later Anya announced his arrival at Katya's door. As Carver watched, a burly man in tactical gear greeted him in stilted English. Carver tensed at the sudden intrusion. This man was a trained soldier.

"Passport please," said the man.

He already held a stack of a dozen or so. Carver handed his over.

"Thank you. Sit tight."

The man continued to the next compartment. Carver wasn't sure whether he should be relieved the man left or concerned he took his passport. But it was evident this was the regular procedure so he did as instructed and waited it out.

The train resumed at a slow crawl until it wheeled under a covered garage. The cars were put on lifts as they changed the trucks to the Russian standard rail gauge. The process took an hour before the train crept out of the garage. It stopped some ways ahead in the dark and the authorities once again boarded. The man with the ballistic vest returned to his compartment and handed the passport back.

"Get some sleep."

The process at the Ukrainian border was a lengthy one. Although Carver's part was done, the train still hadn't budged over an hour later. Some unlucky passengers had been taken off for questioning, and he figured they wouldn't all make it back on. He wasn't sure what he could do if Katya was singled out, but it fortunately never came to that.

After an exhausting wait during which most of the passengers had no doubt fallen asleep, the train resumed its progress into Ukraine. It was almost four in the morning. They would arrive at their destination by eleven.

Carver frowned and waited for any other surprises. The repetitive drone of the tracks was the only thing he heard. It was too dark to see anything out of the window, and his gaze kept returning to the bottle of vodka on the table.

It wasn't really a decision. Carver packed his pistol into the back of his jeans, grabbed the bottle, and went to Katarina's door. She opened up wearing a lace nightie. Her lips parted but she didn't speak. There was nothing more to talk about. He pushed into her, they kissed, and he practically tackled her onto the bed.

16

If the dalliance on the train was ill advised, it at least had the effect of suturing their adversarial relationship. Katya remained just as headstrong and brash as she had ever been, but her challenges to Carver's presence all but disappeared. Instead of trailing her from an unassuming distance, he strolled alongside the exiled dissident in plain sight. She was even beginning to take his advice. Katya had agreed to cancel her reservation at the InterContinental and stay at a hotel of his choosing. They laughed and exchanged small talk as they left the train station.

"You don't have a car waiting?" asked Carver incredulously. "What two-bit security outfit did you hire?"

"I didn't," she said proudly. "You're my security, and you're free."

He grabbed her arm. "Are you being serious right now? You don't have a team lined up in Kyiv?"

"You are my team." She brushed his hand away. "What happened to confidence in your abilities?"

"Ability is no replacement for sufficient manpower."

He bit down as Katya resumed walking. Maybe their relationship was still a tad adversarial. But then, he was at her side and he wouldn't leave it, especially given the news.

They approached the next waiting taxi. It was a white car with fluorescent yellow doors highlighting the company phone number. The driver helped their bags into the trunk and they slipped into the back seat. He didn't speak a word of English.

Katya engaged in an exasperated back and forth. Eventually the car shifted into gear.

"What was that about?" asked Carver once they got going.

"I got a good rate," she answered. "Price is negotiable."

The ride revealed a city that was the opposite of Warsaw. The architecture of Kyiv was steeped in history, with famous churches over a thousand years old. And sure, the package came with a number of brutalist Soviet-era apartment buildings, but even some of those had colorful painted roofs and rustic touches you might find in a country manor. The city was aging in places, but that was part of its charm.

Brand-new signs stood in stark contrast, affixed to walls and on freestanding posts.

"What are those?" Carver asked.

Katya spoke with the driver and he answered with gusto, happy to talk about his city.

"Those are directions to bomb shelters," she translated. "He says there are many Soviet fallout bunkers from when they were afraid America would start nuclear war."

"Does he believe Kyiv will be bombed now?"

Another exchange. "He fought in Donbas. The fighting

is seven hundred kilometers away. He says war will not come to his city in his lifetime, but if it does he will fight to his last breath."

Carver met the man's eye in the mirror and nodded. It was a sentiment he could respect.

As they turned onto the street where their hotel was, Carver noticed a black Mercedes turn after them. It had seemed to follow them in a loop.

"Keep going," said Carver, waving a hand ahead. "Tell him not to stop at the hotel. Keep driving."

Katya explained and then asked, "Where would you like to go?"

"Anywhere local. Go sightseeing."

She sighed as if tired of traveling but told the driver. He complained back to her and there was another back and forth. They were negotiating again. The driver must have gotten the upper hand this time because Katya ended their conversation with a resigned hiss.

They headed toward the water. They passed the Golden Gate, a replica of the medieval city entrance, as well as St. Sophia's Cathedral. That one was real, founded in 1037. On the bank of the Dnieper River, they passed a monument complex that featured the rainbow-shaped Friendship Arch. It was steel-colored except for black graffiti of a jagged fracture at its peak, a symbol of protest on an old Soviet monument.

They passed another old church, St. Michael's Golden-Domed Monastery. Outside was the expansive Wall of Remembrance. Fifteen thousand photographs of Ukrainians killed in battle were plastered across a city block.

With the threat of mounting troops on Ukraine's border, much of the world was paying attention to the conflict now, but the truth was a war had been raging for eight hard years. Countries supplied arms to both sides. Troops had cycled in and out of the fight, creating a weathered army.

Even far away from the conflict zones, the country had essentially been under siege for years. Economically, politically, criminally. The threat to Kyiv was almost invisible as it rebuffed Moscow's entire playbook of unconventional warfare. The bomb-shelter signs were merely the last resort.

Sometime in the middle of their sightseeing, the black Mercedes turned away. Carver kept an eye out for alternating tails but didn't see any. Once he concluded they were safe, he instructed the driver back to their destination.

The Opera Hotel building was a historic monument itself, over a hundred years old. It served a boutique niche in the city center, a crossroads of historic and modern districts, situated close to the National Opera it was named after. The street was narrow and mostly residential, serving a public playground and apartment buildings. As in Warsaw, the hotel's smaller size made it easier to keep tabs on entrances and exits and hotel visitors. It was Security 101. The less crowded a space is, the easier it is to see who doesn't belong.

The taxi dropped them at the curb and Carver unloaded the bags. Morgan was waiting for them and walked them inside.

"This is my associate, Juliette," Carver introduced.

Katya shook her hand and gave him a sidelong smile. "And I was beginning to suspect you worked alone."

"Good for you that I don't. We need all the guns we can get."

They put Katya in a suite themed after a famous Russian composition. It had a separate bedroom and marble master bath, with a large living area and guest bath. It adjoined a separate room for personal assistants. That one contained a pair of queen beds for Morgan and Carver.

They quickly showered and got set up for a new day, but the main thing they needed was food. The night train hadn't served any and wasn't even stocked with bottled water. They found a cafe patio a couple of buildings down and across the street. Soon enough, they enjoyed some much needed sustenance. Carver's sandwich was pulled beef. It wouldn't win any awards but it hit the spot from the first bite.

Katya ate slowly as she leaned back in her seat and basked in the sun. The overcast skies of Berlin and Warsaw were a thing of the past. It was probably about as beautiful as winter could get in Kyiv, with daytime temps in the forties. Anya took up position in the handbag at her owner's feet, head swiveling excitedly at passing pedestrians. Katya was less alert, and it wasn't just the sunglasses that covered half her face. She had navigated the train station and taxi well enough, but by now that half bottle of vodka was catching up to her. Two Advils and a meal were fighting the good fight. This battle, however, threatened to be as protracted as the Russo-Ukrainian War. It was a matter of attrition, and Katya could only last so long.

"I hate Kiev," she groaned.

"Oh?" asked Morgan between bites of her own sandwich. "Have you been before?"

"Not by choice. I was a child. Kiev then is the same as Kiev now."

"Isn't it Kyiv now?" teased Carver. "When in Rome and all that."

"What does it matter? I will still hate it. At least you booked a nice suite."

"Oh, that wasn't Vince," beamed Morgan. "Some things need a woman's touch."

Carver snickered. "It's a great room if you're into the tragedies of Russian royals. I just need three hots and a cot."

"I rest my case, Vince."

Morgan crossed her arms and leaned away from her unfinished plate. Carver kept chewing toward the finish line.

"So what's the next step?" he asked Katya. "This opera of yours is the day after tomorrow?"

Katya spoke without turning her head. "It's at the National Opera of Ukraine, but it's not an opera. It's a benefit for war refugees."

"And you and Pavel are esteemed guest speakers?"

"I'm not in the program yet. Pavel has hinted at me making an appearance, and I've spoken to the organizations running the show. I would like to deliver a speech if they'll have me."

The humble sentiment was part of her innocent act, Carver thought. "And you aren't concerned about attending another public event?"

"Nobody wants to bomb Kiev. It will send the wrong message."

"What message is that?"

A hint of a shrug twitched her shoulder. "That there's something here worth bombing."

A flat-screen above their heads displayed a news anchor going over the week's top stories. Morgan was fixated on it. Parsing the foreign language seemed to take most of her attention.

"I'm going to want to check out the opera house beforehand," said Carver.

"I made some notes," said Morgan. "We can talk shop in the room."

He arched an impressed eyebrow even as she continued to watch the TV. "Okay," he said. Then to Katya, "So do we just show up and meet with Pavel? Where is this guy?"

"I'll call someone after lunch. They'll put me in touch with Pavel, but it will be many hours till they call me back. Maybe tomorrow. Today I'm fine staying in the room. The train was a bad place for sleep. Someone kept waking me up."

She lowered her head so he could see her eyes above the glasses, and wouldn't you know it the TV had picked the wrong time to go to commercial. Morgan caught up fast.

"Something wrong with the bed?" she asked pointedly, gaze darting from Katya to Carver.

"Anya was a little jumpy with the constant ID checks," he said. "I could hear her a car over. Not that I blame her. I've slept in trenches that were more relaxing than that border crossing."

"Mm-hmm."

Morgan knew better than to wait for juicy details. She'd been around him long enough to know he didn't kiss and tell.

Between the awkward moment and Katya drifting off, the table settled into silence. Carver finished his sandwich and they paid the tab. They found themselves too relaxed to move quickly, and Morgan seemed content with the TV. She kicked Carver when a story about Berlin came on. A wide shot of the Stilwerk building and the surrounding police response. Some B-roll of a train. Then the scene flipped to police escorting a man from an apartment building.

"Is that... ?" he asked.

Morgan nodded. German police had arrested the third bomber.

Katya's eyes were closed and they didn't want to arouse suspicion by speaking about the incident in the open. From what Carver could piece together, the three bombers had been officially linked. The third had locked down in a Berlin suburb, though it hadn't kept him from eventually getting caught. Video of the apartment revealed bomb-making materials on site.

All three terrorists were officially accounted for.

While that was a weight off his shoulders, just because Carver had seen three men in a hatchback didn't mean that was the extent of the threat. There was no telling how big the cell was. German police might have more of an indication.

Even then, the situation had shifted past the Libyans with the emergence of the Wagner Group. Legitimate Russian operatives were now in play, and they were a much more dangerous enemy.

As they started across the street, Carver noticed a black car stopped at the end of the block where there were no parking spaces. It was a Mercedes S-Class, the same car he'd suspected was following them earlier.

"We might have a tail," he said. "Get her into the hotel."

"Copy that."

Morgan snapped into protective formation and guided Katya inside. Carver glanced up and down the street and frowned. It was impossible to see through the car's tints. After a moment, he made a beeline for the S-Class, back across the street. As he neared, it pulled out and drove off.

Carver scowled. New hotel or not, somebody knew they were in Kyiv.

17

Katarina retired to her bedroom after making the initial call to someone in touch with Pavel Shishov, the notable Ukrainian activist. Supposedly it was now a matter of waiting for a callback. It was likely Katya would spend that time passed out through the rest of the day and night.

As far as Carver was concerned, this was time gained. They would use it to work through the nitty-gritty of what needed to be done, confident that their resident college kid would safely stay out of trouble.

Morgan started with a primer on the National Opera of Ukraine. She'd had plenty of time to clear the hotel before their arrival so, being Morgan, she'd clocked some overtime to scope out what was likely to be the riskiest point in Katarina's stay in Kyiv. Besides her notes from having personally visited the old building, Morgan had collected various online materials: photos, an overhead map, and even a virtual tour that included areas restricted to the public.

Pavel Shishov was less of an open book. The activist was the founder of the Freedom House of Ukraine. According to the website, they provided support to new arrivals in the form of finding accommodation, job placement, and legal and financial advice. That was Pavel's public persona. Carver suspected there would be more to the former soldier.

Next up was dealing with the local law. Or rather, the lack of it.

"Do you want the bad news or the good?" posed Morgan.

"Always go with the bad news first," Carver said. "Anything else is avoidance."

"I don't even know why I ask," she replied with a playful roll of her eyes. "Okay, handguns aren't strictly allowed in Ukraine. There are exceptions. Target shooting, for one. There are also plenty of people who don't care too much what is technically allowed or not. Ukraine is fast and loose with gun control."

Carver pulled the P320 from his belt and set it on the bed. "Bummer."

"Semiautomatic rifles are a different story. Your Tavor X95 is completely legal."

Carver unzipped his duffel to shake the dust off the bullpup rifle. "I can open carry this?"

"Ukraine is the only country in Europe without firearm laws on the books. Everything is handled by the Ministry of Internal Affairs, but there's no real registry, which makes it easy for anyone with a bit of access to get what they want. I'm in the process of acquiring a local license due to Katarina's high-profile status. I suspect we had a little help from Washington too. So far I've secured preliminary clearance, which you won't really need unless you point the thing at the cops."

"Williams did say she would put in a good word."

"The only catch is they have a ten-round magazine limit."

"Oops."

Carver checked the civilian version of the combat rifle. The mags carried a military load of 5.56x45mm NATO rounds, thirty count. As a security contractor he was cleared with a large-capacity magazine permit. If the state of California could stomach it, Kyiv would have to get with the program too.

"I think that's good for now. I want to get my own eyes on the location while I still have daylight."

The legality may have been in question, but Carver left the rifle and took the SIG to the street. He was figuring on light daytime recon and preferred to remain inconspicuous. He also decided to skip another tense round of haggling with a cab driver. The opera house was only a ten-minute walk, and it never hurt to get to know a neighborhood.

Two unmarked lanes turned into a four-lane highway flanked by wide, active sidewalks. Carver passed various shops and businesses. People of all stripes populated the streets, with light traffic in small vehicles. Railcar wires snaked overhead and met in messy clumps over intersections like the mangled prey of spiders trapped in a web.

The street-facing side of the opera house looked nothing like the online pictures. Carver passed the building and curved around the block before the wide plaza opened up to him. Tickets were dirt cheap. It cost the equivalent of a euro to enter as he didn't much care about the placement of his seat. He was more concerned with the various halls and floors where one could get lost...

The winter sun set early by the time Carver made it back to the hotel. Morgan was happy to see him as she had scoped out a fancy dinner someplace. It was well-earned. She promised to bring something back and he said that sounded good. They only overlapped for about twenty minutes before he was alone again.

He sat on the bed with a heavy sigh. Like Katya, he had drunk more than he should have and not slept nearly enough. The hours were finally catching up to him. He leaned back and closed his eyes for a second. Not five minutes later he was stirred by a quiet knock.

Carver grabbed the SIG, made sure his rifle was secured in its bag, and checked the peephole. An older man who was either in his late fifties or had a rough go into his forties stood outside his door. He wore a black trench coat over a casual shirt.

"I'd like some privacy please," said Carver.

The man had a gaudy handlebar mustache that was black in the middle and white on the fluffy sides. When he frowned the whole affair contorted. "Privacy is good," he said in a thick accent. "That is why I would prefer to do this inside."

Now it was Carver's turn to frown. He twisted the doorknob silently and pulled suddenly. The man barely moved as Carver pointed his weapon, grabbed him, and pulled him inside. No one else was in the hall. He shut the door and spun to his visitor. The older man waited patiently as Carver patted him down. He had no weapons. An erratic sweep of white hair was brushed back on his head while the sides were trimmed above the ears. Wild eyebrows framed hard eyes that were sunken as if they had retreated from the world after seeing too much.

"Who are you?"

The man moved slowly and precisely. He pointed to his jacket and Carver nodded. He pulled out a wallet and unfolded it to present an ID that Carver couldn't read. "My name is Viktor Murayev. I'm with the Security Service."

Carver's eyes narrowed. "Ukrainian SBU?"

He nodded. "We have a friend in common, I think."

"I doubt it."

"Questionable associates, friends in high places. From a fellow three-letter agency."

"I don't know what you're talking about."

He sighed like a man tired of the game. "How about a dark-red leather jacket? Says you are a pain in her ass too."

Carver conceded with a cant of his head. "Okay, you're getting warmer."

"Good. Warm is good. It is too cold outside to shit around. At least for old men like me."

He spoke in a stereotypically thick Slavic accent and seemed to challenge anybody to call him on it, either too rigid or too stubborn to change.

"How long have you been in intelligence?" asked Carver.

"Me? I start as a young man in the party. Independence happens, I know things, and here I am."

That was partly what concerned Carver. Viktor with the

bushy eyebrows and handlebar mustache had at one time served the Communist Party of the USSR before its fall. It was no surprise the SBU was almost completely infiltrated by Russian spies.

"Are you the one tailing me?" asked Carver.

"Tailing?"

"Following me around in the black S-Class."

Viktor wiped his mustache and chuckled. "Ah, this is Belarusian KGB. We have many unofficial police here. Moskals too. The secret police are not so secret in Kyiv."

"You allow them to operate openly?"

"What is open? What is allowed?" he said with a hike of his shoulder. "They are here. We cannot shoot them. But they look and they look. They are nothing to worry for. Do not trust them," he warned with a wag of his finger. "You trust me."

Viktor would have to understand if Carver wasn't quite ready to do that. They might have the same friend in Washington, but the intelligence community was full of pals waiting for the best time to stab each other in the back. The Ukrainian SBU didn't rate as a hard target service and it would be a mistake to rely on them. Which wasn't to say they were incompetent. They were involved in illegal surveillance and eavesdropping to the extent their own population didn't trust them. That wasn't so far off from the CIA...

And it wasn't like they hadn't tried to clean up their ranks. After the ousting of the pro-Russian government in 2014, many intelligence officials were fired or fled into the resistance. The SBU hired a bunch of patriots from western Ukraine, where there were fewer ties to Russia. The new recruits were bright eyed, in their early twenties, with loyalties too fresh to be colored by the past. Viktor Murayev didn't fall into any of those categories.

Carver lowered the weapon to his side as a show of good faith. That was as far as he was willing to go. "How do I know I can trust you?"

Viktor shrugged. "You can't. But I am here. I will run security at opera. This building is a national treasure. We will not let anything happen."

"Are you going to help me then?"

He frowned. "I hear news of Libyan terrorists. I don't ask questions. Maybe you think you did good job, yes? But Libyans are not your problem."

"Neither are Belarusian KGB, apparently."

"No, no. Annoying, yes, but not problem."

They stood there guardedly watching each other. Viktor was fishing. Maybe for something specific, maybe just waiting for the plucky American to spill everything he knew. The only thing Viktor was learning was that Carver didn't talk much.

Viktor's eyes scanned down to the gun and he pointed. "You will need that. No need to worry with permits. You will be fine."

"I have something bigger too."

"Is fine. Is good you have. Moskals have. You need too."

"Moskals?"

His bushy eyebrows jerked up. "This is word for

Moscow people, you know? Bad word. Many moskals come to Kyiv. Some to start new lives, some to start new trouble. They all have guns to protect themselves." He waved an emphatic hand before pausing and sighing. "You know Kyiv, yes?"

Carver frowned. There was no point putting up a bold front and denying access to information. "I'm not really familiar with the lay of the land, so to speak."

He nodded in understanding. "Yes. First thing to know is Ukraine is at war. With Russia, yes, but also with itself. Russian leaders out, Ukrainian leaders in. Russia attempts to get pro-Russian president once more. Everything has two sides, especially government."

"Where do you stand?"

"Bah, do not ask this! I witnessed abuses of the Soviet party."

"So you're on our side?"

"No. United States benefits Americans. You are friends now. Tomorrow, I don't know this. I champion independent Ukraine."

At least he was being honest. Carver chewed his lip and then motioned for the man to sit on the couch. He set the gun on the dresser and rested against it for a more relaxed conversation.

"You must be careful," stressed Viktor. "In Kyiv, you never know which side someone is on. We are like, how you say, the towns with outlaw and sheriff."

"The Wild Wild East," said Carver with a grin.

"Opinions make enemies here. Reporters and politicians

are killed by car bombs. Dissidents are gunned down in broad daylight."

"Who are the ones doing the killing?"

"Not professionals, much of the time. Assassination in Kyiv is... about currying favor. Shoot first, make money after. Lots of criminals here. Ex-soldiers."

"And spies."

He dipped his head. "Many causes intersect in Kyiv. It is not just the capital of Ukraine, it is center for Russian opposition movement. Fighters from the east are starting careers in politics here. This is a war of influence and ideas."

Two world powers fighting by proxy in a neutral state was nothing new to Carver. It was part of what had soured him on the CIA in the first place. But it was an inscrutable problem. Keep the soldiers out and the propaganda goes into overdrive. If you don't play that game, you cede the territory to the other side and the game continues anyway, just along a different border.

There isn't a solution to it anymore than there is a solution to breathing. Rather, these are inevitable facets of life. Violence and power are king. The best you can do is to do your best.

Wasn't that why Carver returned to this line of work? To do his best? Empowered by the CIA, but not beholden to them. He was free to act as he saw fit. He couldn't suddenly make the world a better place—he was too pragmatic to believe that possible—but he could sure as shit put a boot dent into whatever evil crossed his path.

"I'm looking out for a particular class of soldier," Carver

revealed.

Viktor's eyebrows went up expectantly. It was a risk to mention specifics, but Carver had to try to trust somebody. The play here worked either way, even if only to stir the hornet's nest.

"What do you know of the Wagner Group?"

"Ah," said Viktor. "The little green men. They marched into Crimea to protect Russian interests in Sevastopol. They wore green uniforms without the markings of a sovereign state, but we know the state. We know who trains them and supplies them. The soldiers held a referendum to secede at gunpoint, and now they are supporting separatists in the east. Mercenaries in drab outfits."

Carver frowned. "I get that all's not quiet on the eastern front, but I'm concerned with special operations more than tactical support."

"Specifically?"

"I mean operatives sent to extradite or neutralize dissidents in Russian buffer states. I believe the Wagner Group is trying to kidnap or kill Katarina Litvinenko."

"You speak of the ghost soldiers." He released a protracted sigh as if the problem had long troubled him and he had no answer for it. "It begins with the moskals and extends into the puppet state of Belarus. They fly in migrants from Iraq and Afghanistan and Syria. They push them across NATO borders. They wish to weaken your alliance, to stir right-wing sentiment. The people see Middle Easterners moving into their neighborhoods. They see your Libyan bombs on TV. It is all the same to them."

"It's not an easy situation," Carver conceded.

Viktor's grave frown was earned. "It is exceedingly difficult one. Some migrants are Russian plants. More ghost soldiers fighting an invisible war. The little green men have changed uniforms, but they are the same."

Carver was familiar with all manner of ways for operatives to infiltrate countries. With migrant camps becoming overwhelmed, a humanitarian crisis was as good a method as any. The Baltics and, by extension, Europe were a sieve. What did that make Ukraine?

"This Russian you protect," said Viktor. "She has powerful detractors."

"Her uncle, Arkady Malkin."

"Yes. Friends in high places. The highest place. Yachts and mansions paid by government contracts. Arkady is not a man to take lightly. He is very proud, and his pride is a dagger. It is embarrassing for him to have family go against country. More than embarrassing, maybe."

"A personal insult."

"The worst kind."

Carver's arms crossed tightly over his chest. He had long forgotten about the P320. It wasn't necessary here. He couldn't be sure how much Viktor Murayev truly sympathized with his problem, but he wasn't a threat. Not while his country was so reliant on US sympathies.

"How worried do I need to be about the Russians?"

Another sigh. "There is a reason your state department recalled all Americans and their families. The danger of war is ever present, but Russia will not invade Kyiv with an army. They wish to liberate the east to create a new buffer state."

"To reshape a cordon sanitaire and a new Iron Curtain."

Viktor nodded. "As long as the government of Kyiv is friendly with the West, Russia will require an independent state between them. Another puppet."

"I get that. But what kind of threat are we looking at here? How much control do we have over the Wagner Group in Kyiv?"

The old man's sunken eyes darkened in the dim hotel lighting. "The ghost soldiers do not work with intelligence. They are not official, you see? They do anything they want and we cannot stop them. All of Ukraine is effectively non-permissive territory. This is fact for Russian and Belarusian dissidents. This is fact for NATO sympathizers." He lifted his chin at Carver. "This is very much fact for foreign operatives on black operation in Ukraine."

Carver offered a dry grin. "I might as well be in Russia."

"This is not far from the truth. I will try to assist you. I can only do so much. Do not mistake the price of your failure. Aside from our mutual friend, if you die here, nobody in your country will ever know."

18

Pavel Shishov, by all accounts, was secretive and cagey. The nature of his work put a target on his back. The SBU had warned him and his organization about the danger he was in, but he had a history of laughing off such threats. He sounded a lot like someone else Carver knew.

Katarina's prediction of hearing back from Pavel's people in the morning was strangely prescient. It proved she was sharper than the average party girl. That edge was possibly responsible for keeping her alive this long.

The call came from a woman. She was terse, giving only a time and a location to meet. She warned Katya not to be followed but didn't tell her to come alone. It was very cloak and dagger.

Morgan stayed behind with the room and the dog. Carver and Katya hit the street. While relying on taxis was an annoyance, it was prudent given Viktor's warning about car bombs. They hiked a block to a busier intersection to flag a car.

Today Carver carried his Israel Weapon Industries X95 as a test run for the big show. He did attract stares from pedestrians, but they were brief and disinterested. People here understood the need for self defense. And for minding their business.

"You know this city?" Carver asked. "Where we're going?"

"It's a restaurant," Katya answered. "I've never been."

At the corner, Carver clocked the black S-Class again. He slid his rifle into a ready grip with a sigh.

"Wait here."

Six steps toward the vehicle sent it fleeing. While he was still in the middle of the street, one car passed and the next was a cab. Carver swung down the rifle and waved toward Katarina at the corner. The car pulled over. They loaded up and moved on without negotiation so they could avoid prying eyes. Carver thought they got away clean.

The driver knew their destination, but Carver had him divert early, circle a block here, take a detour there, all while promising to pay extra. A fifteen minute drive to the outskirts of the city turned into half an hour. Carver was certain they hadn't been followed. He paid three times the fare.

"Ask him to wait for us."

She made the request and the driver was still wide-eyed at the money. He nodded eagerly, and when they disembarked he pulled into a spot on the side.

The restaurant was a small white building that resembled a French château except with straighter lines. Spanish-style ironwork adorned the exterior wall. The sconces and seals were built strong. So was the foreign alphabet above the heavy wooden door that hung open. It was between lunch and dinner, and it was difficult to tell if the restaurant was open. All Carver could say for sure was that the lot was mostly empty.

He peeked inside first. The welcoming sound of clattering dishware eased his concern. A skeleton staff shuffled in the kitchen while waiters set empty tables. Orange lighting warmed the wood-paneled walls and ceiling. Heavy Russian rugs spanned a room of white table cloths. A small stage at the far wall hosted a man fiddling with cables, but the star of the show was a blond man in a freestanding booth with a wraparound brown Oxford couch.

A woman in green fatigues and an olive-colored hijab pointed a pistol at Carver. She wasn't a large person but looked like she had used a gun before. She spoke with guttural insistence.

Carver kept one hand on the grip of his Tavor, pointed to the floor, and slowly raised his other. "Relax. I don't understand."

"English?" she asked.

Katya nodded. "It's better, I think."

"Why do you bring this gun?"

"The same reason you did," said Carver.

"You must surrender it."

"That's not going to happen."

"Then you go."

That was the first good sign. Instead of taking the gun by force, she left it as a choice: comply or leave. That was a clear signal she was only trying to protect Pavel.

"This is unnecessary," protested Katarina. "What we do

is dangerous. We both need assurances. He's not here to kill you. His name is Vince. He is American and has been with me since Berlin."

The woman glared as if the explanation made her more skeptical of his intentions. But, at least, she conceded that an American had little reason to kill her and wasn't a likely gun for hire in the region. She lowered the pistol to her side. "I am Amina."

"Katya. Nice to meet you."

Amina stared without moving for the extended hand. A laugh came from the central booth and all eyes turned to Pavel Shishov.

"You need to excuse Amina. She is a soldier from the fighting. We're no longer on the front lines, but the war is far from over."

Pavel spoke like an educated youth, nearly a natural at English, with just enough flavor in his twang to peg him as Eastern European. He rounded the leather seat and approached with an eager grin. Pavel was well-muscled with broad shoulders. His hair was short and bleached, and his nose was a little large and surrounded by lines that belied his youth.

"Katarina Litvinenko," he said with pride, kissing her cheeks in succession. "Katya. You are more beautiful in person."

"She is okay," grumbled Amina.

He snorted in laughter. "Amina is my beautiful wife. I was sick of fighting, she was sick of killing. We are a match made in Heaven."

He kissed his wife on the cheek but her frown stayed put.

Pavel shook Carver's hand next. "You are unexpected. Vince... ?" He waited with an open mouth.

"Just Vince for now," returned Carver. "I'm here for Katya's protection."

He blinked twice before deciding he was satisfied. "Okay, Just Vince. Come. Sit with us."

While they moved to the table, Amina peeked out the front door. She reported something in Ukrainian, probably that there was a taxi waiting out front, but Pavel brushed it off. She seemed more worried about Carver and returned to the table, sitting across from them.

"I need to move around a lot," Pavel explained. "I am under constant surveillance. People take shots at me in the street."

"People pretend to be friends," explained Amina, "but turn out to be assassins."

"Who's trying to kill you?" asked Katya.

Pavel spread his hands. "Moscow. Minsk. Get in line."

"I think she's on the same ride you are," said Carver. "Those Libyan bombers were following her."

His expression and his wife's were unmoved. Close encounters in the news didn't impress them. Pavel stretched the collar of his white tee to show off a scar on his clavicle.

"I was shot by a man pretending to be a reporter. This man spent weeks interviewing us, getting to know us,"—he knocked the wood table—"eating with us. His name was not real. He was a criminal boss from Odesa who wanted to score favors from Putin."

Katya sipped her glass of water.

"What happened to the man?" asked Carver.

"I killed him with this gun," said Amina, wagging the pistol before it once again disappeared under the white tablecloth. Carver knew exactly where it was pointed under there. Amina's stare didn't even attempt to disguise it.

"Good," Carver replied. "It's what the bastard deserved."

"What about you, Just Vince?" Pavel prodded. "You look like a man who has seen war. My question is, have you killed anybody who deserved it?"

Katya stared, waiting for his answer. Amina was being Amina and Pavel had a smug grin on his face like he had said something clever. Carver supposed he should have expected this treatment after showing up with the Tavor.

"The German authorities arrested one of the Libyans," he answered. "The reason they didn't arrest the other two is because I killed them first."

Katya's gasp was the only sound from the table, and it was unexpected. Carver had figured she would have put two and two together. Then again she didn't seem the type to stay abreast of the latest news. Amina was a statue but Pavel pressed his lips together and nodded in approval.

"If this is true," he conceded, "they did deserve it. They are cowards with their bombs."

"It means nothing," spat Amina.

"Please," implored Katya, drawing attention away from Carver, "we are all friends here. Everybody at this table lives with worry. My bravery is an act every day. Without it I would break down."

Carver watched her, his turn to be surprised.

"We yearn to be bold," she continued. "We yearn to be strong. The truth is we're all fragile human beings. We have beating hearts that fail with the slightest tremors, and bodies that break under the violence that surrounds us. This is why we're nervous and protective of our own and suspicious of others. It's natural, but it's a weakness."

Again Pavel made a show of nodding. He did that so much it was hard to tell if he was agreeing or just trying to move things along until he could speak again. Amina, for her part, showed understanding in her eyes.

"You have guns," said Katya plainly. "I have guns. It's the only choice we are left with in our countries. This is the way of things. We must find a path to dialog through this."

The two traded a wary glance. Amina nodded. "Okay."

Pavel clapped his hands together as a waiter rolled in a food cart. "Just in time! I hope you forgive the limited menu in the off hour. You can sample some of Ukraine's famous dishes."

A few dishes were placed on the table, far from a full buffet. Pavel offered a plate of shredded pork in little clear domes of gelatin made from fat and bone. They were served cold.

"No thanks," said Carver. "I'll stick with the potato pancakes."

Pavel and Katya snacked with abandon. Even though Carver was hungry, he and Amina were more guarded, picking small bites here and there. Occasional conversation filled the void between passing plates and drinks. Stories of living on the fringes of town and traveling on trains. Not quite small talk but barely flanking purposeful subjects.

Pavel snorted. "Your uncle would not like you to be speaking with me, I know that much. What do you think he would say to you, Katya, if he could see us now?"

She surrendered a hesitant smile. "It cannot possibly be worse than what he has already said. I am disowned because I walked away from him." Her finger traced the condensation on her water glass. "It feels like I no longer have a family, but, in casting them off, I have gained a people."

Pavel rapped the table in excited agreement. "Yes! I like that. This is what I speak of. We need unity in the east. This is why I run Freedom House."

"Freedom House of Ukraine?" prodded Carver.

The supposedly cagey man spoke with gusto. "Yes! I founded the organization with a vision. Freedom House is to be a beacon for a united Eastern Europe, one that extends beyond borders."

"Beyond?" asked Katya.

"Of course. We are not against countries having borders. This is perhaps necessary. But there is so much posturing in the east that we stifle our potential. This conflict in Donetsk and Luhansk. Separatists fight to break away from Kyiv. But what is the point? Is it because some speak Russian and some speak Ukrainian? What they fail to see is we all speak both."

"You're one people," said Carver.

"Exactly right. Render unto Caesar what is his. Eastern

Europe is made of many different authorities. There is no need for one to topple the other. We are stronger together."

"What about NATO?"

He scoffed. "NATO is not the point. You see? This is the problem. There is no reason Ukraine could not be a friend to Russia *and* to NATO. This is the old thinking. It is what I want the world to understand. Borders are real, but our brotherhood extends *over* them. Freedom House is a safe haven for emigrants from Russia, from Belarus, from disputed sections of Ukraine. We take all asylees as we strive to build a responsible Russian diaspora for all of Eastern Europe."

Carver appreciated the new, talkative Pavel Shishov, but most of the words were the same fluff you could get from the website. "But what about the smuggling?" he asked.

Pavel's eyes narrowed.

"What I mean is, you speak of grand ideals. I don't begrudge you that. And getting these people jobs and bunks is great work, but that's not all of it. You and I both know you need to get your hands dirty to make the world clean."

He swallowed a bite and watched Carver, frozen for the briefest of moments, before acknowledging him with a nod. "Yes. We get our hands dirty. Every new arrival has challenges. There is no yellow brick road for them to skip into the capital on."

Although Pavel's agreement was clear, he stopped short of explaining exactly what his operation consisted of.

"What do you say to your detractors?" asked Katya. "You and I are not so different. Well loved by many, but also hated by a mob."

"It is true. Love and hate are two sides of our coin. People resist change. Even good people. Our ideas scare them. That is why we must speak out. Gather our armies on social media. Because our enemies aren't just armed with guns and bombs. Their rhetoric is even more insidious."

Carver was happy to fade into the background as Katya and Pavel chatted. They spoke about more ideals, about loving and hating their countries, about the transitory nature of enemy combatants. While the two had wildly different backgrounds and experiences, he could have envisioned them side by side at a protest on a college campus in America. Pavel was older and more experienced, of course, and this vision would cast him as a mentor of sorts.

The conversation grew more familial. There were fewer challenges besides Amina's continuous glare. Carver didn't take it personally. He was a security contractor who punched in and out, although maybe not so much these days. She lived the life twenty-four seven, day in and out worried about the next stranger or friend turning a gun on them.

Finally, after all the posturing was over, after all the small talk and small plates were out of the way, and once everyone's grand ideals were revealed, the table turned to discussion of the opera event. Freedom House was one sponsor of three humanitarian groups, and Pavel Shishov was making a not-so-surprise appearance.

"I want to help," said Katarina, after he had given an

overview of his message.

"Of course. That is why you are here. Your words will prove my vision. Your heart reaches beyond borders, like mine."

"What kind of security do you have in place?" asked Carver.

"We have friends," said Pavel.

"How many friends?"

"Enough."

"I only ask because—"

"We have enough," cut in Amina. "It is not for you to worry."

Carver bit down. "It is exactly my worry because I have my own people to protect. I'm not asking for operational details. I'd just like an idea of your staffing and if you're cooperating with the SBU."

Pavel's warmth evaporated. "I don't trust the Security Service, and you shouldn't either. They have too many partisans. They spy on me. They tell me it's for my own good, but I don't believe them. Power, you see, must be exercised in order to maintain itself."

"Isn't one of the sides friendly to your cause?"

"Never pick sides," he warned. "Does it matter if it's the left or right hand that strikes you down?"

Carver shrugged. "That sounds good, but in a real fight most opponents have a weak hand."

Pavel showed his teeth. "And which side would the American have me choose?"

"You can start with the side not actively trying to kill

181

you."

He snorted. "You think you know what is happening in my country. Most Americans don't even know what is happening in theirs."

Another shrug. "You've got no disagreement from me there."

Pavel's challenging eyes faltered, frustration at his point not offending Carver.

"Gentlemen, please," said Katya. She reached across the table and rested a hand on each of theirs. "We are friends here, with a common cause. None of us are responsible for the politics of our countries."

Carver blinked at her. It was jarring to see Katya playing the peacemaker. It was like Kyiv was some sort of bizarro world. She wasn't partying, she was subdued and rational. It could be because she hated the place and didn't feel safe. Or maybe she really was passionate about her business here.

Pavel rubbed his large nose while pouting, but he eventually broke out of the glum mood. "I will admit, I am distrustful of Westerners, but Katya is right—this is not your fault." He seemingly nodded to encourage himself. "You are of my people," he told her. "We are brothers and sisters who must settle our differences to grow strong. I would like you at my side at the National Opera."

"Not him," said Amina.

Katya leaned over the table. "He can help us."

"We do not know him," said Pavel. "Who are you, Just Vince?"

"Just Vince for now," he answered.

"That is not good enough. Katya has proven her measure. She takes a stand against her people, *for* her people. This is why I am listening. Why am I listening to you?"

Carver didn't respond immediately. He wasn't sure what to say, for one. There was no expectation that he'd need to prove himself to Pavel. He was just a hired gun, and Katya was his ticket. But that wasn't good enough.

These people didn't trust hired guns. That was evident by his wife acting as his bodyguard. They didn't even trust state security. How then, as an outsider, could he ever have any worth?

"He has contacts," said Katya. "He's here to facilitate." She leaned forward again. "He's CIA."

Carver frowned. "I never said that."

"You didn't need to."

"I'm not CIA."

She turned to Pavel. "This is what they tell him to say. Non-official cover. But he has resources and reach. Vince wants a stable Kyiv. Freedom House relies on it. You can't spit on the hand that supports you."

Pavel worked his lips between his teeth. "Is what she says true, Vince?"

It would have been useless to deny it at this point. Carver wasn't technically CIA, but it was obvious who had sent him. The entire point of his operation was to warm Katarina to the American government. If he had just walked up and stated his affiliation, she wouldn't have listened to another two words. Now, after earning her trust, coming to the conclusion on her own was the best possible outcome.

He was nearing his ultimate objective.

"I can offer resources for rehousing," he said. "Help with visas and funding and red tape. Not just weapons that get resold or dollars that line corrupt pockets. I'm talking about giving locals like you the access you need to make a difference."

"I am worried," said Amina. "With CIA involvement, the opera is too much of a risk."

Pavel leaned back with a sigh. "But think about the reward. We announce a new partnership with Katya. We show the world a new Ukraine. And maybe the Americans offer the tools for change, and maybe they don't. The risk is worth it."

"The opera is too public."

"That is the very reason we will be protected." He shook a fist in the air. "Our righteousness is our armor, and the public is our shield."

Pavel turned to Vince first and then Katya. He nodded once decisively, all doubt left in the dust of a raging steam engine.

"Let us do this thing, together, for a united Eastern Europe."

19

The National Opera House of Kyiv was a grand old building in the Neo-Renaissance style. Striking blue and yellow bands waved on the national flag of Ukraine over the entrance arch. The central dome above was topped with a pair of griffins around a lyre. Carver hoped the guardians would be vigilant today.

Their group navigated the walk-up, celebrities cutting through fervent spectators and press. Pavel and Amina had a sizable escort of ex-soldiers. Katya holding Anya was as photogenic as ever. Carver and Morgan unassumingly melted into the background.

The building loomed like a castle, decorated with an army of busts, composers whose names Carver neither knew nor would be able to pronounce. The modest front door delivered them into a small domed foyer, up white marble steps into an understated entry hall, and through another door before the glamorous splendor of the larger opera house was revealed.

A bustling tile-work hallway rounded the diameter of the theater and featured chandeliers on ornamentally trimmed ceilings. Red velvet benches and standing lamps hugged alcoves along the curvature of the wall. Vendors hawked treats and drinks and merchandise at pop-up tables. With three organizations sponsoring the fundraiser tonight, there was no shortage of wares on display.

Guests filed along the walkway while orchestral accompaniment leaked through small, unassuming doors that provided access to the opera's main floor. Wide stairwells on the opposite wall led to the levels above.

Carver wore his Brooks Brothers tonight. The P320 was holstered under the jacket, with the X95 hooked over his shoulder in plain sight. The Bravo Company blade was slotted onto his weakside hip and the Extrema Ratio everyday carry in his right pocket. Morgan supported with a Glock 17 and Benchmade Griptilian.

Priority one was identifying anyone and everyone who was armed. That started with event security, comprised of an eclectic mix. American-trained Kyiv police officers were posted outside, dark-blue uniforms and high-swept dress hats contrasting with bright metal badges. They wore radios but no sidearms and were mostly for show, though a truck in the plaza likely housed a waiting armed quick-response team.

Pavel's friends were scattered, each with a handgun in a hip holster. While they appeared spottily trained, they were at least properly paranoid for security, taking no chances and stopping to vet various guests with friendly questions. One man with a Kalashnikov stood out, but Pavel hugged each of his people in turn, including this one, signaling that he was trusted.

Carver also spotted who he presumed were SBU agents with concealed carries. They were overweight and wore cheap suits and couldn't be more obvious if they tried. Perhaps that was the point. With the police outside and the Security Service pacing the halls, the message was clear. All bases were covered.

Amina was uncomfortable with the crowd. The SBU hadn't cleared their presence with the showrunners and she felt surrounded. Words of warning turned into a tense disagreement as she and Pavel clashed in the grand hallway. Katya employed her calming influence again, but this time Amina pushed back and soon they were all talking over each other.

Carver grabbed a few beers from a nearby booth, wincing as the disagreement escalated. He just had to get through this event, admittedly a tall order, and then he would introduce Katya to the CIA. After her public commitment, she would need them to follow through on the promise of aid. Carver would hold Williams to it too, as much as any citizen could hold the CIA to anything. The way he saw things, it wasn't a lot to ask considering how much taxpayer money was lost in the name of defense. Grift and lack of capable oversight were inherent anytime large amounts of money moved between governments. The least the united States could do was give Pavel and Freedom House a chance.

"That's enough of that," interrupted Carver, shoving his large frame into the middle of the scrum and passing around beer bottles of goodwill. "We're in the public eye now and need a united front. How are you supposed to unite Eastern Europe if you can't unite yourselves?"

The others accepted the peace offering with mollified pouts. Katya frowned especially hard at her beer and Carver grinned. The label read, "Kyiv Not Kiev." The city's tourism agency was apparently a fan of outside-the-box marketing.

"Very funny," she groaned, but the first sip did its job of appeasement. "What other choice do we have?" she asked Amina. "Vince is right. We're here now. What's done is done. Would you have the people see us run?"

Amina handed her beer to a friend. While she didn't concede the argument, her resigned silence was answer enough.

In the distance, Carver's gaze passed over Viktor Murayev. The older man nodded and Carver nodded back. Then he followed as Katya and Pavel turned on their smiles and mingled.

They weren't the only stars of the hour. Others guest speakers of various standing and fame were in attendance. Carver didn't know them and instead focused on the crowd that was growing more dense by the minute. Amina's concerns turned out to be well founded. It was increasingly difficult to maintain a sterile area around his principal. The threat level only amplified when he clocked a man from the Belarusian KGB perched against a wall with a wire in his ear.

This was like one big spy party.

The background music crescendoed, and a man with a

pleasant voice cordially requested that guests take their seats. Lines formed at doorways and stairwells. Stragglers rushed to purchase additional drinks. Katarina clinked her empty bottle to Carver's, still half full. He tossed them in the trash as their group clumped toward a door.

"Katya."

Carver pulled the girl back to let Pavel's crew lead.

"You don't need to go through with this," he said under the bustle of background movement. Now that CIA involvement was out of the bag, this was a card he was compelled to play. "If you're at all concerned with your safety, we can skip the theatrics. We can get out of Kyiv, you and me, right now, and I can introduce you to some friends of mine."

A burgeoning smile played on her lips. "You would do that... You would really do that, for me."

He nodded. "You don't need live publicity to make a difference. This part can be done with social media."

She half stifled a snort. "Your concern is admirable, Vince, but you and I both know that's not my style. I want it all. I can make the announcement *and* meet your friends. I'd be happy to. But I won't back down from this when I'm so close." She stood on her tiptoes and kissed him on the lips. "Injustices grow stronger by gestating in the dark."

Morgan aimed a pointed eyebrow as Katya headed in.

"Don't say it," warned Carver.

They stepped through the door and onto the red carpet. Rows of chairs arrayed the large space, filling fast. The low ceiling remained overhead for all of ten steps before the opera house mushroomed into a massive domed area with a shining central light, a private sun in a microcosm of grandeur. The circular white walls were adorned with red-velvet-trimmed balconies five stories high. The band tuned instruments in the sunken orchestra pit before a grand stage framed by lustrous scarlet curtains. Custom-made pipes from the organ were fitted into the walls. Their hums and the low pull of violins penetrated flesh and bone.

Katya followed Pavel's people toward the stage. Rather than walk through the orchestra pit, they were escorted to one of the side doors. Morgan stuck with Katya. Amina was with them, as was their friend with the Kalashnikov. Carver remained standing at the rear of the theater, back against the wall, and watched the chaos of the crowd settle into something eager and ordered.

It was apparent the presentation was not well-rehearsed when it started with awkward muttering as the speakers hesitated to introduce themselves. The heads of two humanitarian orgs apologized and briefly spoke about putting the fundraiser together. They thanked everyone for contributing and attending. Their platitudes were clearly a buildup to the man of the hour, a refugee from Eastern Ukraine with many notable stints in the news.

Pavel Shishov entered the stage to rabid applause. His activism was well regarded as being practical and effective in a country that was often opaque and corrupt. Despite the positive mood of his introduction, Pavel began his speech on a sober note, overseeing a moment of silence for the victims of the Russo-Ukrainian war. The names and faces posted on the Wall of Remembrance weren't just photographs, they were fathers and sons and brothers and uncles. He criticized the need for a Russian superpower, for there to be any one leader of the Slavic people. Killing people to save a nation was backwards, he insisted, and it was the nations that should put themselves in harm's way for the people.

Carver was only mildly surprised when Pavel's criticism of the violence extended to the progressive wing of the Ukrainian government. The activist had proved he was willing to rub anyone and everyone the wrong way in the name of justice, taking sides be damned. With what must have been a preplanned jab, his eyes locked on Carver's across the theater when he called out the United States by name for engaging in an ideological power struggle that did no more for the people than any other hard-line approach. Carver didn't take the bait and watched the proceedings with professional detachment before deciding to have a look around.

He retreated to the outer hallway and found a well-lit stairwell. The elaborate wall molding, chandeliers, and porcelain lamps were more impressive in the bright space. Half a flight up, the large window revealed a busy but controlled scene in the plaza. The second-floor hallway was much the same as the first except slightly narrower, wood floor lined with carpet in place of tiles. Carver did a lap and popped into the mezzanines before heading up another flight.

The next hall overlooked the last one and was greatly

scaled down in width and flair. This was the top hallway, with the second and third floors each servicing two levels of theater balconies. After Carver had checked various nooks and rooms to his satisfaction, he settled onto an empty top floor balcony at the back to watch the conclusion of Pavel's speech.

Several minutes along, Viktor Murayev shuffled onto the balcony and posted beside him at the rail.

"Young people and their ideals, hmm?"

Carver studied the old man. "He's only a little younger than I am."

"So maybe you are not as naive as he, and not as jaded as I."

"That's cynical."

"Is it wrong?"

"It's a cynical world."

Viktor nodded and clenched his jaw as he watched the emphatic younger man on stage.

This was a fundraising event, not a packed show, so many of the higher balconies were empty. Most of the lower ones were sparsely seated. From their vantage at the very top, they could see everyone except for the seats directly beneath them, all the way in the back.

"Your Belarusian spooks are here," noted Carver.

"Yes, this is good. They are known."

"Known enemies."

He shrugged. "I would be concerned if Pavel was from Belarus and speaking out against Lukashenko. He is not."

"It would still be easier if you escorted them out."

"This is not the way, my friend. Better to be cordial with your enemy than adversarial."

"Up to a point."

He conceded with another nod. "Up to a point. But look at this. You have already seen government men, yes? Friendship comes with many benefits. For example, I know who is Belarus and they know who is Ukraine."

"Your point?"

He clasped his hands in front of him, low and behind the balcony railing where he could point discreetly. "That man. Lower left balcony, brown coat, sitting alone. He is neither Belarus nor Ukraine."

Carver worked his jaw. The man was almost definitely an Eastern European operative. If he didn't work for one of the expected intelligence services, that left Russia as the likely culprit.

"Wagner Group?" he asked.

"Because I have not seen him before, I would assume so. There is another." Viktor pointed out a similar man on the right balcony. "They signal each other when Pavel took the stage. Just once, but I see it."

"Can you arrest them?"

His face was a hardened mask. "These men do not get arrested."

Carver thought of the encounter in the Warsaw alley, operating outside the confines of police and civil consequence, and tended to agree. "Can you kick them out?"

"I can try, but these men are connected. They are not

alone. And I cannot guarantee any of my men do not sympathize with them."

Corruption within the SBU. Who would have guessed? "How many do you trust?"

For the first time, a hint of a smile formed under his mustache. "There is one who I believe I can count on, and he is standing on this balcony with me."

Carver grimaced. He had just been told in not so many words that Ukrainian State Security was useless. Through that lens, it was hard to imagine the police outside being any more dependable.

"I take one, you take the other?" suggested Carver.

"You see?" Viktor replied with a boisterous grin. "Not so jaded, not so naive. But I must warn you. They will not talk."

"Then neither will I."

They split off, Carver heading for the west stairwell and Viktor for the east. This was where the Maxim 9 would have come in handy. In a large acoustic space with laughter and music, a single well-timed report might go unnoticed. The P320 was more of a risk.

Carver unbuttoned his jacket and loosened the pistol in its holster. He descended one level and followed the sound of Pavel's voice back toward the balconies. The upper mezzanine was a few carpeted steps up. He covered the ground, light steps in heavy boots, and peeked into the dark space. The operative was seated alone and preoccupied by the proceedings onstage.

Pavel worked up the crowd, building into a dramatic

coda, but the opera house was too quiet to act just yet. After a minute on his perch, Carver watched as Viktor Murayev made his presence known on the opposite balcony. He seemed to be asking the Russian man for an aside.

It was too early. Carver didn't like the timing but had no choice but to move before his guy noticed the distant interaction. Carver switched the rifle to his left shoulder and drew the SIG. He held that with his left hand under the right lapel of his jacket. Then, just as the Russian noticed his friend on the opposite balcony standing up, Carver sat to his left.

"Thought you might want some company, comrade."

The operative went rigid with the realization that a pistol was pointed at his chest and the slightest move could see him bleeding out. "I do not—"

"Can it. I want to know what you're doing here."

"I am watching show."

"It's not the watching I'm concerned with."

The man's face twitched. Across the theater, his friend stepped out of the balcony with Viktor. Carver's Russian looked very concerned about this fact, and he coiled like a snake ready to strike.

"What are you planning?" demanded Carver. "You going to shoot somebody?"

The operator was unfazed as Carver reached into his jacket to search him.

"Blow them up?"

The man's eyes twitched, a five-year-old caught with the cookie jar. Not a good liar, this one, which meant he was muscle. Carver located his gun and pulled it away.

"So there's a bomb," he concluded.

But Viktor Murayev was right. These men didn't talk. They were professionals. They were violent men. And when violent men were backed into a corner, violence ensued.

As Carver's right hand threw the pistol aside, the Russian twisted off the chair and pounded the SIG into Carver's chest. The move was so fast, it twisted Carver's aim toward the chair as the operator hopped out of it, escaping the kill zone.

So not a good liar but a capable fighter.

Instead of firing in the relatively quiet theater, Carver kicked his knees up to fend off his attacker. Both his arms twisted out of position as the Russian attempted to grapple. Carver succeeded in kicking him away and creating space, but his opponent yanked his SIG up and out of his jacket. Neither man would let go.

Carver shoved again and pressed to his feet, putting his shoulder into the guy's ribs and lifting. His pistol caught between the seat backs and dropped to the floor. Now no one had it.

It was better this way.

Pavel's fists shot to the air. Applause erupted as Carver pitched the man into the wall and onto the floor. They twisted and fought for position in a booming theater. Carver thought he picked out the crack of a distant gun under thunderous clapping. The operator reached for his grounded pistol, and Carver let him turn around and surrender his back. The man's fingertips brushed the grip.

"Where's the bomb?" pressed Carver through gritted teeth.

The operator didn't answer. With single-minded zeal, he succeeded in tugging his weapon closer. The Russian's grip tightened around his weapon. Carver jerked his head backward until his neck snapped, and he was dead before his finger could find the trigger.

Carver sat up, cursing silently and checking his six. He put on his gloves and slipped the pistol back into the man's holster. He recovered his weapon and checked the opposite balcony. It was still empty. Carver frowned and surveyed the damage. He considered lifting the dead Russian back into his seat so he would appear to be sleeping, but the corpse was less visible on the floor.

Across the opera house, Viktor Murayev trudged back onto the opposite balcony. They locked eyes and something unspoken conveyed their similar predicaments. Carver made a wiping motion at his cheek. Murayev pulled a handkerchief, wiped the spatter of blood off his face, and nodded thanks as the roar of the crowd found a second life.

Katya strolled onto the stage, and they had a bomb to find.

20

Katarina Litvinenko waved to a mixed crowd that wasn't yet sold on her message. She blew kisses, having ears only for the applause. Anya the toy terrier wasn't as pleased with the noisy welcome. She barked and cowered into her protective handbag, and Katya did her best to calm her. After several failed attempts, she pleaded with the audience to quiet and, when they did, she set the bag down and hugged Anya to her chest beside the freestanding microphone. A single satisfied yip resonated through the opera speakers.

"She is as fervent as you," remarked Katya with a grin, and the crowd laughed.

Katarina's face went flat and she began her address with a childhood story. The words faded into the background as Carver scanned the audience for anyone out of place. His vantage near the front allowed examination of the faces affixed on the beautiful speaker, but it also made him stand out like a sore thumb. He caught a man watching him from among a group on a lower back balcony. Carver spun on his boots and headed into the hall.

As he rounded to the rear of the theater, the same suspicious man exited his perch. He saw Carver and turned around.

"Hey."

The man kept walking so Carver tackled him into the wall.

"Please," he cried. "I do not do anything."

"You're from Belarus, right? KGB?"

The man's cheek pressed into the ornate molding. "I work for government, yes. You cannot do this."

"I don't like being told what I can and can't do, comrade."

Carver checked up and down the hallway. It was empty and he figured it would mostly stay that way during Katya's address. If Wagner operatives were planning to bomb the theater, they wouldn't engage in open combat that would scare the crowd away.

"What do you know of a bomb?" he demanded.

"What bomb?" whined the man. "I do not know this."

Viktor Murayev sprinted over and pulled Carver away. "No, he is Belarus."

"I know who he is," spat Carver. "There's a bomb here and we need to find it before it explodes."

"What?" asked Viktor, shocked and more than a little out of breath. The Belarusian watched like a wounded animal backed against a wall.

"It explains a lot," said Carver. "The Libyans in Berlin. They found bomb-making materials at their apartment but no bombs. One of them traveled on the train. He didn't have a bomb on him either, but he did make a call to Warsaw where Wagner operatives were in wait. This is an op to blow a Kyiv opera house and blame it on immigration. A casus belli to incriminate the new government."

Grim faces processed Carver's information.

"I did not know this!" claimed the Belarusian.

Carver took a menacing step toward him. "Then what *do* you know?"

"Nothing! I swear it!"

Viktor weakly pulled at Carver as he grabbed the man's jacket and shook him violently. "Stop it," pleaded Viktor. "This is no use. Wagner Group does not operate with Belarusian approval. This man, I do not trust him but I know him, you understand? He is not assassin."

"How can you be sure?"

Viktor sighed. "If his men do this, they are implicated. Belarus is responsible. It does not work this way."

Carver winced. He didn't like it, but there was sense in what Viktor said. This sniveling man was ready to piss his underwear. He was lost and confused, not running a clandestine op.

"Fine," spat Carver, shoving the man away. He wagged a finger in the air. "I want you and your men out of here. Understand?"

He nodded anxiously. "Yes. We leave now. Yes."

Carver turned away and the man took off at a near run. Viktor stifled a groan that sounded equal parts angry and amused. "You are fun, you know this?"

"Let's find that bomb."

"Yes. Where is it?"

Carver bit down in thought. "If their aim is to assassinate

Pavel and Katarina, it would be backstage."

They marched downstairs and found the Belarusian contingent scurrying out the front door. That made things cleaner.

"We need to keep an eye out for enemy operators," said Carver. "Anyone who's here that we don't know."

Viktor frowned. "I will need to check with my men too."

"You think they could be involved?"

"No, but I must confirm their movements and positions."

He split off while Carver took the hall all the way to the door at the end. Katya's voice traveled the halls. She was speaking like Pavel now, about how dreams transcended borders. It was a little heavier than her usual schtick. One of Pavel's people watched the entrance and let him backstage. In the green room, Pavel joked with one of the other org presidents while a few other speakers went over their notes. Amina and the man with the Kalashnikov watched Carver pass and converge on Morgan at the side of the stage.

"Wagner is here," he said in her ear. "They're planting a bomb. A false flag or something."

"Should we extract the principal?"

"I don't know just yet. Whoever has their fingers on the detonator will have eyes on the stage. It would go a long way if we could locate the bomb first."

"What the fuck, Vince? How are we supposed to find that now?"

"Is there anybody back here that isn't supposed to be? Any deliveries or items out of place?"

Morgan stepped away from the stage to look over the back room. "Pavel's people have been surprisingly tight."

"Do we trust them all? Amina and this other guy?"

"They've been targeted themselves. They've saved Pavel's life. They have history."

He knew it too. As paranoid as security was at Freedom House, Carver had little option but to trust Pavel's judgment of his old friends. There simply wasn't time to start an investigation from square one. Focusing on them was a waste when they were much more likely to find the threat among active Wagner agents. With what may have been a literal ticking clock, they had to move as fast as possible.

"Let's do a sweep," suggested Morgan.

There were a few other rooms behind the stage for changing, props, and that sort of thing. As this wasn't a full-scale production, these areas had all been closed off. Carver and Morgan dug through them anyway. Throughout audience claps and laughs and other sounds of Katya winning over the crowd, they came up empty and met on the opposite, empty, side of the stage.

The audience was now captivated by the beaming young woman and her toy terrier. When Katya noticed Carver behind the curtain and winked, it was easy to imagine why. It was also easy to imagine her body ripped apart by an amateur explosive.

But then, as crowd members smiled and chuckled and cheered, Carver imagined something else. A dense crowd of Ukrainian citizens caught in a devastating blast. If this was a false flag to sway public sentiment against an incompetent or malicious government, killing Katya wouldn't be the death stroke. Dozens of dead everyday Ukrainians on the news would be.

His mission was the girl. By all accounts he should already be evacuating the principal to safety. But the gleaming faces of proud Ukrainians bubbling with laughter and hope was hard to dismiss. He couldn't abandon them to a senseless fate.

With this many government operatives around, he also couldn't send Morgan and Katya off alone.

"Watch her," said Carver. "Warn Pavel and the others. We might need a united effort sooner than we thought."

He strode clear across the stage. Katya faltered as he hopped down into the orchestra pit. A nervous laugh and a joke about him needing the bathroom put her speech back on track. Carver checked the musicians for anyone or anything out of place. On a recessed floor and behind a wall, the spectators were not privy to his search. Failing to find anything suspicious, Carver vaulted over that wall and into the audience.

He was close to ground zero now. He could feel it. And while the bomb could be anywhere, there was one fact working in his favor: Wagner operatives weren't Libyans. They weren't suicide bombers who would panic and detonate at his approach. That said, when he did approach, they would almost certainly be compelled to act.

"All people were immigrants at one point in history," pronounced Katya, hugging her dog with pride. "Now we fight over who is chosen and who isn't. Who deserves one thing or another. My path has been long and confusing. Only now I realize this is a fight for our identity."

Carver walked up the aisle, scanning the rows of seats. His behavior only earned a few curious looks. Katya's speech enraptured most of the spectators, and it wasn't that strange for a security guard to be doing the rounds.

"I had the good fortune of meeting a man," continued Katya. "You all know and love Pavel, and I am quite taken with him too. But he is wrong. He speaks falsely."

A few skeptical audience members booed.

Katya doubled down. "All of you are wrong too. Immigration is not a problem to be fixed."

Others joined in and stood to shout. A pair of men in long coats exited a row of chairs, walking away from Carver to the opposite aisle. They were able-bodied, of fighting age. One peeked over his shoulder but stopped short of eyeballing Carver directly.

They were suspicious. Without the chance for a quiet chat, with the threat of a ticking clock, he made the field decision to treat them as Wagner operatives. He could come back from a presumptuous mistake. Underestimating them? Not so much.

"Hear me out. Please. Pavel Shishov is intelligent. He wants peace, but he is blinded by idealism. You must see this. There can be no peace when we think of ourselves as a separate people."

More boos. More spectators took to their feet. Carver was only half paying attention, but it sounded like Katya was burning Pavel's goodwill for a sound bite.

In the rear of the theater, at the end of his aisle, a man with a dark-blue overcoat watched him instead of the show.

It was Roman.

Carver glanced down the aisle the men had left. He had almost missed it in the commotion. A jacket partially protruded from beneath the chair a row ahead. The corresponding seats where the men had been sitting were empty.

Roman sneered at him and nodded upward in open challenge. What are you gonna do? They locked eyes for a tense moment.

Carver scowled in frustration. He wanted a second go at Roman but knew when he was being baited. He turned on his boot and advanced down the row of chairs. It was hard going now with half the audience standing and jeering. He brusquely pushed past people on his way to the vacated seats.

"Borders are a problem of the West's making," proclaimed Katarina above the discord. "We are one people. There is much history to prove this. The truth is hard yet beautiful. The truth is that Ukraine is not a separate state, it is a Russian one!"

Everyone jolted to their feet in raucous anger. Cups and bottles flew. Nervous shouting joined the fray as people pressed into each other.

What the hell was wrong with Katya? Her message was suddenly pro Russian. He wondered if they had somehow gotten to her. If she had been threatened and he had missed it. They had been in her hotel room.

Carver knelt and pulled the jacket from under the seat. The revealed yellow Semtex was compact but more than enough to make a statement. While it wouldn't bring the building down, it would obliterate anything centered on the main floor.

The audience was livid now, stomping and screaming and working themselves into a general frenzy. Pavel and another man stormed onto the stage and angrily faced Katya. The dog was frightened again. Morgan entered the stage, caught between competing desires. Carver tried to get her attention. He wanted to tell her to get Katya out of here. It was too difficult to gain notice among the animated crowd.

Carver pulled his Extrema Ratio and unfolded the squared blade. As he leaned down to disarm the explosive device, a woman stumbled on him from behind. Carver turned to help and found a man shoving her aside. Carver jumped back just as a thin dagger punched into his previous position.

The woman screamed and the operative shoved past her. He was high and Carver was low with a shorter weapon. Fortunately, the angry woman smacked him on the back of his head with a purse. The blow was cosmetic, but it was enough of a distraction. Carver batted the man's weapon hand upward and buried the police blade into his chest. Keeping his off hand on the man's wrist, Carver tugged him to the floor.

The woman screamed again and retreated down the row,

though no one seemed to notice. The crowd chanted something in Ukrainian, and it didn't sound nice.

With no active threats incoming, Carver cut the wires on the detonator. He removed the assembly so it couldn't be reactivated and crushed it under his boot.

Spectators filled the aisles. Some pushed forward but the wall of the orchestra pit was an effective enough barrier to prevent a full rush of the stage. At least for the moment. Things could quickly spiral to the point that a waist-high wall would no longer serve as a suitable barrier.

Pavel was red-faced. Katya's message had gone too far. More of his people congregated onstage now, including Amina and the guy with the Kalashnikov. Katya appeared daunted and hugged Anya close. The entire opera house was devolving into chaos as Carver pushed back into the main aisle.

He finally locked eyes with Morgan. She rushed to the front of the stage and raised her Glock. Carver spun to follow her aim. Despite all the yelling and shouting, the pistol's reports cut through the space like thunder.

A Wagner operative dropped to the floor. Another jumped behind a low wall. Carver tried swing his rifle up but there was no room. They were packed like sardines. He clenched his jaw and pulled the SIG. Too many spectators crossed his field of fire. The crowd had already been active and belligerent. After Morgan's gunshots, panic was now introduced into the equation.

Without many tactical options, Carver rushed toward the operative's entrenched position, opting for speed over prudence. He caught the Russian looking toward the back wall. The guy barely had his gun raised before Carver put two in his head at close range.

Five tangos down. That matched the number left alive in Warsaw, but that failed to account for Roman. Which meant their numbers had been reinforced. Carver followed the final gaze of the operative he had just killed to see what he was looking at. Nothing stood out.

Panicking people kicked at and shoved Carver as they scrambled for the exits. There weren't enough doors in the old theater to make that easy. Bottlenecks filled up fast and Carver was momentarily pinned.

Gunfire erupted from the stage. The man with the Kalashnikov went down. Amina stepped forward and fired into the orchestra pit, putting someone down. Morgan jumped down there now, scanning the fleeing crowd for anyone still advancing. Viktor Murayev and two SBU guys forced their way onstage. They moved hesitantly, perhaps unaccustomed to a firefight, yet also showed serious grit in joining the fray.

Somewhere, another gun sounded. Everyone on stage cowered. People scattered in all directions, fish desperately looking to escape the rounded barrel of the opera house.

Carver was nearly trampled. He crawled out from under pounding feet to find another operative ten feet away with his gun drawn. It was the driver of the Land Rover in Warsaw. Carver had seen him up close right before their car went over the bridge.

The man had the drop on him. He fired twice before

Carver could fire back. They expelled rounds in a simultaneous barrage, with Carver lying low on his left shoulder. Bullets pounded the seat beside him. A bystander took a tumble and cried in pain. Both their weapons barked until empty.

Carver was unscathed. The same couldn't be said of the driver. All but two rounds had penetrated the target. The 9mm jacketed hollow points expanded and broke apart, doing maximum internal damage without enough follow-through force to create an exit wound. The operative listed to the ground, and panicked audience members ran right over him on their way outside.

Finally, as the rush of people hit the walls of the opera house, he had a bit of breathing room. Carver turned back to the packed stage to finally exfiltrate Katya. He took a single step before a sudden explosion and wave of pressure smacked him to the carpet.

21

Carver pushed to his feet. His ears weren't ringing but he was slightly confused. It might have been shock. After a few blinks, he felt sufficiently in control of his faculties to assess the situation.

The bomb he had disarmed had not exploded. There must have been a secondary explosive, not as large but centered onstage. The huddling, cowering group was no more. In its place was smoke and ash and mangled people.

Carver holstered his P320, swung the X95 off his shoulder, and clicked off the LUMA safety. He hurried forward, scanning for Morgan and Katya. The SBU guys were injured and down. He saw that much. On the edge of the stage, Amina crawled toward where the microphone had been. She wasn't the only one moving. A few disfigured forms on the edges of the isolated blast radius squirmed and whimpered. He still didn't have eyes on Morgan.

Amina converged on the broken torso of her husband and wailed. Pavel was in pieces. She cradled his head and shoulders into her lap and sobbed. Her cry cut out when her head burst in blood timed to the crack of a pistol. Another operative was firing from the orchestra pit. Morgan came up behind him and put four in his back. She pulled the mag release and slipped a fresh set of rounds into the Glock.

"There's more of them," warned Carver as he hopped into the pit with her.

Just as his boots hit the floor, a round of gunfire erupted from the green room. A Wagner operative emerged onto the stage and found one of the younger SBU guys struggling to sit up. The PMC pointed the gun at his head and executed him. He moved to check the next SBU officer. When he was about to shoot, Viktor Murayev emptied his magazine into the man. Viktor spat and said something in Ukrainian, and then his head sagged to the floor. There was still shooting backstage.

"Where's Katya?" Carver barked.

Morgan shook her head. "I was engaging active threats. I saw you were in trouble."

"Damn it. Did you see what happened?"

She glanced at the center of the stage. "She was with Pavel."

Carver vaulted onto the stage. "Eyes forward. They might have her."

He knew it was stupid. Katya had been worried about kidnapping while he'd been uncovering bombs. Still, he had to hold out hope. The girl didn't turn up in his quick survey of the bodies, but it was admittedly hard to identify some of the pieces. He paused by Viktor to find him bleeding from the stomach. The SBU officer had no detectable pulse. Carver advanced to the green room as Morgan rushed to back him up.

A few of Pavel's people were dead and two more were pinned down. Carver wished he'd sent Morgan around the front. He considered doing it himself but didn't think there was time. He held the rifle to his shoulder and readied just outside the field of oncoming fire. As soon as a bout paused, he swung into the doorway and fired into the hall. The Tavor battered the fancy walls and decorations. Halfway through the military load, he'd succeeded in tagging one Russian and suppressing another.

With the hallway temporarily clear, he pressed forward and measured the remainder of his magazine. With three rounds left, he reached the alcove the operative was hiding in. Carver killed him and took cover in the same space, swapping the magazine and peeking out as a last Russian retreated around the curved hall.

Morgan stopped at his side, covering him. "She wasn't there, Vince."

He grunted and raced toward the front door. More gunfire came from ahead, though most of the screaming seemed to be outdoors now. Carver turned the bend to find the last Wagner operative taking cover at the front door. The police outside shouted what he took as orders to surrender. The Russian grimaced and checked his weapon before noticing Carver. His eyes widened. The operative swiveled his arm but Carver was already in firing position. Seven M855A1 Enhanced Performance NATO rounds tore into him at close to three thousand feet per second. It was over.

* * *

Katarina hadn't made it outside. The last Russian Carver neutralized had been alone, hesitating at the prospect of an impossible exit through a line of police. The entrance plaza was now a disordered henhouse after the fox had split. No more threat, only panicking hens and the farmers desperately trying to restore order.

Kyiv police entered and Carver and Morgan were disabused of their weapons and taken into custody. Those of Pavel's men who were fortunate enough to still be alive were detained as well. The authorities quickly came to the correct conclusion that they were private security. That truth was not enough to set them free. The defenders against the Wagner attack stood half forgotten in the hall as the quick-response team cleared the opera house.

"Viktor Murayev," stressed Carver. "He's SBU and he's hurt on the stage."

He managed to stray into the theater as he gave the instructions, and the police seemed to take his concern to heart. It wasn't until five minutes later that medical responders arrived to attend to the wounded.

Because Carver had disarmed the larger bomb, no audience members were wounded besides two from stray gunfire. An investigator entered the scene. She identified herself as Captain Popova from the Ministry of Internal Affairs and soon singled out Carver as a level head who could explain what happened. He stuck with the private security story and identified the Wagner Group operatives as unknown shooters.

Carver waited by the stage as Popova surveyed the damage. A couple of men were put on stretchers. One was the survivor from among the three SBU officers onstage. Viktor Murayev was dead, which meant Carver had nobody to vouch for him. That was why he straddled the line between being helpful and being *too* helpful. If the authorities knew he was an illegal Western asset, there was no telling what repercussions he would face or who would try to get to him.

About the only good news coming from the search was that Katya's body had not yet been identified. Unless she had disintegrated in the blast, the implication was that she was still alive. Carver scanned the wreckage for Anya or other clues. Under state custody, his mobility was limited and he had no luck.

Popova tersely thanked him for his help with the investigation. She ordered officers to take him outside, where he joined the others. The police in the plaza had been unable to contain the bulk of the fleeing spectators. As expected, no enemy combatants had been taken into custody. This was a concern as Carver was pretty sure Roman had slipped the noose.

Since no effective perimeter had been established around the National Opera, there were two possibilities regarding Katya's fate. Either she had gotten away, or she had been taken.

For the time being it was out of Carver's hands. He and

Morgan were loaded into the back of a police wagon with three of Pavel's friends. During a thirty-minute wait, two more prisoners were dumped in with them. More of Pavel's people, and still more questions than answers. Eventually, the police muttered something in Ukrainian before loading into the front cab and driving off.

"What did he say?" Carver asked.

"I didn't catch all of it," muttered Morgan. "Something about enjoying dinner. Maybe that means we'll be released before tonight."

One of Pavel's men snickered. "No. He said he hopes we like dinner in jail." His buddies laughed, though their faces were painted with defeat. Classic stress mitigation. Their fearless leader had just been killed before their eyes, and their fate and future were question marks.

The ride to the police station was not long. They were unloaded and split up. Carver's remaining possessions were taken. He wasn't given a phone call or lawyer or even an explanation as to what was going on. A junior officer took him to a private cell and locked him in all by himself. Carver waited hours in silence, listening for clues as to what had happened to Morgan and the others.

At some point, the guards called out and the lights shut off. It was obvious he wasn't a priority. He had not even gotten the jail dinner he'd been sarcastically promised. Carver sighed and settled in for a long night. If he was lucky, that was all it would be.

22

The guards finally fed him in the morning, delivering some kind of bread cakes filled with questionable meat. Carver readily devoured them. They weren't great but they got the job done. He couldn't say the same about his attempts to communicate with the junior officers posted in the jail. His requests to speak to Captain Popova were ignored. The one officer who did speak English simply told him to be quiet and wait.

While Carver didn't have his watch, he had been in custody less than twenty-four hours and still had a pretty good sense of time. It was at what he judged to be about noon that he heard the ring of his own phone outside his cell. He turned to find a man in a suit, with one arm in a splint, holding his burner. The man answered it.

"If you want to talk to your agent, call back in exactly ten minutes."

He hung up.

Carver deflated with his back against the cell wall. "They won't call back."

The other man was young, in his twenties, but he didn't look like a cop. His English was nearly perfect but he was a local, a new generation of Ukrainian. He shook his head, confident that Carver was wrong. "They'll call back. They want to know what the fuck happened, no?"

Carver idly shook his head. He wasn't counting on it.

The man gave orders in his language and two guards opened the cell to secure Carver. They fitted him with handcuffs behind his back and guided him down a boring hallway and into a quaint if unimaginative office. The suited man sat behind a sparse desk with a laptop while the guards escorted him to a chair. Carver was keeping his eye out for openings but figured, for now, his best bet was to behave.

The man set the burner phone on the desk. He didn't say anything and just watched, eyes glued to his subject as the guards finished locking him down, exited the room, and shut the door.

"You were in the opera," said Carver. "Onstage. You're SBU."

The man dipped his head once. "My name is Georgi. You?"

"Vince."

Another nod. "Vince and Georgi. Good. First names are good. I grew up in Lviv. Are you in the CIA?"

The sudden pivot caught Carver off guard so he didn't say anything.

The man raised a hand. "That's okay. I don't want to know. Here, in Kyiv, we don't have many friends. We stand alone. That is why, if you are truly a friend, I may decide to rely on you."

Again, Carver wasn't sure how to respond. Since he

thought remaining silent would come off as surly, he simply asked, "Why?"

Georgi hiked his good shoulder. "You know who else was a friend? Viktor Murayev. He saved my life on that stage. I lost my weapon. I was about to be shot. Viktor saved me with his last bullets and his last breath."

Carver bit down and nodded in grim agreement. "He was a good man."

"He thought good of you too. He told me what you were doing there. I tried to help and look what that got me." He nodded toward his arm splint. Georgi had probably caught some shrapnel from the blast. "I apologize for your treatment so far, but nobody knows anything about you besides me, and I was in the hospital. Honestly, I did not think you were still alive."

"That's all right. I don't need a vote of confidence, I just need to get out of these cuffs."

"Not so fast, Vince. You're here for a reason. You and I need to talk."

Carver couldn't begrudge the man that much, though he wasn't about to spill the beans about the CIA either. It seemed Georgi already had an inkling of what was going on, including whatever details Viktor had shared. It would be understood that he wasn't in a position to say much.

"What should we talk about?" asked Carver.

"This woman you were protecting, Katarina Litvinenko."

"Do you know where she is?"

"I do not, but I would very much like to."

Carver swallowed. "You and me both."

The man's expression was flat. "I suspect our motivations for finding her are very different."

"Georgi, what can I say? I was left behind, just like you. I defused that bomb in the seats that would have killed a bunch of innocent civilians. Why don't we just call this a wash and you let me get out of here already?"

He stared for a beat. "No, no, no, I think you misunderstand me. You see, Viktor told me about Katarina, and you told him about Katarina. I'm here to tell you it has come to light that you were both very wrong."

"What are you talking about?"

He took in a breath and glanced at the closed door. Apparently satisfied it wasn't going to open, he spun the laptop around on the desk. "I'm not supposed to show you this, so let's call it a secret between friends."

He played a video taken from the audience in the National Opera. The video showed an angry crowd chanting. It showed Katya onstage, arguing with Pavel. Everyone cowered at the sound of gunfire. The camera twirled around as the owner of the phone succumbed to panic. The picture blurred and had trouble correcting the zoom and lighting levels, but it eventually settled again. The camera moved as its owner ran along the aisle. Carver recognized the string of gunshots as he and the Wagner operative fired at each other. The camera retreated from that position and captured events onstage.

Katya bent down to the red handbag at her feet and retrieved a phone. Then, hugging Anya to her chest, she scurried to the empty side of the backstage area opposite the main green room. The explosion occurred seconds later.

"Play that back," said Carver, leaning closer to the screen.

Georgi complied, and the repeat showed the same sequence of events, plain as day. Katarina pulled out her phone, began to dial a number, and ran offstage. The explosion came from the handbag she had left behind.

Carver immediately understood what he had just watched twice over, but processing it was another matter. This was clear evidence that Katarina was an integral party to the bombings. He'd known she was manipulative. He had been confident he could stay ahead of that. Instead he had wholly underestimated her drive and ambition to please the people in power in Moscow.

"She always worked for Russia," realized Carver aloud.

Georgi replied with a glum nod. "You thought she was kidnapped, I bet? It was my first thought after we didn't find her. It is now more likely she fled back to her uncle and guardian, Arkady Malkin."

"How easy is the border crossing?"

He stared at Carver for a minute. "You're serious?"

"Yes."

Georgi closed the laptop and leaned back in his chair. "Normally, it is laughably easy to cross. She could take a car east to Kharkiv. But now there are several obstacles. First, the National Opera of Ukraine is a monument of personal pride. A bomb on its stage is an insult to everyone in the country. Authorities set roadblocks on all the highways out of the city."

"Could she have beat the perimeter?"

"Doubtful. The Ministry of Defense and Kyiv's Territorial Defense Force acted quickly."

"But Katya has powerful friends."

"I agree, and we can't rule out some level of assistance. But the roadblocks are secure. There are too many men to be bought off, especially after striking at the city's heart. The second concern is the situation at the border. Your government warned of an imminent invasion. Heavily armed soldiers guard the border on both sides. People are wary and on edge. A high-profile figure like Ms. Litvinenko would be smart to avoid such checkpoints."

Carver nodded, surprised to be slightly encouraged by the developments that occurred while he was in jail. "So where did she go?"

"No one knows. I believe she's still hiding in Kyiv."

That was what one of the Libyan bombers had done in Berlin and it hadn't worked out for him. Still, it was a possibility, if only for a day or two. But something told Carver that time was working against Katarina. She couldn't stay in a city under threat of impending invasion. Darling or not, the Red Army would not wait for her. At the same time, the looming invasion was the perfect distraction from her capture. Ukrainian authorities could only devote so much attention to her.

The burner phone on the desk rang. The CIA had actually called back.

Georgi smiled. "Go ahead. Say hello." He answered the

phone, set it on speaker, and slid it to the center of the table.

Carver cleared his throat. "Right now I'm sitting in a room with someone in the Security Service."

Silence answered and the two men watched each other.

"Viktor Murayev is dead," Carver added.

"Shit," said Williams. "I've been trying to call you. What happened?"

"I've been in jail. I was just tentatively released by—"

Georgi covered the phone and shook his head.

"Um... a friend of Viktor's."

"He's listening now?" asked Williams.

"He is."

"I'm not sure you can trust him."

Just like that. She didn't care that he could hear her.

"He's young," explained Carver, "from Lviv, out west. These guys don't have strong Russian ties."

"Well," she hedged, "without any intelligence on him, you need to go with your gut."

"What else is new?"

"Why don't you tell me?"

Williams had a way of answering questions with questions. Carver proceeded to go over the broad points, hyperaware that any information he conveyed would now be known by the SBU. When he described shooting the Wagner operatives and the last bomb going off, he paused and said, "A lot of people died. Pavel Shishov, his wife Amina in the shooting that followed. Viktor."

"It's the reality on the ground, Vince," she consoled. "You can't save everybody."

He winced. "Especially when our intel was bad to begin with?"

"Meaning?"

"We have evidence that Katya set off the last bomb. That's why I missed it."

Williams was surprised but unruffled. "Was her body recovered?" Another question.

"It won't be. She was an enemy asset from the start. Raising awareness on European immigration, breaking bread with like-minded people, and then having Libyans bomb sympathetic audiences and sway public opinion. She spread terror through Russian proxies, destabilized NATO partners by presenting the idea of civil borders as a risky proposition. The attacks only made her more popular, more of a folk hero, which gained her more access to do it all over again."

Georgi cut in. "Culminating with a false flag in the Ukrainian capital to turn our people against the government."

Williams waited a beat. "Who am I speaking with?"

"You aren't," he said.

"Katya came out with pro Russian rhetoric at the end," explained Carver. "Out of nowhere, she said Ukraine should be one with Russia. The whole place was heckling her. She wanted to make it look like the SBU tried to silence her. Maybe to give Russia casus belli to invade."

Williams grunted. "As if they need a pretext. The false flag might explain one of our findings. The bomb we recovered from the dead Libyan in Berlin matched the residue from the blast in Rome, but it doesn't match the materials we recovered in the apartment. It was clearly the same bomb maker, but they didn't want the signatures to be an exact match."

"Wait," stopped Carver. "Are you saying the Wagner bombs are from the Libyans?"

"It would explain the discrepancy."

"So the bomb maker was on the train to pass them off to Katya. She smuggled them across the border in her bags. That explains why Wagner Group broke into her apartment to recover the large bomb. Katya kept the small one. But why the different signature from the previous Libyan bombs?"

"So sympathizers within the government could leak that they weren't an exact match. They could say the bombs were built to look like Libyan bombs but they weren't, and they would have the proof. That would support the false flag theory, that it was really a setup. Which it was, of course, just not by the SBU."

"Ugh," said Carver. "My head hurts."

"Have you considered seeking medical attention for a concussion?" she asked drily. "I suppose you'll have plenty of time for that now. Are you cleared to get out of there?"

Georgi said, "Vince is on his way out."

"Good. Troop movements have intensified the last two days. This thing is going to happen. Kyiv isn't safe anymore. I'm sorry."

"Wait," said Carver. "We believe Katya might still be in the city."

"Doubtful," countered Williams. "This was a planned operation. It may have hit some snags, but she would have had an exfil in place."

"It's not a sure thing she got out."

"It never is, but it's a long shot that she didn't. You've done your part. We gave you bad intel and a flawed directive. You ran with that and minimized a lot of damage. It's a win, considering."

Carver grimaced. "It doesn't feel like a win."

"Come home, Vince. The job's over."

He took a long breath. Since staring at the phone didn't seem very persuasive, his determined gaze moved to Georgi. The security officer's eye twinkled with recognition and he returned a nod.

"What if the job's not over?" Carver asked.

Williams had been waiting for that. "It most certainly is," she admonished. "Take the train back to Warsaw where I'll have assets meet and debrief you. Fill me in on your arrival details before the fact."

"And if I don't?" he challenged.

"I'm already supposed to be disavowing you, Vince. Don't make me rethink my choice." The line clicked dead.

The two men appraised each other for a moment. Georgi dismissively flicked his working hand. "I am learning this about the intelligence services. It is a job filled with disappointments."

"Maybe," said Carver, "but I'm still not sure I'm ready to leave."

Georgi grinned. "I see why Viktor liked you."

The goodwill wasn't just for show. Georgi got him and Morgan released. He even returned their weapons. He knew where they were staying, got his phone number, and said he would look into Katya's location. Long shot or no, it was still a shot.

Carver rejoined a newly released Morgan outside the police station and explained the situation on the walk home.

"Are you sure about staying in Kyiv?" she asked. She seemed exhausted after the night in jail. "It sounds like we're getting a pass here."

"I don't want a pass, Jules. I want to complete the mission."

"The CIA ended the mission. Like it or not, they're our employer."

"And they knew the deal from go. I made myself very clear on this point. It's my way or the highway."

Morgan huffed and rolled her eyes. Deep down, she must have known he would say that.

23

Carver's firearms and knives were arrayed in orderly fashion atop the comforter of his hotel bed. He was in the process of cleaning the X95's flash hider when there was a knock at the door. He glanced up expectantly as Morgan answered. The mahogany bush of Shaw's beard gave the fellow operator away before Morgan assaulted him with a hug.

"Nick!"

"Easy, Jules. Easy."

She had nearly tumbled him over before realizing his right shoulder was supported by a crutch. Shaw limped in. A splint on his right thigh limited the motion of his knee.

"Sorry," she said. "You surprised me is all. We were expecting someone else."

"Yeah?"

She canted her head. "Ukrainian Security Service."

"Moving up in the world, I see. Sorry to disappoint."

"You all right there, brother?" asked Carver, eyes back on his work.

"Nothing a little R and R won't fix. What did I miss?" Shaw waited as Morgan checked the hall and closed the door. His anxious gaze swiveled from Carver to Morgan.

"Jules?"

She sighed. "Vince has been like this for hours. You'd think he recovered his guns from the tar pits given how long he's been cleaning them."

Shaw snorted like it was old hat. "A little antsy. I get it."

"It's more than that," said Carver belligerently.

Morgan frowned and lowered her voice. "He's not square with how things went down."

"People died," boomed Carver, still able to hear her.

She spun to him. "You stopped the main bomb from going off, Vince. The secondary explosive was much smaller."

"It still killed people. I could have evacuated them. I should have ordered you to evacuate them, Jules."

She rolled her eyes, upset at his continued insistence to circle the drain. "You can't see everything in the fog of war, Vince."

"This isn't theory. A more traditional SWAT response would have evacuated them immediately."

She huffed loudly and stormed into the adjoining room. Shaw limped to the doorway and took off his sunglasses to admire Katya's suite. An impressed whistle escaped his lips.

Nick Shaw wasn't one to meddle, but there was a difference between meddling and support. After a few minutes of standing around in contemptible silence, he shuffled to the queen bed beside Carver's and gently eased himself down. He leaned the crutch against the bed and mopped a hand over his beard.

"You're right. SWAT would have evacuated

immediately. But you're here, Vince, because a more traditional SWAT response doesn't work in all situations. You know this. It doesn't matter if you're Delta or SEALs, guys like us are needed precisely because we go off book and take independent action. You stopped a bomb in Berlin. You tracked the bomb maker on the train. Time and again you've operated in the margins that SWAT can't penetrate. Most of those decisions have been good ones. Even this one. It's impossible to save everybody."

"You think I don't know that, Nick?"

"Then let's cut the shit and get to what this is really about. Katya's in the wind and that pisses you off."

Carver tightened a fist of fingers slick with Hoppe's Black Precision Oil.

"You were too trusting," said Shaw.

"I never trusted her."

"Fine, but you played into her hands. Katya acts a little defenseless, a little risque, and it was enough to distract you from the real play."

Carver worked his jaw. "Nobody saw the big picture on this one, not even the CIA. You were as concerned about her well-being as anyone."

"Hey, brother, you're right on that point. I'm not saying I knew the score. But I did know she couldn't be trusted."

"You here to rub it in?"

"I'm here to help a friend."

Carver continued wiping his rifle. "I'm not sure it matters anymore. The CIA pulled support and the SBU doesn't have a lead on Katya."

"Then it's a perfect time to show our value to your employer."

For the first time in the conversation, Carver broke his gaze away from his guns. "What are you saying?"

Shaw shrugged innocently. "Only that I figured anything the CIA was looking at was interesting. And with Katya sneaking out and not being where she said she would be more times than not... and with me in charge of her security... I did what any responsible CPO would do. I put a tracker on the bitch."

Carver's eyes twitched, somber mood tempering true excitement. "Katya was exfilled by a Wagner operative. She changes clothes three times a day and doesn't have a regular car. What did you tag?"

"That's the beauty, Vince. I didn't tag her. She would notice it, especially if she were a Russian asset. But there's one thing that's always hanging from her elbow..."

"The dog handbag," he said glumly. "It's a nice thought, but it's blown to bits and ashes."

"Nah, you're not using your imagination," countered Shaw. "She goes through those bags every week too. I put the tracker on the back of that little terrier's diamond-encrusted bow. And it's still active."

The excitement hit him then. "Nick, you beautiful bastard."

Shaw didn't have the military tracking equipment locally and it wasn't as simple as an app on his phone. He made a call to a friend out of state. Katya's latest location was confirmed. Combined with a string of previous positions, her exfil came into focus.

After the blast in the opera house, the police outside moved to full alert but had to deal with a fleeing crowd. Katya unassumingly slipped out while authorities were overwhelmed.

Meanwhile, the Ministry of Defense took action against an act of terrorism. They immediately locked down the city, placing checkpoints on the highways out of town.

Only Katya didn't attempt to flee by car.

The Dnieper River sits two kilometers from the National Opera of Ukraine. Fleet feet could take her to a waiting boat in minutes. A shipping vessel would blend in and be difficult to search. Traveling by river was slow, but it immediately slipped the noose. Katya was now more than halfway to the Black Sea, no longer in Kyiv but still very much in Ukraine.

Morgan returned as they discussed options. There was another knock and she let Georgi inside.

"Nick's with me," Carver said in greeting. Then, to Shaw, "Georgi's the friend I told you about."

The young SBU officer picked up on the excitement of the group. "There was a development?"

"We have her," said Carver. "Katya's not going for the Russian border. She's traveling downriver."

He clasped his hands together. "This tracks with my latest intelligence. Arkady Malkin has a yacht approaching in the Black Sea."

Carver stood in anticipation. "Is he on it?"

"It's impossible to say."

"Do you think they'll split the difference and meet in

Crimea?"

"It's one contingency," he hedged, "but, with an increased presence of Russian warships performing naval exercises and a heavy troop buildup in Sevastopol, it's unlikely. The real problem is the blockade of Ukrainian ports, preventing trade and military movements, but personal friends of the Russian president enjoy certain benefits. I believe Malkin will dock in Odesa. It is a popular destination of his."

Carver, Morgan, and Shaw looked at each other like they had just been informed it was Christmas.

"Can you intercept her there?" asked Morgan.

"If Ms. Litvinenko is smart, she will stay on the docks. Ship to ship transfer without leaving the port."

"Does that matter?" asked Carver. "Arkady Malkin is the mastermind of this plot. You should nab him as well."

Georgi grunted. "This will not happen. He is a powerful man and there is no proof."

"You can question him. Make sure Katya doesn't disappear."

"We have no power to do so. Odesa is heavily regulated by the mafia. They are a powerful *malina* network with strong Russian ties and are paid handsomely by Arkady for protection. That is why, even with current events as they are, he confidently heads to port in Odesa."

"What authorities can we count on?" asked Shaw.

"The local police are paid off, as are members of the Security Service."

"Are you kidding me?" he replied. "You're saying the

SBU is going to sit this out?"

"Guys," tempered Carver. "This can work for us." His funk was gone and he gazed encouragingly at each person in turn. "Georgi's right. Involving the authorities is a mistake. There's no paper trail to Arkady and there are too many tripwires. One whisper of an operation would tip him off. He won't dock in Odesa, and then Katya won't either. There are lots of other safe havens on the Black Sea and we might lose her for good."

"So we're screwed," said Morgan.

"Not as long as Arkady is confident. These types of guys think they're untouchable. The man is sailing past warships to Odesa. If we play this right, we can not only intercept Katya quietly, we can also get the oligarch bastard who orchestrated this madness."

Stunned silence was broken by Morgan. "Are you crazy, Vince?"

Shaw nodded. "A quiet insertion is about as risky as it gets, but the payoff is huge."

Morgan threw her hands in the air. "I can't believe I'm hearing this."

"We'll need some ordnance," added Carver. "A vehicle. Maybe some access for passing checkpoints."

Georgi nodded. "I have some ideas."

"What about Odesa?" asked Shaw. "The thing about corruption is it cuts both ways. Can we find a friend or two at the docks?"

Georgi grinned. "Anything can be found when you're willing to pay a premium. Give me one hour to get everything together."

* * *

They were packed and geared up. The mood of the room had changed considerably. It was one of resolute efficiency. One way or another, this was going to get done. Sometimes going above and beyond was the only way to turn the wheel.

True justice is as terrifying and staggering as a mountain. It's up there, at the peak, and hard to reach. It's easy to turn around early, to think it can't be surmounted, and to walk away patting yourself on the back for a minor victory. But when that rare moment presents itself, when the weather conditions are perfect and you have the strength and oxygen and grit to keep climbing, that's when something special is possible.

Carver knew Shaw was on board. Even wounded, he was willing to go the distance. Realistically, they also had to acknowledge he could only go so far. It was while pondering that same dose of reality that he made another decision.

"How're you holding up, Jules?" he asked. She stood by the window watching the street for their SBU contact.

"I'm good," she replied, arms crossed in an attempt at casual cool.

Carver worked his lips. "You're right about us being happy with what we've accomplished. About it making sense to follow CIA orders."

She arched a skeptical eyebrow. "You had a change of

heart?"

"You could say that."

"That's not like you." There was still doubt in her voice.

"I just booked a ride back to Warsaw."

"That's... good, I guess. I just..."

"What are you going to tell Frank at your next therapy session?"

She blinked, taken aback by the turn of conversation. "My mission statement?"

He nodded. "Your mission statement."

Morgan took a breath and composed herself. "I'm going to tell him that sometimes the operation takes me overseas, and when it does it's because it's important, but when I'm home my sole mission is to be a present mother who spends quality time with my kids. They need me, Vince. And Frank needs me, even if we don't get along like we used to. So *his* mission is to suck it up and stop bickering. And if he doesn't like it, I can knee him in the kidney."

He laughed. "Maybe omit that last part, but everything else reads A-OK."

"Thanks, Vince. It helps to have a sounding board."

"And since Kinetic National Security doesn't have strict paperwork requirements, you'll practically be on vacation as soon as you get home. You know, after you debrief the CIA for us."

Her features went rigid as she realized his meaning. "No, Vince. I'm not leaving Kyiv without you."

"Yes you are. I can't order you to go but I can fire you if you don't."

"Screw the job," she hissed.

"Then think about your kids."

"No. You don't get to use them against me. I'm a soldier. My job has risks. I signed up for those risks."

He grabbed her shoulders to look her in the eye. "Jules, listen to me. You served your country doing Special Reconnaissance in the Army Special Forces. You were a damn good soldier, and that's the only reason you're on my team. You're used to going behind enemy lines without reinforcements, but..." He drifted off because he didn't want to cross the line with her. "Look, our work puts us in the line of fire. That's a fact. And I respect your decision to live or die with that fact every day. We all do it. But what I'm doing next is beyond the pale... Shaw and I, we're killers."

She swallowed. Carver loosened his grip because he was getting through to her. "You don't think you're coming back," she said.

"I always think I'm coming back. This isn't some planned suicide mission, but I'm not fooling myself about the risks here."

"Then why do it?"

"Because I *need* to. And it's not just because I screwed up. There's a chance here, a chance to take out the trash, to hit someone unspeakably evil who believes himself invincible. And I don't blame you if your heart isn't in this part. It wasn't what you signed up for. It's not what we're authorized for. I won't drag you down because of my personal mission."

Morgan frowned. She wanted to object, but she also saw

the truth in what he was saying. Letting her go made the most sense all around, for everyone.

"Tell me you'll get on that train," said Carver.

"I'll get on the damn train," she relented. "But only to convince the CIA to help you get out of there."

Carver nodded and gave her a hug. There was a fat chance the Agency would reverse course on this, but he didn't dissuade her of the notion.

24

Carver and Shaw may have been a whole day behind Katarina, but an unassuming vessel on the Dnieper would be forced to take an extremely roundabout path toward its destination. The boat would head southeast over most of its journey before looping back west. That bend was more or less where Katarina was now. Soon the vessel would emerge in the Black Sea and follow a short coastline to the city of Odesa.

Driving would take them to the same port. The difference was their route was a six-hour jaunt on Highway M05. It was a modern four-lane affair, part of European Route E95 that bisected Ukraine in two from Chernihiv to Odesa.

Georgi saw them off with parting gifts. Carver now drove an aging Jeep Renegade. Georgi led them two miles out of Kyiv to clear them past two checkpoints. The first was the police net that had been set up to capture Katya. While it was no longer needed, due to public sentiment Georgi would be slow about calling off the search and taking it down. Security theater was one facet of security, after all.

The second checkpoint was run by the 112th Territorial Defense Brigade for the purpose of vetting vehicles headed in and out of the capital. Carver and Shaw weren't the most inconspicuous pair around. The stockpile of firearms and ammunition in the back seat didn't help.

Carver had only been in Kyiv for a short time and already appreciated its nostalgic charm. While it was undeniably lawless in areas, it was jarring to see a city he only just started getting to know readying for a military invasion. Carver watched the armed soldiers in camo helmets and combat fatigues. Surprisingly well outfitted, they didn't look so different from a NATO detachment at a glance. They had no doubt spent the last several years trained up by America and other Western powers.

That said, being supplied and trained by NATO was very different from being a card-carrying member. There were no Western boots on the ground. Ukraine was a country pitted against all odds, a people in a fight they had to wage themselves. Only time would tell if they were ready.

Once their cars were past the troops, Georgi pulled away and waved them off. From here, Carver and Shaw were on their own.

A few hours into a quiet drive, all thoughts remained on the mission, which involved the other of Georgi's gifts in a bag on the back seat. It contained the large explosive Carver had defused at the opera house. The public didn't know about the bomb that hadn't gone off and they didn't need to. The narrative was simpler that way. On top of that, keeping the bomb a secret made it the perfect weapon to repurpose. It had traveled a long way from Berlin and was almost at its final destination.

They stopped at a gas station an hour out from Odesa and filled the tank. It was a lot more fuel than they needed. In operations like this, if you could spend a few dollars to be more prepared, you didn't skimp. There was always the chance they would fall back to the vehicle if things went sideways.

While Shaw pumped, Carver leaned on the front bumper and called Williams.

"Here," she said.

"The train arrives in Warsaw West tomorrow at 7:30 pm."

"We'll be waiting for you," she said matter-of-factly. "I'm glad you made the right decision."

"You're damn right I did." He flexed his jaw and decided to go against his gut. "Morgan will be available for debrief, but I won't be on that train."

A moment of silence. "Why not?"

He told her the plan. They had a shot, not just at Katarina, but at Arkady Malkin. This was the chance of a lifetime. They weren't likely to get this close again, especially if Russia did the unthinkable and actually initiated a war. This, he said, was their moment.

"I appreciate the tactical opportunity," said Williams, "but I can't condone that course of action."

Carver winked at the phone. "Uh-huh, I read you. Plausible deniability and all that."

"I'm being serious, Vince. I can't green-light this

operation."

"It's *my* operation, officer. The question is, are you going to stop me?"

Her reply was a boilerplate denial. "The CIA and its associated assets have no ongoing operations in Ukraine at this time."

Carver snorted. He wasn't sure if she was now doing her own nudge-wink thing or washing her hands of him. "I can get her, Lanelle. I can do it without your knowledge or oversight or orders. Everybody wins."

She sighed loudly into the microphone. "If you even think about doing this, you need to destroy this phone the second you hang up with me. That's non-negotiable."

"Copy that."

"That's not just an empty metaphor, either. You need to ditch the phone and any hope of future support. That means you're on your own. Completely disavowed."

"I understand."

She hissed in frustration and maybe something else. "Do you have any idea where that ship is headed after pickup?"

"Speculation is Sochi, that Olympic village. Malkin has vacation properties there and it's the farthest Russian coast from Ukraine."

"On the Black Sea anyway, right on the border with Georgia. You can attempt to disappear there, but I wouldn't recommend it. If it's in any way possible, you should head further south. Turkey has a long stretch of coast, and their officers should take care of you if you're caught. But I can't give them a heads up or acknowledge your operation."

"What operation?"

She grunted in resignation. "You know, it's just like you to plan an international incident."

Carver smiled. "Thanks, Lanelle."

"Don't thank me. Don't even call me. You're done..." It sounded like she was trying to catch her breath. He reminded himself that she wasn't accustomed to battle and was probably experiencing jitters. "Good luck, Vince."

"Take care of Morgan, all right?"

"It's the least we can do."

When they disconnected, he removed the sim and snapped the phone in half. He ground the pieces under his boot and dropped them in separate trash cans. Then they once again hit the road.

* * *

The Odesa Sea Port is one of the largest on the Black Sea, serving multiple terminals and acting as a transport hub to all of Ukraine and Eastern Europe. Its valuable commerce and traffic lanes make it the ideal center for certain extra-legal organizations to grift the public twice, first on the front end and then through government contracts on the back. Being a major hub for both freight and passengers, very little goes in or out without the okay of the Odesa mafia.

This de facto *malina*, this underworld, creates the perfect haven for smugglers, whether trafficking people or Afghan heroin and meth. It is no coincidence the coastal city also serves as the Miami Beach for ultra-wealthy Russians.

The greater port complex consists of a number of harbors set behind multiple jetties in the bay. The passenger terminal features bars, restaurants, and entertainment venues; a diving center and marina complex; a church; and an officially closed but unofficially repurposed four-star hotel. Carver knew better than to ask questions about its current purpose. He was singularly focused now.

Carver and Shaw parked the Renegade in a long-term lot with eyes on Malkin's docked superyacht, the *Mat' Drakonov*. They traded binoculars as they studied the three-hundred-foot monstrosity which was worth 250 million American dollars and featured a six-deck interior and Rolls-Royce engines. Believe it or not, it was a modest flagship by modern oligarch standards. To make up for that deficit in status, the gaudy yacht came with its own support vessel for additional staff and recreational equipment. That support vessel was itself a superyacht.

"That's got to be him on deck," said Shaw, passing the binocs.

Carver located and confirmed the identification of Arkady Malkin, wearing baggy sweatpants and an unbuttoned shirt that blew in the wind like a cape. His shaded glasses were suave, but the spare tire around his waist, not so much.

"Looks like Arkady's living his best life," observed Carver. He handed off the binocs and checked the parking lot. "Where is this guy? If he doesn't get here soon I need to infil on my own."

"Relax," said Shaw. "That Georgi fellow seemed to be on top of things, and I talked to this guy on the phone. Sounded like a straight shooter. We have time as long as Katya doesn't show."

There was no telling which vessel she was on in the busy port. Her tracker had been deactivated somewhere around Kherson, near the end of the river. It could have been a technical malfunction, or the collar could have been removed or lost. There was also the possibility it was discovered by Katya or her Wagner escort.

If the escaping assets were spooked, it sure didn't show on Malkin's face. Carver hoped that ditching the tracker would fool their prey into believing they were home free. That they wouldn't put the dots together about their target destination already being compromised. Which meant Arkady waited, and they waited.

"Security is real," noted Shaw. "The PPO on deck is carrying a Kord 6P67. Those are the new assault rifles reserved for airborne. Selective fire with a two-round burst."

"Fan of Eastern European ordnance, are we?"

"I've been known to dabble," he said with a grin.

Carver had seen the bodyguard. With Malkin's connections to the government and military complex, there was no question he was elite Spetsnaz. Likely the best of the best Wagner Group had to offer.

"The other guard on the dock makes two bad boys. Plus whoever's escorting Katya."

"I know," said Carver. "That's why this needs to be

quiet."

"Everything's quiet until it's not."

"Go big or go home."

Their levity was standard practice for operations like this. When a soldier faced harsh odds and likely death, it didn't help to be scared. Mindful, sure, but fear of your own mortality was a crutch in a firefight. You worried about living when you prepped the gear and planned the op. When it was time to fight, you shut down any contemplation of failure.

"You know," mused Shaw, "this is good. Getting the band back together again. It feels right."

Carver nodded. The mutual feeling just made what he had to say worse. Shaw was wounded. He could walk but not easily. Shaw didn't have fear as a crutch but he did have an actual crutch. There was no way an operative in his condition could sneak onto a boat and engage in close-quarters battle. It was especially tragic because Shaw was a SEAL—maritime ops were his specialty.

"I know you made mistakes, Vince. No op goes perfectly."

"I'm past that. We have a chance to catch Katya and more."

"I'm talking about Taipei. About keeping that intel from me."

Carver turned to study his friend.

Shaw waved dismissively. "There's no need to get into all that again. I get why you did what you did. I'm just a stubborn asshole. But you've been straight with me this go around."

Carver nodded warily. It was an odd time for Shaw to get sentimental.

"I just mention all this to say bygones are bygones and all that, and to ask if there was any chance Kinetic National Security was still hiring?"

That was a sudden turn. "I thought you had no interest in working for the CIA?"

"Wasn't that their phone you smashed back there? Doesn't look like you're beholden to me."

"You know what I mean."

He nodded. "Screw it. This extracurricular stuff is more fun than vanilla security work any day. When you showed up in Berlin I knew it was on. And everything that happened since just shows I may be a CIA asset whether I work for them or not. I might as well sign up for the pleasure."

Carver blinked. "What will you tell Iris Executive Protection?"

"Toss them. I already quit. You think I'd let you save the world without me?"

Carver laughed. "Then welcome to the team, brother." They bumped fists. "If you're already unemployed, I'll see about securing back pay for you when we hit stateside." He nodded toward Shaw's leg. "Sick pay, too."

"That sounds mighty good," said his friend. His camaraderie quickly evaporated and his features went stern. "You know I can't go in there with you. I would just hold you back."

Carver bit down. "I know."

That was Shaw again, ever the professional soldier. Carver shouldn't have bothered preparing the talk because an operative like Shaw knew combat and knew the score. If they were holding a position Carver would take Shaw's gun over a pristine soldier's every day of the week, but this wasn't that.

Before they could say anything else, a crappy Euro car with peeling paint rounded into the lot, paused for a moment, and then made a bead for them. They held their pistols low as the tiny car parked and a fat man got out. His shirt stretched tight and his pants ended high over socks and sandals. They disembarked to greet him.

"You are the Americans?" he asked in a thick accent. He was mostly bald with a horrible comb-over that only added to his mafioso image.

Shaw circled the car with an extended hand. "Nick. We spoke on the phone."

"Yes, yes, the Americans. I am Olek. You still want to do this?"

"The question is, do you?"

The man waited an extended beat as his frown deepened. Carver grabbed a bag from the back seat and handed it to Olek, who unzipped it halfway to reveal the colorful local currency of Ukraine. "I trust you. Besides, I don't do this for the money."

Despite the declaration, he set the bag of loot in his car. Carver and Shaw eyed each other like who is this guy? Olek turned around, planted his hands on wide hips, and watched them with an appraising eye.

"I could get trouble for this," he said, "but I don't care fucks, you understand me?"

Carver allowed himself to smile. "I think we do."

Olek nodded back, satisfied. "Good. I will get you in. Then you teach those moskals a lesson they cannot forget. For Ukraine."

25

Carver lingered outside a marina-complex warehouse wearing flip flops, waterproof trainer pants, and a black Adidas windbreaker to fight off the coastal breeze. He felt ridiculous but needed to look the part, and it was all Olek had on short notice. A stripped-down bag with minimal gear for the op sat in the back of a golf cart. Hitched to its trailer were a pair of pristine Jet Skis to be loaded into Malkin's inventory.

The support vessel was a 140-foot catamaran, its two well-spaced hulls supporting a large, flat deck. It essentially amounted to a giant floating garage, space for all the crafts and toys, and for extra stores of food and fuel. The thinking was not to burden the main yacht with such trivialities when there was extra recreational space to be had. Two smaller, faster vessels can fit into more ports worldwide than a single huge monstrosity.

A dockworker whose name he didn't catch strolled up and said, "Let's go." He sat behind the wheel of the golf cart and was apparently prepped not to ask questions. Carver sat in the passenger seat and they pulled toward the boats.

The *Mat' Drakonov* grew more impressive as they

neared. Now late in the day, the shadow it cast was tremendous. The main section of hull was a striking black, with an imposing straight vertical bow, and the white superstructure protruding above. According to deck plans obtained online, the vessel featured a pair of Jacuzzis, a helipad, spa, gym, and eight staterooms. Their recon led them to believe there were no guests on board.

At a cruising speed of fifteen knots, it was a thirty-eight-hour trip from Odesa to Sochi. It was almost too much time.

The dockworker stopped the cart beside the support vessel. Beneath the elaborately styled text *Viserion* lay the open aft hatch. Carver wasn't sure what they were waiting for. A minute later two matte-black dune buggies drove up under their own power and took the lead, entering the vehicle deck. As he passed, the second driver smiled behind a mahogany beard.

"Shaw..." muttered Carver under his breath.

He couldn't believe it. He had been played.

As he waited, Malkin's main superyacht departed the dock. The quick exit was either a sign that Katya had already boarded while he had been busy in the warehouse, or that the oligarch had been warned about the tracker and was cutting ties. Not knowing Katya's location added a level of guesswork he would have preferred not to deal with. Carver often chided the CIA for unreliable intel and here he was, in the same boat so to speak. Then again, he wasn't working with satellite imagery and spy drones.

At any rate, it was too late to alter the plan. Arkady Malkin was the tango they had confirmed so all they could do was move ahead.

Once the dune buggies were clear, the golf cart towed the Jet Skis in. While the tenders, the larger watercraft, were secured topside where they were exposed to the elements, the underdeck garage was storage for vehicles, motorcycles, and smaller craft like the Jet Skis. Aluminum beams stretched overhead in the same gray color as the *Viserion's* exterior, giving the feel of a military installation able to withstand a twelve-megaton nuke.

Carver helped ease the trailer into place. The dockworker unhitched it and nearly drove away before Carver could grab his gear. That was it then.

He wandered deeper into the vehicle deck, checking that all the vehicles were tightly stowed, and met Shaw tying down the dune buggy.

"Nice speech about staying behind," skewered Carver.

"I meant it at the time. Honest. But then I saw this bad boy and knew I had to give it a test drive."

The former SEAL also grabbed a bag of gear and hooked it over his shoulder. They assessed the garage and their eyes landed on a gloss-black Hummer EV Edition 1 pickup. Carver signaled toward it, and the two surreptitiously made their way over as personnel finished loading the aft of the garage. The truck's doors were unlocked and the keys were in the cupholder. They slipped inside the back, and just like that they were out of sight.

Shaw whistled. "I didn't even know these were out yet. You know this thing can drive diagonally?"

"Let me know when it can drive upside down," muttered

Carver, unimpressed.

An anxious ten minutes passed as various workers cleared out. Carver and Shaw were free to watch from behind the black windows without being seen. In that time they couldn't locate any security cameras. Plenty of objects were stowed in the overhead atop aluminum grates between the beams. Tarps, canisters, manual rafts and paddles. Snaking pipes supported a number of fire suppression nozzles, but there wasn't a single camera.

"I don't like this," said Carver. "Arkady's ship has sailed but we're not moving."

"It's standard," tempered Shaw. "Support vessels have higher cruising speeds than their mother ships so they can catch up. They linger at the port loading supplies, and then they beat the rich bastards to the destination port so they can unload and be ready for them. You think Malkin's the type of guy who likes to wait?"

Carver supposed he could see the sense in that. "Let's just hope he at least waited for his niece."

"That's a different kind of patience," harrumphed Shaw.

After a while there was some movement on the vehicle deck. A guard with an assault rifle boarded from the port. The last dockworker waved him off. Two members of the crew, identified by their stark white uniforms, secured the aft ramp. Carver and Shaw were officially sealed behind enemy lines.

They waited until the deck was clear to open their bags. They checked the pistols first before going for their rifles. Shaw produced a used M4. Carver was happy to throw off the flip flops and put socks and boots back on. They had also packed ballistic vests, knives, plastic flex-cuffs, and flare guns. Carver fit the vest nicely under the windbreaker while a separate sling held the prepped explosive around his neck. That was pretty much it with the limited space they had.

As the engines of the *Viserion* spun up, Carver snapped a quick-attach Griffin Armament M4SD II suppressor to the paired flash hider of his X95. He was locked and loaded.

"We have about a day and a half," conveyed Carver in a discreet voice. "I figured we'd wait the crew out and make our move after midnight."

"Yup," was Shaw's curt answer.

The soft infil had been successful. The beauty of the two-yacht setup was that Arkady's bodyguards were with him. Their state of heightened alert would be reserved for their time at port. All the two of them needed to do was sit quietly and wait for the sun to retreat. Later, at night and with the vessels alone in the Black Sea, security would grow lax. That was when they would strike and make the transfer to the *Mat' Drakonov*.

"Wake me in three hours," said Carver.

It wasn't much, but Shaw needed the same amount of time to sleep afterward. Maybe it was the hum of the engines or maybe it was a plan coming together, but Carver slept like a baby.

Shaw gave him an extra hour so Carver returned the favor. His watch read 1 am as they both finally readied to make their move.

"You know the downside to this plan, right?" asked

Shaw.

"What's that?"

"These two ships will have an easy line of communication between them. We do anything splashy and they warn Arkady."

"If it comes to that, we'll have control of this vessel. You said we're faster than them, right?"

"What are you gonna do, ram him?"

Carver grinned. "Might be fun. But you're right. We'll do what we can with knives first."

"Hooyah."

"Hooah."

They slipped out of the fancy Hummer. Shaw had ditched his crutch on the mainland and limped gingerly. If Carver could, he would beat his friend to any action. He marched for the internal stairway, leading with his rifle. He peeked along the metal railing to moonlight above and didn't see any movement. He stepped back and proceeded to an open doorway by the aft hatch. A guard stood outside watching the catamaran's twin wakes. The boxy rear of the stern was overshadowed by a wide helipad above. No one could see him from the upper deck.

Carver signaled the tango to Shaw. He pulled his fixed blade and advanced, driving water concealing the sound of his boots. He wrapped a hand around the guard's mouth and slit his throat with a quick, tearing motion. Before the man could mount a response, Carver shoved him over the railing and into the foamy sea. He subsequently retreated into the garage and signaled to Shaw. One tango down.

His friend didn't have eyes on anyone. Though there were no port or starboard exterior decks on this level, the wide windows showed only black water. Carver moved 120 feet to a hatch at the bow. Moonlight bathed a small utilitarian sundeck. It was brighter outside than Carver would have liked. No one was outside. Malkin's ship was some distance ahead and to their left. The *Viserion* was offset to avoid its wake, reminiscent of a squire taking position behind his knight. Between the drone of the engines, water, and wind, he judged the superyacht to be outside the audible range of gunfire.

While an exterior set of stairs led to the main deck above, it would put them in sight of the bridge and any lookouts within. They retreated back to the central stairway inside.

"You'd better take the lead up the ladder," said Shaw.

He did. While his friend used common Navy terminology, the stairways on these yachts were anything but ladders. It brought him right behind the main superstructure of the upper deck. Carver remained low among the top steps to survey the scene. Speedboats, motorized rafts, and even a beautiful competition cutter were tied down on the weather deck. Cranes with folded booms sat to either side, ready to lower the tenders to the water. The helipad at the stern was empty. Shaw hopped up behind him.

"I don't see anyone," Carver whispered. "There's got to be one more guard on this boat."

His friend completed his own scan. "Maybe Arkady's

cocky. Could just be one man watching his toys."

"That's not cocky, that's stupid."

They waited ten minutes to assess the situation. They could only observe the open-air afterdeck of the vessel as they were backed right up against the wall of the deckhouse. It would consist of the shared cabins, galley, and bridge. This was a multihull ship, touching the water along the port and starboard lengths with an empty center to easier cut through the water. That meant the crew cabins were belowdecks.

They couldn't risk securing the separate hulls until they had seized command of the ship. If Shaw were at full strength, one of them could go down while the other waited topside. Then, if trouble sounded, one could rush the bridge. With their current status it was best to bum-rush the primary objective first.

"Okay, we go in hot. We don't kill anybody in white unless they give us cause. All bets are off for the Spetsnaz and anyone holding a gun."

"Copy that," said Shaw.

Carver spun around the railing and moved to the hatch. Staying low, he waited till Shaw was in position before breaching into a carpeted living room with a wraparound couch and roller blinds. Finding it empty, he marched forward with the Tavor braced against his shoulder.

The next cabin had a pair of high tables, eight stools each. A guard with a Kord 6P67 swiveled from a television on the wall, chocolate bar in hand. He raised the rifle and Carver popped two round into his chest and neck. Carver moved for the starboard doorway. Another guard alerted by the suppressed fire rushed in through the port side. Carver turned but Shaw lit him up with the M4. Knowing speed was vital, Carver continued ahead without pause.

He entered a posh command cabin with a wood floor and blue faux leather captain's chairs. Three crew members in white uniforms cowered around a low wall. An assault rifle double-tapped and Carver dove to the deck. He fired blindly once, twice to suppress. The guard returned with fully automatic fire. Carver scrambled on all fours to retreat.

The man shouted in Russian. Carver waited for the magazine switch. He attempted to pop up but the wallpaper around him shredded to pieces and he thought better of it. The trained operator had reloaded in a snap. Luckily, Shaw's M4 let loose from the opposite doorway and the barrage immediately cut out. The guard cried in pain.

Carver spun through the doorway and advanced on the downed guard. He put a quick one in the suffering man's head as Shaw limped over. The captain reached for the navigation console. Carver's rifle snapped to him.

"Stoy!" shouted Carver. "Stop! *Stoy!*"

The captain froze.

"Reloading," called Shaw. Carver waited with his weapon trained until Shaw said, "Ready."

"Reloading," repeated Carver in turn.

He replaced his partial mag while Shaw covered the crew. When he was done he pulled the captain away from the nav station and sat him on the deck beside the other two crew members. Shaw pulled flex-cuffs and secured their hands behind their backs.

"Where the hell did they come from?" snarled Shaw after the bridge was secure.

Carver kept his weapon on the captain. "You. You speak English?"

The man nodded, eyes wide yet somewhat defiant.

"How many Spetsnaz are on this ship?"

The captain bit down.

"You and the crew are safe if you don't lie to me," said Carver. "You have my word. How many Spetsnaz?"

The captain looked at his men and swallowed. "There are six," he said. "Four on and two off, in three shifts."

"The last two are belowdecks?"

The captain paled when he realized four were already dead. "Yes."

"Where?"

The captain answered and Carver nodded to his friend.

"Gentlemen," announced Shaw as Carver walked back through the bullet-shredded path he had come by, "this vessel is now the property of Black Sea pirates. Any attempt to resist will be met with deadly force. Any attempt to communicate..."

His voice faded as Carver went outside through a side hatch and moved around to the bow of the boat. As he had suspected, a small deck encircled the superstructure and overlooked the forward sundeck. Carver used those stairs to start at the head of the vessel and moved down into one of the two hulls.

"My sdaemsya!" called a man.

The X95 lasered down the narrow passageway.

"You have got to be kidding me," Carver muttered.

Two Russian guards wearing all black lay prone with their hands on their heads. Their rifles rested on the deck behind them. Carver watched the space for a full minute before making his decision.

"Nobody move!"

"Okay!" they each called.

Carver advanced down the passage, wary of an ambush. There were four doors. Rather than turn his back to them, he opened each sequentially. The cabins were small. The first two had made beds with sparse belongings. The second pair were where these men had been sleeping. The bedsheets were akimbo in what must have been panic at waking up to gunfire.

With this deck clear, he warned the guards once again not to move before putting a knee on their backs and slapping cuffs on them. He retrieved their weapons, hooking them over his off shoulder, and instructed them to stand. It was mildly humorous to watch a few failed attempts as they had to roll to their sides and get their feet under them without using their hands. Once up, he had them lead the way to the sundeck, where he threw their rifles overboard. He then pushed them up the exterior set of stairs and back to the bridge.

"Are you kidding me, Vince?" groaned Shaw.

Carver hiked a shoulder. "They surrendered."

His friend sighed at the added hassle and Carver lay them on their stomachs. "You good here?"

"As long as everybody behaves," he warned.

Carver nodded. "I'm going to clear the other hull."

The second set of cabins averaged one crew member each, with one being empty because he caught a man and woman doubled up in a bunk. None had weapons. He confiscated their phones and warned them not to leave their cabins. Upstairs, he realized in their haste they had passed the officer's quarters. The two staterooms were empty because their owners had been manning the ship.

The *Viserion* was secure. All things considered, they were lucky. Carver returned to Shaw and relieved the officers of their phones as well.

"Do any of the crew have weapons?" Carver asked the captain.

He vehemently shook his head. "Excepting security, Arkady doesn't trust anybody with guns on either vessel. Not even me. It is a strict requirement."

"Hey," prodded Shaw with an encouraging wave of his rifle, "tell him what you told me."

The Russian wore a defeated expression but answered helpfully. Carver figured seeing the two captured Spetsnaz gave him confidence that they would survive this ordeal.

"I told him there is only a skeleton crew on the other ship," relayed the captain. "Arkady's personal bodyguard only."

"Are you serious?" asked Carver in disbelief.

"Most of the crew and security are here when not needed. Arkady likes his privacy."

It was sensible enough. Despite Shaw's previous joke,

Carver was aware of no pirates on the Black Sea who would dare attack a Russian vessel. While they were on the water, Arkady was presumed safe.

Carver had believed securing the support vessel first was the smart play, but it turned out to be the more difficult one. He couldn't say he was angry about the miscalculation. Now the hard part was over with.

"What about Katarina Litvinenko?" he asked.

The captain's brow furrowed. "Ms. Litvinenko is not here."

"She boarded the other boat. That's why Arkady docked, isn't it?"

He shook his head. "I don't know anything about that. She may have, but I was overseeing the *Viserion*."

"What's your heading?"

"The Port of Sochi. We're to trail the *Mat' Drakonov* until dawn before pulling ahead to arrive before them in a little over a day."

"How little?"

"Twenty-seven hours from now."

It was still 2 am according to Odesa. That gave them plenty of time to iron out a plan.

26

A few hours later, their preparation was complete. Most of the work was getting the go-fast boat ready on the crane. Inside the bridge, the crew was lined up in more comfortable sitting positions along the back wall. Doubled-up flex-cuffs bound the ankles of the two living guards. The captain was cooperating and manning the navigation station. His priority was the safety of his crew. Shaw kept a close eye as he steered the *Viserion* along the Crimean coast.

Several Russian naval ships skirted the stretch of land. It was difficult not to be nervous. The *Mat' Dragonov* sailed confidently between the warships, and they followed in the standard cruising formation. They would be safe in the wake of the powerful oligarch.

Carver wondered why the Crimean coast was so dark. As far as they were from the Ukrainian mainland, a glow of lights hovered over the horizon like candles lost in shadow. But not in Crimea. It was as if the entire peninsula had lost power.

Moving to the outer deck with binoculars, he thought he could make out military vehicles mobilizing. It was impossible to identify which vehicles comprised the convoy, but the signature of roving headlights was unmistakable. There were a lot of them.

Carver's bad feeling deepened as they rounded the base on Sevastopol.

"I don't understand it," said the captain on his return to the bridge. "Their beacons went black."

"Arkady's?" asked Carver.

"No, not our ships. The navy's."

Carver and Shaw turned with trepidation toward the only vessels in their vicinity.

"If the Russian Navy turned off their locators," said Shaw, "they're initiating an op."

"How could they know about us?" asked Carver.

Shaw shook his head. "I don't think it's us they're after."

The timing was disastrous. Carver wanted nothing more than to transfer to the *Mat' Dragonov*, but that was suicide around the Russian warships.

He was forced to delay an hour as they rounded the southern coastline of Crimea. Once they left the navy behind, the mysteries were answered. Sporadic drums echoed in the distance. Back in the open air, Carver scanned for light. They were too far away, but he swore he caught flashes every minute or two. Maybe his eyes were playing tricks on him, filling the void with something tangible.

He returned to Shaw and the boom of navy cannons resounded. This time the light was unmistakable.

"They're shelling the cities," said Carver. "The crazy bastards are actually starting a war."

"Perfect," muttered Shaw.

Carver checked his watch and did the math, accounting for the time zone change moving toward Sochi. They were only an hour ahead, but that was more than enough to squeeze his window. "I have half an hour before sunrise. I need to get on Arkady's ship now and hope he's not an early riser."

Shaw worked his lips. "I suppose if the navy's looking north, they don't have time to deal with you."

Carver had been thinking the same thing. As important as Arkady was, his presence wouldn't draw the Russian military away from their mission. The oligarch had timed his excursion just before the invasion. He would be expected to protect himself.

"I should be the one going," said Shaw.

"I know."

"Remember, if you're thrown in the water, don't fight the current."

Carver nodded.

"It can be disorienting when you first go under. Just hold fast and look for the light. That's up."

"It won't come to that," said Carver. The SEAL was trying to give him months of training in the final minutes. "Look, there's something you can do for me." Carver offered the new detonator paired with the Libyan bomb in his satchel. "There's a considerable chance I manage to plant the explosive but can't set it off. If something happens to me, you need to do it."

Shaw waved off the device. "You'll be fine, Vince."

"It's for mission integrity. It's safer with you. I'll place and activate the bomb as soon as possible. If the worst case happens after that, if I'm unaccounted for, you need to blow the ship."

Shaw frowned.

"Just try to wait for my signal, will you?"

Shaw answered with a grim nod and took the device.

Carver moved to the vehicle deck while Shaw remained at the console with the captain of the ship. Aside from overseeing the explosion and getting out of Dodge afterward, his part in the action was over.

Carver studied the white wake through the *Viserion's* open aft hatch. The water blazed by at a daunting speed, so he would need to be faster. A high-performance Jet Ski could travel about four times faster than the fifteen-knot cruising speed of the superyacht. This was a case where Malkin's taste for quality would work against him. Carver pushed the personal watercraft into the darkness of the sea and plunged in behind.

The cold water revitalized his body. He climbed onto his craft and inserted the key. Jet Skis generally don't have lights. In most places it's illegal because headlights flipping around would confuse boaters. Arkady's Jet Skis featured instrument lights over the gauges. These Carver had covered with black electrical tape. Now, on the water in the predawn hours, he was nearly a ghost.

He pulled the throttle and shot forward. The high whine of the engine was a concern, but as long as he didn't go too fast, he believed it was manageably hidden under the roar of the superyachts.

Mist peppered his face as he gained on his target. Once past the *Viserion*, he stared out into the massive galaxy before him. The muted lights of the *Mat' Dragonov* were a beacon, drawing him in like the gravitational pull of a dying sun.

Carver bounced on the rolling wake of his target. The watercraft leapt into the air twice before landing smoothly. Then he was between the wedges of foamy water. He sped forward and watched the upper decks for any spotters.

The stern of the superyacht, where it touched the water, was a flat platform and swimming deck. Carver reached for the metal railing at one side. The choppy sea forced several attempts. The water was loud, and he was sure he could not be heard. He found his grip. Keeping one hand on the Jet Ski, he transferred to the deck and tried to pull the light craft up after him. It was heavy and the next bounce ripped it from his grip. The Jet Ski idled sideways as the *Mat* left it, lost and adrift in space.

Carver abandoned further thought of it and hurried to the sealed aft hatch. He knelt by the wall, pulled the pack from his shoulder, and removed garbage bags containing his gear. As he unwrapped them, he tossed the black plastic to the wind. It flapped on the water and disappeared.

The pistol went into his holster, the Tavor over his shoulder, and the spare mags in his pockets. He checked the hatch. It was unlocked. Carver snuck over teak floorboards and secured himself inside.

The overhead lights were shut off. He made his way by the dim glow of track lights lining the walls. The cabana-styled cabin had changing closets, wicker patio furniture, and a party bar with five stools. Carver advanced low between the wall and the bar and listened for anyone who may have detected his entry.

After he was satisfied, he moved to the wide double doors and cracked one open. There was a small storage area with a fancy-but-small motorboat and a genuine personal submersible. Its glass dome revealed tight seating for four. Between it and the helicopter pad on the bow, Carver counted possible escape crafts in case of danger. He was sure Arkady had done the same.

Instead of heading upstairs, Carver moved to the maintenance room ahead. The next thin passageway led past compartments with humming machinery and culminated with the ship's central stairwell. It was spacious, with several landings at each corner as it rounded. He descended, listening for movement. He had no knowledge of how closely or often the engines needed to be monitored or if anyone would be around. He just knew he had to be ready.

The last step left him on the bottom deck. The engines were toward the aft, but he heard a sound behind the door leading the opposite direction. He opened it slowly, pushing with the X95, and found backlit designer tiles forming the curve of a wall. A slatted door hid a toilet and sink and stacked clothes. Stark blue lights traced rounded steps which Carver followed. They led him right into the spa. Through the open door he saw the profile of a woman's legs as she lay on a wooden bed. One more step confirmed it was Katya. She hummed a pop melody, oblivious to his presence.

Despite the rifle being equipped with a suppressor, the last thing he wanted to do was alert the crew by firing it early. He frowned at the thought of using the knife now. He urged himself not to be emotional but it was ultimately logic that convinced him not to make a move yet. His primary objective was the bomb. Failing that, if he was going to announce his presence by making noise, it was better to start by targeting the largest threats.

He backed out of the spa, past the stairwell and into the much more prosaic machinery compartments that took up the majority of the deck. The presence of Katya readied him for more. Sure enough, as he rounded an industrial bilge pump, he came face-to-face with a shocked engineer. Carver slammed the butt of his rifle into his crown and pulled him behind the pump. The crewman groaned as Carver tied a cuff around his wrist. He didn't have any gags.

"Don't scream. Don't move. Or you die."

The engineer nodded. Carver rolled him to his stomach and proceeded past the Rolls-Royce engines to the fuel tanks. He had to move fast now.

A ship this size had a capacity of at least ten thousand gallons of fuel. It could be twice that. Carver hadn't been able to pinpoint the tank size for this particular vessel online, but he ballparked its range at seven thousand nautical miles.

As his first order of business on the boat, Carver set the large explosive where he thought it would do the most critical damage. He placed it near the hull in hopes that it would blow through the steel, but he knew that unlikely.

Still, the resulting leaks and fire would cripple the superyacht.

Carver turned back to the tied-up engineer and cursed. He stopped beside him on his way back. "Count to six hundred in your head," he instructed. "That's ten minutes. When you get there, stand up and head to a lifeboat. Copy?"

The man nodded.

A door slammed ahead. Carver stayed low and moved back to the stairs, pressing against the wall as he watched Katya exit the spa wearing a towel. He supposed the staff would take care of her left-behind clothes. He waited for her to ascend before silently following.

She climbed two decks to the main living quarters with the large hot tub and party area to the aft. Katya strolled down a long passageway toward the bow and entered a private stateroom.

Carver waited a moment. Seeing no follow-up movement, he backtracked in case anyone was in the lounge area. Sunlight spilled over the luxurious interior as the day broke. He wouldn't be able to hide for long.

He passed through a break room of sorts. There was a sleek table and fridge that serviced the adjoining entertainment space, though it wasn't a full-service galley. An expansive, double-height atrium showed off the size of the superyacht. Two sofas and leather chairs circled a central marble table, with a pool table to one side and ping pong on the other. Neither this room nor the exterior pool deck were occupied.

Carver doubled back to the stairs and proceeded into the passage Katya had used. He walked its full length, listening at each door without opening any. At the end of the hall, a small circular stairway rose to a personal sundeck above. Carver poked his head out and the direct sunlight was blinding. He worked his eyelids as he retreated.

Now he had a dilemma. There were six staterooms in this passage. Arkady would be in the master above. His bodyguard could be in the single supporting stateroom above or in one of these. There were also additional guests to account for. As much as he hated it, it was too dangerous to move on without clearing these cabins.

Carver figured the two at the head, including Katya's, would be the nicest. He opened the door opposite hers and found it empty. There were some signs of it being lived in but the bed was made. The private bathroom was likewise unused. Still, the pair of men's boots in the corner stood out.

He moved down the passage to check the middle cabins, and then the ones in the rear. As he had suspected, the other staterooms, while nice, were not as premium as the ones at the head. So far they were all empty. He wasn't sure if that was lucky or not.

Three of the six decks were cleared, not counting the crew quarters and the full extent of the maintenance areas, which he would ignore. Carver lingered at Katya's door and considered the VIPs left aboard. Each upper deck from here grew progressively smaller. There was vanishingly little place for the boat's remaining passengers to be. It was beginning to look like the intelligence from the captain of the *Viserion* was accurate. As he pondered his next move, Katya opened her door and almost walked into him.

Carver put his hand to the towel at her chest, said, "Surprise," and shoved her into the stateroom. He secured the door behind him. The cabin was a mirror image of the one opposite except Katya had made herself at home. Carver aimed the Tavor at her, and she took a couple of reflexive steps away.

"What are you doing here?" she asked, completely caught off balance.

"Shouldn't I be asking you that?"

She pouted.

"Where are you headed?"

She glanced at the white bath towel fitted snugly to her body. Her cheeks and neck were tense, a deer caught in headlights. He almost felt sorry for her.

"To the spa," she answered. "I think I left my phone down there."

"No need for that now." His voice was icy but he made sure not to shout or otherwise attract attention. "You thought you could play me? No, you thought you could *kill* me."

Her head shook with urgency. "No, you don't understand. My uncle took me."

"It's not going to work, Katya. The bomb was in your bag."

"The bomb... What?" She huffed like she was trying to think of something to say. To come up with a lie. "My

Gucci?"

"No more playing dumb. You showed your true intentions in the opera house. You announced to the world that Ukraine should unite with Russia."

She stepped forward and Carver shook the gun once for effect. He stepped into her threateningly and she backed up, bare heels hitting the platform of the bed.

Katya hissed. "That's what I'm trying to tell you!"

"Keep your voice down!" he warned.

She swallowed and lowered to a whisper. "Would you just let me talk?"

Her voice was low and her eyes keyed on his weapon. She was scared to death. Instead of telling her to go on, he took a step toward her with the weapon and waited.

"Thank you," she said under her breath. "My uncle... PMC Wagner... they got to me. It was backstage. One of Pavel's men, I think. He searched my bag. After that he warned me. He showed me a gun and said my words had consequences."

"What gun?"

"The big one. The rifle."

Carver shook his head. The only rifle in the opera house was the one belonging to the man with Amina. The Kalashnikov. Carver tried to recall how he had died and who had killed him, but he wasn't sure that he ever knew.

"You're scaring me, Vince."

She took a gentle step forward to lay a hand on his arm. He shook her off and she flinched. The sudden movement caused the towel to unfold and drop to the floor. She covered herself with her hands and shivered. She looked like she was about to cry.

There was shuffling from the half-open closet and Carver pivoted his rifle. Anya jumped and barked. The little terrier was shaking and growling as if she were ten times bigger. Carver dipped the gun lower and turned to Katya, who failed to stifle a giggle. Her hand left her chest and went to her mouth, and then she remembered her bare breasts and dropped her arm back over them.

And that was it for the floodgates. The laughter came and it wouldn't stop.

Carver bit down. "Katya, quiet down."

"What? It's funny."

Her chest heaved up and down as she laughed, and she didn't bother covering herself anymore. Carver had seen it before anyway. Here, in the privacy of her room, she shook her head, sat on her bed, and leaned back, arms behind propping her up.

"You're crazy," she chided. Her nude body swayed back and forth in playful anticipation. "You were always so serious, Vince. I'm glad you're safe. How's Juliette?"

"Alive. Put some clothes on."

She sucked her teeth. "Or what?" She lay back on the bed and arched her back. "Are you going to make me?"

"Stop it."

"Or what?"

Carver stepped into her and grabbed her wrist. And damn if he didn't see it a split second before it happened. A light in the cabin shifted. A cast shadow. Carver spun as

Roman grabbed his rifle and tackled him. Anya barked as they crashed down. Roman was only wearing boxer shorts but he was strong. He landed on top of Carver with his knee and full weight pinning the Tavor to the carpet.

His fist struck Carver in the cheek. It was a hard hit that made him dizzy for half a second. As the daze melted away, Carver saw Roman pulling his SIG from its holster.

"What do we have here?" taunted the Russian.

Carver released the pinned rifle to control the new threat. He twisted the pistol up with one hand and peeled Roman's fingers back with the other. The Russian screamed and the SIG fired once into the overhead.

Rather than fight for the weapon, Roman twisted his body and released it. The P320 bounced away and his weight shifted. His leg came down on Carver's neck.

In that split second, the Tavor was free. Carver reached but Roman kicked it away. Two more fists rained down and the Russian laughed. He was enjoying this. Carver went for the Colonel on his belt but found it missing. It was in Roman's hand.

"You see this little piece of shit?" he needled. "That's why it didn't go through my vest. Now I have two of them."

Carver bucked his back off the floor and wrapped a leg around the Russian's head. Roman slashed with the knife as Carver kicked him away. He tumbled on the floor and Carver rolled backward. They jumped to their feet simultaneously as Katya watched from the bed.

Roman flipped the blade in his hand and secured it in a proper grip. He tested by punching the air a few times.

"Actually, I might like this."

Carver pulled the Police III from his pocket and unfolded the square blade. Roman frowned at his oversight and glanced at the rifle against the wall. If he made a move for it Carver would gut him.

His opponent had the same realization. They were only a few yards from each other. Each with a knife. Granted, they were both small blades, but that didn't mean they weren't lethal. It only meant this was going to get messy.

"Me and you then," Roman decided. "The way it should be."

He lunged. Carver sidestepped the stab, grabbed his wrist, and punched his blade into Roman's eye. The Russian convulsed on his feet as Carver released the handle and jammed it with the butt of his hand straight into Roman's brain.

There were no more wiggles. Roman dropped to the ground and his lung emptied with a heavy sigh.

"What an idiot," exclaimed Katya.

Carver turned. She was still naked, only now she was holding his pistol, and it was pointed directly at him.

27

Carver stood motionless, slate eyes fixed on the truth. "Does this mean we're past the part where you care about my safety?"

Katya grinned ruefully. "I think it means I never did."

He clenched his jaw and searched the stateroom. His X95 was against the wall. One knife was in Roman's eye socket and the other had his fat digits stuck through the finger holes. The Russian only wore underwear. His clothes were piled on the bathroom he had just come out of, and if he had a gun it wasn't in sight.

"The damn boots," Carver muttered.

"What's that?"

He shook his head. It would just give Katya satisfaction to hear that bunking with Roman had saved her life.

"Are you sleeping with everyone these days?" he grumbled.

Her smile might as well have been painted on. "Only big, strong men. You know my type."

"Well I'm sorry to get in the middle of true love."

She chortled at that one.

"Give me the gun, Katya."

She transformed her voice into a playful damsel's. "Or what? Are you going to make me?"

He sneered at the mockery. It was what he deserved. His eye darted to the Extrema Ratio sticking up like Excalibur in Roman's skull.

"I will shoot you," Katya warned.

She probably would. The Police III was his closest weapon, but his best strategy was to take a bullet, tackle her, and hope for the best.

"Let's just talk about this," he said.

Carver leaned forward to make a move and the pistol rose to his head. He winced and backed off. There was no hoping for the best with a hollow point bouncing around the inside of his skull.

He had to wait for an opening.

"Why get mixed up in this, Katya?" he appealed. "I get the loyalty to your uncle, but why become a terrorist?"

She hiked a shoulder, unashamed about her nudity. "There are no free rides, Vince."

"I guess Roman found that out the hard way."

Her features tightened.

"Why don't you get dressed?" he suggested.

She sighed. "It's too bad. Not that he's dead—he was a meathead. But you, you were actually interesting. Granted, you don't like to let loose. It was obvious you never learned how to have fun. But I could have worked with that. Now... Such a waste."

"You wanna hit the sack once more for old time's sake?"

She snorted and her aim lowered slightly to his neck. "It

is tempting, but you've proved impossible to control."

"Some might call that an attribute."

"I wouldn't." She frowned introspectively. "If it means anything, I did sort of like you."

"Be still my achy-breaky heart."

The gun drooped as she stared wistfully. It was now pointed at his heart. Wearing a ballistic vest under the windbreaker, that was as good as it was going to get. Carver's legs tensed and his fingers closed into a fist.

The door crashed open and Arkady's bald security guard barreled into the stateroom.

"Boris!" said a startled Katya.

The bodyguard must have been mobilized as soon as he heard the gunshot. Carver was suddenly outnumbered, and it wouldn't be so easy to close the distance on the professional soldier. His vest, likewise, wouldn't fare so well against the fully automatic Kord 6P67.

This guy was serious, too. Boris held position on Carver without a peek at Katya's lithe body as she slipped on a bikini and put a wrap around her waist. Then he searched Carver for weapons and found him already disarmed. Boris tossed leftover flex-cuffs on the carpet and paused to study the signal pistol recovered from Carver's ankle.

"It's just a flare gun," protested Carver.

Boris kept it anyway. He held the flare gun and Tavor in one hand and the Kord in his other. It wasn't the best setup for tactical readiness but the odds were still heavily in his corner.

"Let's go," said the bodyguard.

"I don't suppose I'll be walking the plank?"

He didn't react. "Let's go."

Carver was hoping Boris would attempt to juggle the SIG too, but he seemed content to leave that with Katya. That in itself could turn in his favor, except Boris sent Carver ahead first. The bodyguard followed at a safe distance and Katya trailed behind. They went back to the passageway and the same stairwell.

"Up."

Carver climbed one flight and found a similar layout, except the passage was cut short as it led to the expansive master. Instead of going to the stateroom, Boris motioned him into the living area. They passed a formal dining table set for fourteen and a cozy lounge that smelled of cigar smoke. Another short passage led to a modest den with large glass doors slid open. The sunlit deck featured white floorboards, a luncheon table, and lounge chairs. The sea was calm and the horizon flat. Long gone were signs of land, the booming staccato of artillery, and the politics of nations. All that remained in the middle of the Black Sea was intimate and personal.

Arkady Malkin sat at the table alone. He wasn't entirely what Carver had expected. A pudgy little man up close, with beady eyes and unassuming rectangular glasses. He wasn't yet bald or gray, though he was getting a healthy start at both, and his thin lips seemed equally suited to smile or sneer. Arkady wore an elaborate scarlet dressing gown with open-toed Adidas sandals, and he busily puffed a cigar, giving it more outward attention than his prisoner.

"How did you get on my boat?" he asked without a hint of animosity. He had no accent, revealing his Western education.

"Oh-dark-thirty insertion. I parachuted onto your deck."

He was unimpressed. "Is that why my captain is unable to reach the *Viserion*?"

Arkady had him there. Carver waited as the middle-aged man enjoyed a long drag. His exhale was immediately swept away by the brisk maritime air. "This is the only reason you're still alive. Is my property compromised? How many operatives are on board?"

Carver gazed at the support vessel on the edge of their wake. With any luck, Shaw could see him right now, but he didn't bet on it.

"Sit down," instructed Arkady.

Boris pointed to a seat on the opposite side of the round table. "I found these on him," reported the bodyguard. He placed the Tavor and flare gun on the table, well out of Carver's reach.

The oligarch picked up the rifle with practiced hands. "Israel Weapon Industries Tavor. The civilian version of the TAR-21. Yet you are not a civilian."

Carver canted his head. "I'm not officially employed by any government on Earth. I think you're familiar with the concept of plausible deniability."

The head of the Wagner Group laughed. "Yes. You would condemn me for my actions while participating in the same charade. This is geopolitics."

"We're not the same."

"Of course not. You're the one who follows orders and I'm the one who gives them." He finished admiring the Tavor. Instead of setting it back on the table, he rested it across his lap. "I have an illustrious legacy and you might as well not even have a name. But if you believe there's a fundamental difference between you and Roman, you're fooling yourself."

"He's dead, for a start."

An amused snort. "There is that. You are a ghost soldier while he is a ghost. However, you may soon be following him into those Elysian Fields. If you decide to be of no use to me, then I no longer need you alive."

"Trust me, I understand the implications of my situation better than you do. Maybe you were familiar with battle at one time, but you're too disconnected to know it now."

Arkady nodded along as he puffed his cigar. He wasn't angry with the statement. He was maybe even entertaining it. "Tell me," he said, "what did you hope to accomplish out here?"

Carver hiked a shoulder. "Besides killing you, you mean?"

A chuckle and a nod.

"To make a statement that people like you aren't untouchable. That your perverse actions can come back to bite."

"And you would risk starting a war?"

"Isn't that what you just did?"

The oligarch grinned. "I started nothing. What you are witnessing is the continuation of the Great Game, Britain's failing attempt to curb Russia's expansion. The politics started long before us."

Carver snorted. "Katya already gave me the Third Rome bullet points."

Arkady appraised his niece who silently watched the exchange. "The concept of greatness is a formative tool," he explained. "Third Rome is not meant to be taken literally."

"Tell that to the Third Reich."

"What do they have to do with it?"

Carver twisted his lips. "Generalmajor Karl Haushofer said: 'It is a great mistake, world-politically, to consider borders as unchangeable, rigid lines. Borders are anything but dead—they are living organisms extending and recoiling like the skin and other protective organs of the human body.' It's said he influenced Hitler."

"You would compare us to our oppressors?" Arkady chuckled. "This is Ratzel's theory of the organic state. Countries are alive and must consume like all animals. Such nonsense doesn't drive the present."

"Then consider the words of his Russian successor, Aleksandr Dugin. 'My heart beats with the same rhythm as the heart of my country, my people. I waited for the diastoles and systoles, the ebb and the flow, contraction and expansion.' "

Arkady Malkin laughed. It was a genuine, full-throated guffaw without a trace of mockery. "Dugin is little more than a court jester but you..."—the oligarch wagged his finger affectionately—"you are something else. A well-read assassin. Out of everything you've blathered on about, you are right about one thing. You are not the same as Roman."

He became silent for a minute to study Carver as he smoked the cigar. Carver waited and assessed his opponent. He'd expected an ideologue, a man blinded by grandiose nationalism, but true visionary evil is hard to come by. Usually it's just a man who has everything and still wants more.

"You never answered my question about what killing me would accomplish," pivoted Arkady. "I'm one man. A man with a great legacy, yes, but still just one. Even if, against all odds, you were successful with your pitiful attempt to snuff me out, there will always be other men of power and means to pick up the torch."

"But they'd be on notice," Carver assured. "Your death might be lost among the countless others, but it would never be forgotten. You'll be a Wikipedia footnote for the rest of history. How's that for legacy?"

If anything irked Arkady slightly, it was this. His cheek twitched and he skipped his rhythmic drag of tobacco. Boris and Katya watched quietly from the side. Carver decided he had nothing to lose and continued to push.

"What about a legacy of blowing up innocent civilians?"

Arkady snorted. "Civilians, yes. Innocent, not even close. The West believes in the power of words, but then pretends they don't have consequences."

"Says the man who has never seen a consequence in his life. Unless that's no longer true? Your false flag in Kyiv was a non-starter. No one will pin the bomb on Ukraine. Will you need to answer for your failure in the motherland?"

His voice found a grating edge. "Do not place the failures of my whore niece upon me."

"I did my part," insisted the girl.

"Did you?" he snarled. "Or did you allow your lust to get in the way of a simple job?"

"He's CIA," said Katya. "I kept him close."

"Is that a euphemism for spreading your legs?"

She grimaced and pointed the P320 at her uncle. "I did what I did for my country."

Arkady may have been out-of-shape and unfamiliar with battle, but he blinked back supreme calm. "You, my Katya, aren't very different from a spoiled Western prostitute. Is there a single true loyalty inside you?"

His niece trembled at the insult. She battled her will to pull the trigger but couldn't do it. She lowered the gun. In a flash Boris had her. He twisted her arm behind her back. She cried out as he snatched for the pistol.

Carver stood and shoved the round table into Arkady's chest, cutting off access to the Tavor. Boris shoved Katya to the deck and fumbled with the two weapons. Carver reached across the table for the flare gun.

He had an opening, a single moment where he could have fired the flare right into the oligarch's smarmy smile. Instead he pointed both arms high and launched it vertically. Boris dropped the SIG to the deck to regain control of his rifle. The 6P67 locked on Carver as both arms stretched to the sky in surrender.

"*Nyet!*" shouted Arkady.

The oligarch had dropped his cigar and pushed away

from the table, holding the X95 by the barrel. With Carver frozen and Boris covering, he didn't bother to properly point the thing. He searched the deck and retrieved his burning cigar. Then he frowned at the overhead trail of red light fighting against the sun.

"That was very stupid!" he admonished. "You have no chance of rescue. Even if you have a team of SEALs on the *Viserion*, they're not getting on my ship." His breathing slowed and his eyes narrowed. "But you've already shown your hand, haven't you? There is no team of SEALs. This is an off-book operation. You said it yourself. Plausible deniability. Tell me, since you're the one so familiar with battle: if I shoot you in the head and throw you into the sea, would anyone ever care to look?"

Carver sucked his lips and slowly lowered his hands to brace against the table. "You know what's funny?" he mused. "I'm here to kill you and I don't even know you. I'd expected a lofty speech about Third Rome and the provenance of Russia, but the truth is you don't believe in anything consequential. You're nothing more than a bureaucrat counting his money. At the end of the day, you don't matter. You're just another in a long line of greedy assholes."

The *Mat' Dragonov* shuddered as a huge blast rocked its depths. Lower-deck windows shattered. Katya was still on the floor but Boris and Arkady were standing without support. They lost their balance and stumbled with the ship's sudden jerk.

Carver lunged from the table, grabbing the Kord assault

rifle and slamming a fist into the bodyguard's kidney. As he winced in pain, Carver shoved Boris forward. Arkady twisted the Tavor in his hand but Carver beat him to the punch. Holding the barrel of the 6P67, he pressed Boris' trigger finger and a volley of rounds peppered Arkady's chest.

Carver's legs kept pumping as he wrapped around Boris, running with him all the way to the edge of the deck. Carver flipped him over the railing. The assault rifle was still strapped to Boris as he banged against the hull and plunged into the Black Sea.

Carver spun. Arkady was prostrate on the deck, fingers weakly playing on the Tavor. Katya lunged for the downed SIG Sauer. Carver dove forward and slid into his rifle, flipping it around and pulling the trigger before she could get into shooting position. The look of shock on her face as a bullet split her eyes was one he would never forget.

As she collapsed to the deck, Carver turned to Arkady. His eyes were wide and his breathing strained. He tried to mouth something but sounds of thunder roared belowdecks. The alarmed shouts of the crew followed.

They watched each other as Arkady bled on the sun-faded teak floorboards. His suffering came to an end. Carver checked the deck for any threats and then set the safety of his rifle and stood. He recovered the P320.

The *Mat' Dragonov* slowed to an emergency stop. The vessel listed in the sea as the hull took on water. It didn't matter if it was enough to ultimately sink the ship or not. His work was done. The fire would manage the rest.

He watched the go-fast boat disconnect from the *Viserion* and head his way as the last light of the flare faded overhead. Carver holstered the pistol and dove off the side of the deck and into the water. He surfaced and swam away from the ailing vessel. Shaw helped him out of the water a minute later.

"You were still on the boat," hissed Shaw, palpably relieved to see his friend still in one piece.

Carver glanced back at his handiwork. "What boat?"

From their position on the water, the fire wasn't visible, but a clear plume of smoke grew on the ship's port side. The crew scrambled for lifeboats. An older woman flashed by holding a blue Gucci handbag with a toy terrier peeking out.

Carver smiled. The *Mat' Dragonov* would appear to have been scuttled in the center of the Black Sea. If its wreckage was recovered, the source of the explosion would be revealed to have been Libyan rebels. That detail would probably never make the newswires because it was a personal message sent directly to Russia.

They would recover the bomb fragments and know exactly where it came from, because they were the ones who had made it.

Shaw turned the wheel of the go-fast boat. It was a sport catamaran with twin outboard racing engines that topped out at well over a hundred miles per hour. They sped from the wreckage under a brightening cerulean sky, toward a horizon still tinged orange by dawn, and Carver wondered what the beaches in Turkey were like.

Afterword

I hope you enjoyed Vince Carver's upgrade as a full-fledged independent asset of the CIA! This book was a lot of fun to write and had me daydreaming about European vacations. As is probably obvious, there's a lot that rings true in this adventure.

Unfortunately, much of it for the wrong reasons...

The post-WWII Cold War ended December 1991 with the dissolution of the USSR. It concluded with a clear victor and dark days for the loser, but just because wars end doesn't mean conflicts do. Economic and social tensions continued to spark throughout Europe, and NATO and Russia still push for their versions of empire building.

This ensuing ideological battle between traditional superpowers is the basis for *Ghost Soldiers*, a reimagining of recent historical events.

At the heart of the novel is Russia's stance on a modernizing Ukraine. They see the state as a puppet of the West, the

Revolution of Dignity as a CIA coup. The Kremlin increasingly views Ukraine as a Western aircraft carrier parked at their border. Years of Russian soft power have failed, and they're now forced to take a hard line.

Russia's specialty has been what is termed hybrid warfare, the use of unconventional methods to disrupt or disable opponents without engaging in open hostilities. They focus on gray-zone operations that are meant to intimidate but fall short of a physical conflict. They even engage in lawfare, using the law as a weapon. This is apparent in Russia's migration war, where an influx of smuggled Middle East nationals put a strain on NATO's humanitarian efforts.

Given Russia's penchant for unconventional warfare, imagine my shock upon completing the chapter set in the National Opera in Kyiv and to then see Ukraine invaded that same night! The escalation into total war had to be written into the closing chapters.

The Wagner Group features heavily in Russia's military operations, clandestine or otherwise. From the little green men who marched into Crimea to the ghost soldiers sneaking across borders, and even to the saboteurs hunting President Zelensky in Kyiv as I write this, these specialty units are adept at fomenting unrest. As with any intelligence fieldwork, deniability is the strongest asset.

Arkady Malkin is inspired by the real billionaire oligarch who is friends with Vladimir Putin and rumored to own the

Wagner Group.

There are plenty of other depictions of real people in this novel, many of them tragic.

Last year, an Olympic sprinter fled Tokyo after speaking out against her home country of Belarus.

Assassinations in Kyiv are likewise not exaggerated. Pavel Shishov's two names are taken from a Kyiv journalist killed in a car bomb and an actual Belarusian dissident who went for a jog one day in Kyiv and was found beaten and hanged in a park.

Amina's story is real. A veteran of the fighting in Donetsk, she really did shoot her husband's would-be assassin. He lived and went to prison. Her husband recovered, but Amina was killed months later when their car was ambushed by a gang with automatic weapons. The Ministry of Internal Affairs suspects the Russian military.

My desire is to highlight these tragic figures instead of painting them as disposable characters in an espionage thriller. There is a very real human cost to these barbaric tactics. Somewhere, some day, this needs to end.

I'd love to hear your feedback on Vince Carver's continuing adventures! If you'd like to chat, or if you have a special skill set and would like to set me straight about an error in my story, feel free to email me at matt@matt-sloane.com. Writing is a lonely business, and I welcome collaboration and corrections from readers.

On that note, if you appreciated the story, you can help the book succeed by leaving an online review. Simply put, your opinions are powerful. The more you give voice to good stories, the more of them you'll find. Whether it's a few words or an essay, every five-star rating increases our visibility together. Think of it as a vote of confidence in me and Vince.

Thanks again for reading.

-Matt

Read Next:

The Service of Wolves
Vince Carver Book Three

Continue the Vince Carver series
where Matt Sloane books are sold.

Matt-Sloane.com

Be notified when new Vince Carver
thrillers are released, right to your inbox.
Sign up at the website and never miss another book.

A Favor

It's not always easy to ask for a favor, even a small one, but I'm going to do it.

As an author, it's impossible to understate how much my career relies on you, the reader. Every purchase supports me. Every kind word helps my work flourish.

For that all I can say is thank you, from the bottom of my heart.

I know you're ready to dive into the next book, the next adventure, whether by me or another author, but it would be an incredible kindness if you could spend another single minute in the world of Vince Carver to leave me a review wherever you bought the book.

I guarantee that your words will make a difference. Not just to me, but to a random stranger stuck deciding what to read next and wondering if an author they've never heard of is worth their valuable time.

For that one guy, your input means everything in the world.

Preview:

The Service of Wolves
Vince Carver Book Three

A rare and fortunate isolation followed Carver on his run along Coyote Creek Trail. The morning air invigorated his lungs while the cloud cover kept the sun from doing its worst. The scenic beauty of the water was so inviting that he extended his usual distance of five miles, content to exercise in a peaceful trance interrupted only by the occasional errant bicyclist and ornery duck.

Carver caught himself twenty minutes past his mark. He slowed but didn't stop, took a gulp from his water bottle, and turned around to resume his pace. By the time he made it back to the bridge over the creek, a pleasant burn sapped every muscle in his body. He had a few ideas for how to cap off such a perfect morning, but meeting CIA Officer Lanelle Williams was not among them.

Under the enclosed metal frame of the pedestrian bridge, Carver slowed to a stop beside the woman and reopened his water bottle. It was a shame, he thought as he watched the creek through the links of the fence. His private paradise had become routine to the point of predictable. He would need to change his habits.

"I'm still mad at you," said Lanelle curtly.

Carver's heavy hand hung on his hip. "Mad-mad or mad-ha-ha?"

"You're not making it better."

He killed off the remaining water in the plastic bottle, crushed it, and screwed the lid shut. He hadn't seen the case officer since his debrief some months ago. It was in her nature to only be around when she needed something, which suited Carver just fine. Theirs was a working relationship.

At least it had been until Carver veered off-script.

"Are you trying to tell me I'm in the doghouse, Laney? Because months of neglect clued me in."

"Don't look at me. There are a few others within our ranks who discovered your indiscretions."

"Only a few? Isn't that a saying, a few can keep a secret?"

"I'm pretty sure that's not right."

Carver crossed his arms and leaned on the fence. "I can't believe anyone's crying over a corrupt Russian oligarch."

"It's not about crying, Vince, it's about exposure, and there's not enough deniability in the world to pretend you didn't cross a red line. What you did was reckless. It could have come back on us."

He tried not to shrug his shoulder. "Luckily bigger boats have since sunk in the Black Sea."

"There's the greater good to think about."

"I noticed. From where I sit, Ukraine is still under the gun, and Russian citizens are suffering for their government's greed."

She nodded. "Lucky for you the world has gone crazy. All the chaos has made Malkin's death little more than a footnote."

Carver grinned at that characterization. He had said as much to the smug bastard himself. As far as the lack of CIA contact, Carver understood what he had signed up for. Besides, every intelligence agency in the world was now focused on analyzing ground combat in the modern era. The NSA was working overtime for Kyiv as well as keeping tabs on similar prospects in Taipei, both cities Carver had recently visited. He wasn't sure if that made him good or bad luck.

"Long story short," continued Lanelle, "I'm not even supposed to be talking to you right now. Hence this... clandestine ambush in the boonies."

"And I always took you for the outdoorsy type. Although I doubt those flats would make it half a mile."

Her expression withered. "Vince, if you see me running, it's only because I've lost my gun and there's a homicidal clown after me. Are you done being cute or do you need to go a few more laps to burn off the testosterone? I'm here as a courtesy."

This time Carver kept his mouth shut and waved an upward palm in invitation for her to continue.

"You're a good guy, when you get over yourself," she said, which might have been the most magnanimous thing to ever come out of her mouth. "I know you've got mouths to feed. The problem is no one can touch you with a ten-foot pole right now. So I found you some work outside the Agency."

"I can find private security work on my own. Hollywood's been hounding me for a consulting gig, but I'd rather not pander."

That prospect earned an amused chuckle. "It's nothing like that. This is for a three-letter agency—just not the CIA. See, you may be persona non grata right now, but the DEA has it worse in Mexico."

Carver groaned. "The War on Drugs? Really?"

His pain had the opposite effect of lightening her expression. "I'm aware Mexico isn't as splashy as your last two destinations, but it's real work with genuine national security ramifications. We can't fix the cartels and we can't stop the drugs, but we can shield the government and police from corruption. As you know, it's a dangerous time to be a reporter or politician in Mexico."

"Only if you're honest," he interjected.

"So here I am, keeping my distance from you like a respectable intelligence officer, and a contact in the DEA throws out a feeler. He's a field guy, a real grit and grindstone type who sees rules as suggestions. You'd like him."

Carver ignored the implicit jab. "I get private enterprise in Mexico is booming these days, but my understanding was the DEA kept out of that."

"Your understanding might be outdated. Have you heard of the Merida Initiative?"

He nodded. "Financial support by the United States to take on the cartels."

"More than a billion dollars worth over a decade, for aircraft and materiel to engage transnational criminal organizations, to retrain police forces, and to revamp the justice system. And what do we have to show for it? Spiking levels of violence, trafficking, and drug abuse. Kidnappings and homicides are at an all-time high. It turns out American defense contractors got the brunt of that money. The Merida Initiative is dead in the water, with politicians now placing their hopes in the new Bicentennial Framework for Security."

Carver conclusively clapped his hands together. "Problem solved then."

"The problem's not too big with the right allies, but those are few and far between. In 2018, Mexico elected a populist president on promises to combat corruption. This guy threw the three previous presidents under the bus. He overrode the power of local corrupt police forces by creating a new national guard that answers to him."

"Meanwhile we've taken a hard line at the border."

Lanelle nodded. "If this ever was a marriage, there sure wasn't a honeymoon. The US recently arrested their former secretary of national defense in Los Angeles for drug trafficking. Mexico responded by limiting our federal powers in the country. And when we released their general, they leaked US intelligence anyway, effectively warning the cartels about everything we knew. It was an operational disaster."

"Were agents compromised?"

"No casualties to speak of unless you count their balls being snipped. The DEA's operational capacity in Mexico has been vastly reduced."

"And, due to your recommendation, the Drug Enforcement Agency believes I can be an asset?"

She returned a sly smile. "Seemed to me like the perfect time to inject new testosterone into the mix. Unless you're not interested... ?"

Carver showed his teeth. Case officers were expertly trained to wiggle the line just enough to ensure a bite, and Carver was, if nothing else, a shark. "Cut the crap, Williams. What's the job?"

She handed over a business card. "I'll let Pineda explain that himself. I'm not talking to you, remember?"

Special Agent Albert Pineda was printed beside the official DEA seal on cheap card stock. The reverse side had handwriting with a time and location.

"Get out of town," urged Williams. "Sit down with him. If you like what you hear, take the job. No need to run it by me. I won't be in San Jose for a while."

She retreated from the bridge, and he studied the card a second before casting one last longing look at the fading tranquility of Coyote Creek.

Also by Matt Sloane

VINCE CARVER THRILLERS
National Security
Ghost Soldiers
The Service of Wolves
Project Sundown

The latest books and information will always be on
Matt-Sloane.com

Made in the USA
Middletown, DE
14 December 2023

45589825R00184